MY FRIEND JESUS CHRIST

s HUSUM was born in West Jutland, Denmark in 1974. After
lying drama and literature at the University of Aarhus, he
ked as a dramatist for the Van Baden theatre company before
king as a writer and developer for Zentropa. *My Friend Jesus
ist* is his first book.

1 in 1977, METTE PETERSEN grew up in Copenhagen and
sels. She lives in Copenhagen where she teaches English and
rature at a Steiner school. This is her first translation.

MY FRIEND JESUS CHRIST

Lars Husum

TRANSLATED FROM THE DANISH BY
Mette Petersen

Portobello
BOOKS

First published by Portobello Books 2010
Paperback edition published 2011

Portobello Books
12 Addison Avenue
London
W11 4QR
United Kingdom

A CIP catalogue record is available from the British Library

9 8 7 6 5 4 3 2 1

ISBN 978 1 84627 210 3

www.portobellobooks.com

Printed and bound in Great Britain by CPI Bookmarque, Croydon

Part One

MOTHER, SISTER, GIRLFRIEND, JESUS

In the bathtub

I'm fifteen the first time. I do it because I'm in love with Miriam with the red hair. She has large breasts, four freckles on her nose, and what's more she's a Jehovah's Witness. I wish I were brave enough to speak to her, but I don't utter a single word in all of Year Ten. She knows how I feel about her because I follow her around, even when we're not at school. In the beginning, I hide behind bushes and trees, throwing myself to the ground whenever she turns to face me. Of course, she notices that I'm stalking her – I'm not really that good at hiding – but I have a reputation for being odd that makes her afraid to do anything about it. She tries to ignore me, but the more she ignores me, the closer I get. One fair May evening I even sneak into her garden and peep through her window. She is lying in bed, reading, while I stand outside in a flowerbed. Then she puts down her book, yawns, and suddenly our eyes meet. She is silent and terrified as she stares at me, and I give her a small, confused wave before I make a run for it.

I do know that we'll never be a couple, but the fact that she doesn't want me is actually part of why I love her. I wank five or

3

six times a day around this time. Actually, I wank just about everywhere, including in the flowerbed in her garden. Sis is worried because I shut myself in and seem so secretive, but really I am just randy.

I gawp at Miriam in a Danish lesson, and she looks back at me nervously. My Danish teacher has told me off several times, not for gawping at Miriam but because I don't pay attention. I can just make out her knicker line, and if there's a knicker line then there must be knickers, and if there are knickers then there has to be a bottom and a cunt. Without even knowing it, my hand slides down to my groin, I unbutton my trousers and pull it out. She is the first one to notice. Her face contracts in disgust. In a split-second she overcomes her fear of me. Running straight across the room, she slaps me resoundingly – SMACK! – and storms out. There I am, confused and disconsolate, with a flaming cheek, and I just don't get why the others say I'm a creep. All of a sudden my Danish teacher grabs hold of me. He shakes me.

'Put it away, you little perv!'

I'm baffled. 'Put what away?'

He assumes it's a provocation, loses his cool and slaps me on the same cheek that Miriam slapped: SMACK! I haven't done anything! Why are they hitting me? I jump up from my chair and thump him. I'm not a big lad, but I am strong and my aim is perfect. POP! and his nose splatters. Blood is spraying all over the place. That paralyses him. I hit him again, aiming for his temple – POW! – and he keels over. I turn around and see my classmates' bewildered faces. The girls are wailing; some of them are running

4

away. I stare aggressively at them, and then I bellow, 'You nits!' After all, I have to scream something.

Then I'm tackled from behind by Jesper, who is the class hero because he plays on the U18 handball team, and we tussle for a bit. He's bigger than me, but I end up on top anyway. I manage to lock his arms with my legs, and I am sitting on his chest, about to pummel him when I notice that my cock is jutting in across his face. That's when I realize what I have done. I get up, tuck my cock away and hurry out. No-one follows me or tries to stop me. Why would they? They're just glad the little pervert is running away. I want to go home so that I can erase the humiliation.

The next thing I remember is being in the bath, slitting my wrist. I look with surprise at the blood running down my hands, but then I sink into the water with a nice feeling of calm. Sis hasn't heard from the school yet, so she doesn't know what I've done. She comes home, and as usual she heads straight for the bathroom. Sis will often wait for longer than necessary if it means she can wee in her own bathroom. I have forgotten to lock the door. She slams it open, heads for the loo and screams. She wees on the floor and stands, rocking back and forth in wee, water and blood for a bit. And then she gets started. Sis saves my life, as she has done many times since. I am in hospital for three days due to the massive blood loss, and not for one minute does Sis leave my side.

It is a long time before I fall in love again.

Because I can't be orphaned at thirteen

Dad torpedoes another car when I am thirteen, and Sis is twenty. Nothing serious happens to the driver of the other car – a broken leg, that's all – but Mum and Dad both die. Mum dies on the spot. Her neck is broken, and she looks almost untouched. Dad, on the other hand, dies of terrible injuries, but only after several hours on the operating table. He is one big bloody mess. We are at the hospital and, unlike Sis, I'm as cool as a cucumber. I don't for a second worry whether Dad will survive. Of course he will, because if he doesn't then we won't have any parents. I refuse to believe it when they say he's dead. They *must* go back and check, because I can't be orphaned at thirteen. But they have not made a mistake, and that's when my stomach ache starts. Often it's not an intense pain, merely a feeling of a knot tightening. When the knot becomes too tight, I whimper and growl. I don't tell Sis about the knot, because she's got quite enough to worry about as it is.

Review from *Jyllands-Posten*

Grith Okholm: Surrender Myself to You

by Henrik Vestergaard Nielsen

Talent on the rise. Beautiful songs from the greatest beauty on the Danish music scene.

Last year Grith Okholm came soaring out of musical nothingness with her debut album *Everything is Changing*. With her frail girlish charms and a sex appeal likened to that of Brigitte Bardot, the singer-songwriter was suddenly hailed as the greatest talent of Danish music. She has been awarded a special place in the musical hearts of the Danes, who have always had trouble resisting a pedigree beauty.

This album, then, is the difficult second album which is going to make clear whether the talent is real or just a fluke. *Surrender Myself to You* stands head and shoulders above her otherwise very successful debut. In terms of music, lyrics and atmosphere it is on an accomplished international level. Everything has improved in an album everyone by rights should fall in love with.

Surrender Myself to You consists of eleven beautiful songs, which we will be singing along to on a hot summer's night and then will warm ourselves by when the temperature begins to cool. Charm is perhaps the greatest asset of these songs which elegantly explore the byroads and banalities of love. Grith Okholm has very quickly become a household name and on this album she shows why she will go on being one in the years to come. She is already a giant on the Danish music scene. I humbly bow down before her.

Mum releases twelve studio albums plus a couple of live albums, all of which go on to sell at least 100,000 copies. *Surrender Myself to You* was her great breakthrough. So far it has sold 493,000 copies, plus many more in Norway and Sweden. Last Christmas, a boxed set came out with a price tag of 399 kroner, containing all Mum's records and one with previously unreleased tracks. In other words, demo versions and scrapped songs. The box becomes the Christmas present of the year, selling damn near 200,000 copies, more than ten years after Mum's death, making me even richer. Sis and I inherit millions when Mum (and Dad) dies, but what good are millions to us? So Sis invests the money in flats all over Copenhagen. She buys the flats before the huge hike in the property market, and suddenly the flats are worth four times what she paid for them. I am, to put it plainly, rich, owning property and stuff, but I've never really cared about the money I had, because I've never had to.

Mum

It doesn't hurt Mum's reputation that she's only forty-one when she dies, but she would have been equally beloved today if she had still been alive. After all, she has created some of the catchiest and best-loved songs in Denmark. There was a poll of the 50 best Danish pop songs three years ago in a national newspaper. 'Kvinde Min' by Gasolin won, but Mum had nine songs on the list, three of which ('With You', 'What the Heart Holds' and 'Storm') were in the Top Ten – at Number 3, 7 and 8, respectively.

Mum wants to make the most of her career, so she performs constantly and absolutely everywhere. Even when we go on holiday, it's connected to some tour in Norway or Sweden where she is also insanely popular. We never just go on holiday, only to lie on the beach or look at ruins. Of course, there are days off when we are in Norway, but we go because of Mum. The reviews are almost always good, because she gives her all when she's on stage. She had one bad review on her last tour, written by a young reviewer, Hans Henrik Fahrendorff, in the magazine *Gaffa*. He called her concert 'lazy and slovenly'. There were probably twenty other reviews of the same concert, calling it 'amazing and captivating', but Mum started crying because of that one bad review. Dad waited until he was alone, and then he called the reviewer and explained to him that he was never to review anything of Mum's ever again.

When Mum isn't doing her stuff, she relaxes to save her strength. She watches a lot of television or shuts herself in and listens to loud music. Mum listens to music that is totally different from what she's playing. She likes Iron Maiden, AC/DC and late Metallica. We're not to be difficult, because Mum needs to relax. Sis takes it very seriously. She makes sure I never go to Mum for no reason, because I'm not to go to Mum at all. I'm to go to Sis. I've frequently knocked on the door to Mum's office, only to have Sis pull me away at once, sit me down and say, 'What is it, sweetie?' It's strange the first time she calls me sweetie (she must have been around eleven), but I soon get used to it.

The only place Mum never performs is in Tarm, where she grew up. She refuses, even though they try to tempt her. She's offered outrageous sums for a single concert in the Tarm Arena, but she never ever wants to return to that town. When they realize they can't tempt her with money, they try various alternatives. The entire town means to celebrate her career with a huge party. Plans for the event are well under way before they tell her, and she informs them that she isn't interested in participating. Of course, the party doesn't takes place, what with the guest of honour not coming. The people of Tarm are very disappointed. After a number of failed attempts to lure Mum to Tarm, the then mayor – an elderly, greying pig farmer – comes to see us. He leaves Tarm and comes to Copenhagen and rings our doorbell.

'Hello, my name is Bjarne Andersen. I'm the mayor of Tarm.'

Mum looks surprised at him and asks, 'Where did you get our address?'

He blushes and says, 'A secretary at your record label gave it to me. I thought it was better to speak face to face than to communicate by letter.'

He's very humble, an elderly man who blushes, and Mum feels sorry for him. She asks him to come in and listens to him politely. He even stays for supper. She gives him hope, but in the end she has to say no, and he returns home with yet another failure. I'm told that it made him give up politics.

Dad

Dad only sees one single colleague outside work. That's Uncle John. They're both postmen. Ending up as a postman in Nørrebro, while Mum is beloved by all of Denmark annoys Dad. Especially because the magazines always show him in his postman's uniform. Dad is stalked by paparazzi, who knock over his bike just to get a picture of him chasing letters blowing in the wind. He feels pathetic, but Mum doesn't think he's pathetic. She doesn't care what he does, as long as he's there for her, and he is – every second, every breath is for Mum.

Uncle John is not our uncle – both Mum and Dad are only children – but John wants us to call him uncle.

'I think it's nice that they call me uncle – it's almost as if we're a family, Allan.'

Dad doesn't respond, which makes John repeat, 'Almost as if we're a family, Allan.'

He's a chubby man, around Dad's age, who lives with his parents, and he's utterly devoted to Dad, but John isn't Dad's friend. He's a bit more than a colleague and a bit less than a friend. Dad listens, but he never speaks of his own problems, and he doesn't like to meddle. Nevertheless, John is the closest thing Dad has to a friend. But Dad's like that with everyone, except Mum. Once I tell Dad that I'm being bullied at school. He listens, nods gravely, and says, 'That's not very nice of them, Nikolaj,' and that's all he says.

This is how they meet

Mum's parents are devoutly evangelical, and she's been raised with Jesus and a stern God.

According to Mum, Grandad's primary reason for being evangelical is that it gives him a reason for scolding. To Grandad's never-ending vexation, Mum snogs boys (quite a bit) – partly as a protest, but also because she loves it when people tell her she's lovely. She dreams of running off to New York or London, but Copenhagen would be fine, too, as long as she gets away from Grandad.

Dad is from Tarm as well, but he has decided to move to Copenhagen. He's an only child, both his parents are dead, and he has no close friends, so why stay in a small town like Tarm where options are so limited? He isn't exactly planning on becoming a comical sidekick to Mum.

He meets Mum at his leaving party. They don't know each other, except by sight. Mum has invited herself. Dad is twenty-two, good-looking, he's going places and he's the official centre of attention at the party. Mum is sixteen, beautiful, supposed to be in her room but she has snuck out, and straight away she has become the unofficial centre of attention at the party. All parties have a tendency to centre on Mum. Mum and Dad hadn't spoken to each other before that night, but now they don't speak to anyone else. Mum doesn't let him out of her sight, because he's going to save her. When everyone leaves, Mum stays, and Dad can't believe he's suddenly alone with this beautiful girl with the happy tits.

'Allan, won't you take me with you to Copenhagen?'

'Of course I will,' he says, surprised at how easy it is to make that decision.

She relaxes, and he notices how small and defenceless she is in his big manly arms. They have known each other for eight hours when they decide to move in together. He kisses her, and she holds her breath when he unbuttons her trousers. She's snogged a lot of boys, but the only man she ever goes all the way with is Dad.

When Mum tells her parents that she's moving out (and she does that with surprising confidence, because she has Dad to fight for her), Grandad is furious. She's only sixteen. She is certainly not moving to Copenhagen. He calls her things a father shouldn't call his daughter. He's done that often enough, but things are getting worse now. Mum runs away several times, escaping to Dad's. Dad hates it being so difficult, because, of course, she must come with him, but he demands that Mum returns to her parents every time to work it out in a proper manner. You are supposed to honour your parents, even Grandad and Granny. The fifth time she goes back downcast, Grandad is waiting for her, bloody murder in his eyes. It starts out with yelling and threats, but does he really think he can scare her into submission with just words? She been threatened with damnation all of her life. Mum simply yells back at him, and then Grandad takes off his belt. Grandad isn't in the habit of beating Mum. He slaps her when she's naughty or talks back, but he's never done anything as violent as this. Grandad whips Mum, while Granny stands by and whimpers. Granny isn't mean. She is weak.

SMACK!

'You ask for forgiveness right now!'

SMACK! SMACK! SMACK! SMACK! SMACK!

'Get stuffed!'

SMACK! SMACK!

'Ask for forgiveness!'

SMACK! SMACK! SMACK! SMACK! SMACK! SMACK! SMACK! SMACK!

'Get stuffed!'

SMACK! SMACK! SMACK! SMACK! SMACK! SMACK! SMACK!

13

SMACK! SMACK! SMACK! SMACK! SMACK! SMACK! SMACK! and then the door slams open. It's Dad. He's walked Mum home and has decided to stick around. He's in no doubt that her screams are meant for him, and he responds in exactly the right manner. He yanks the belt out of Grandad's hands and flings him across the room. This is when Mum really falls in love with Dad, because she's never felt as happy as when Dad thrashes Grandad with his own belt. When he stops beating him – and it's a long time before he does – he breathes out and squares his shoulders manfully.

'We'll be off now. You'll never see Grith again. She's mine, and you two just stay away from her,' and with that, they leave.

Mum takes nothing with her except the love of her life and her daily evening prayer. She despises people who are openly devout, but she still prays. Maybe it's just a habit she can't shake off, but she prays every night because it makes her calm enough to sleep.

Mum and Dad expect my grandparents to set the police on them, but they seem to decide that Mum isn't worth the trouble. At all events we don't see them again until after Mum's death, and then it's not Mum they are interested in but me.

Mum loves Copenhagen, and she does nothing for the first couple of weeks except go to different places, sit down and watch passers-by. She loves to watch strangers passing. Every day a kindly soul cautiously asks her, 'Are you okay?' and Mum says with a smile, 'Yes, I'm fine.'

One day, while she is watching people, she's humming. Then she attaches words to her humming, and with that 'With You' is born. She has made an entire song, and it is easy! A couple of days pass before she decides to sing it to her boyfriend. The song is for him, but she doesn't think it's good enough, because she loves him more than her little song can express. When Dad comes home from work, Mum says she has a present for him. He is to sit down and say nothing. She is nervous, shaking all over. Dad on the other hand is confused. He doesn't understand what present requires him to be silent, especially because Mum's afraid to take the plunge.

'Where's my present?'

Mum is hopping mad.

'I told you to shut up. Now you're spoiling it.'

'Sorry,' says Dad, feeling even more confused.

It's another five minutes of awkward silence. This is the weirdest present anyone has ever given him, and then he hears the first nervous notes come out of Mum's mouth. Mum is singing with her eyes closed, so she can't see the expression on Dad's face. She finishes her song and sits for a bit, hoping Dad will say something nice, but he doesn't say anything. That stupid boor, why can't he just pretend? She opens her eyes. She wants to apologize for the rubbish song, and then she sees Dad crying. And finally Dad manages to stammer, 'I bloody love you. Bloody hell, you're amazing.'

Mum doesn't think he means it. She shrugs off the compliment with a goofy smile, but Dad holds her gaze and says with great strength, 'That is the most beautiful thing I have ever heard.'

Mum senses the earnestness of the words, and she doesn't know what to do with herself.

*

Five months later the song is Number 1 in the Danish charts. She has Dad to thank for that. She would never have done anything about it herself. Dad is proud, but he is also increasingly annoyed that her needs are constantly put before his. When he finally complains, they have a violent row, ending with Mum slamming the door. She leaves and is gone for two days. Dad's a mess, but of course Mum comes back, and everything is the same as before. She does that often enough, leaves and is gone until Dad's a broken man. Once she is gone for an entire week, and Dad doesn't sleep for seven nights straight. Are Mum and Dad happy? No, but they can't bear to be apart. Being together is just not enough to make them happy.

School

My sister is born when Mum is twenty-one. They just don't have the time before that. They start talking about having kids when Mum is seventeen, but then her career gets in the way. After a couple of years of concerts she is tired, and then it's time for a baby. Sis is born in a kind of creative intermission. She soon learns that there's no-one to straighten things out for her. That's why Sis always insists on straightening things out herself. Unlike Sis, I have never had to sort things out myself. I have Sis.

Mum has always handled her fame with the utmost ease. I on the other hand have let it weigh me down. On the first day of school Kathrine and little Vibeke discover who I am, and then they sing 'What the Heart Holds' in a mocking way. I get upset, and when the other kids see this, I'm doomed to be forever jeered at. I get used to the pain of it. It becomes a routine, because it is almost always the same things that happen. I know that when Morten sees me, I am about to get punched on the arm. I know that when Pernille opens her mouth, she's going to tell me her dad says my mum's a slag. I know that when they whisper, it is because they're scheming. I stop reacting to it, even when they beat me, because if I can make myself numb it won't hurt. That my sister is a vengeful angel is also helpful. If Morten punches me, Sis gives him a dead leg. This beautiful girl from Year Seven goes up purposefully to the dirty boy from Year Two.

'Hiya, did you hit my brother?', and before Morten can even answer, he tumbles to the ground, screaming.

In Year Ten Sis is sent to a boarding school near Frederikshavn. She doesn't want to leave me alone at the mercy of my bullies; she pleads with Mum and Dad to be allowed to stay at home, but it's no good, because the teachers say that she's a difficult child, and Mum and Dad do as they suggest.

She calls me every night, and I tell her that I have made friends, that the bullying has stopped and that school is cool. Sis is astonished as I tell her about my new friend with whom I've just seen *Terminator 2*.

'What's his name?'

'Kenneth. It's Kenneth from number 16.'

'But he's older than you, isn't he?'

'Only two years.'

Sis thinks this over, but happily she decides to say, 'I'm so glad that you've found a friend, sweetie.'

I make more friends while she is away at school, amazing friends who protect me, and she wants so fervently to believe it's true. I do it for Sis, so she won't be ashamed of not being there to protect me. It's the first time that I really feel lonely and alone.

It's a blessing when Sis returns home. We are inseparable the following summer holiday. I see no-one but Sis, and she sees no-one but me. I even sleep in her room. We lie buried under the duvet, as she hugs me tight. It doesn't help me at school, because she begins at the local college, but she's there when I get home from school, and time flies.

Tue

In the second year of college she falls in love with Tue. He is laid-back, smiling and kind, all the things I'm not. Naturally I detest him. He comes and goes as he pleases, kissing my sister and making her smile in a way I haven't seen her smile before, taking her out of the house for hours and days, staying the night. Tue is there all of the time. He is always nice to me, and when he meddles, he does it because he worries about Sis's confused little brother, but I want my sister to myself.

The showdown is inevitable. I just have no idea how, because Sis is in love and it's not at all inconceivable that I could lose it. It happens suddenly and is as surprising to me as it is to him.

18

His cousin has died that day, and he is in Sis's room crying. His levity is of no use to him now. They have played with each other since they were in their nursery, and now his cousin is dead of leukaemia. I have no idea. I know that I have had a miserable day at school. Not five minutes have passed before someone flicks a glob of snot down my neck. I would far rather get a beating, because it's really humiliating that I am counted for so little that people can flob snot at me. Apparently, they have agreed to give me a good going over today. I am wearing my jeans jacket. Dad's had it custom-made for me; my initials are on the breast pocket. It's really cool. He rarely says anything to me, but he gives me a jacket that is one of a kind. To my mind that speaks volumes. They throw it in the urinal, and three of them get over there and piss on it. People gather round and howl with laughter, while I just bawl my eyes out. Piss can be washed out, but I never put on the jacket again, because they have ruined the feeling it gave me. I come home with my piss-soaked jacket in my bag. I need Sis and only Sis, and then Tue is there. I don't even notice that he's crying. I just hear Sis saying, 'Not now, Niko.'

'Yes, right now. He's always here. I want him to leave.' But Sis shakes her head and that's when I start screaming at Tue until I'm quite out of breath, and when I stop to inhale, he takes over. He takes it all out on me. He knows all of my tender spots, and he makes sure to hit each one in turn. He finishes it off by saying, 'And you reek of piss.'

For ten seconds no-one says anything, and then Sis tells Tue with equal measures of anger and misery, 'Get out. I don't want to see you again.' Tue is confused. He tries to touch her, but she pulls away. No-one is to attack me.

Singer Grith Okholm dies in traffic accident

Denmark's most beloved singer, Grith Okholm, passed away in a tragic car crash. Her husband, Allan Jensen, who was driving the car, is still fighting for his life.

Grith Okholm, known for countless classic pop songs – such as 'With You' and 'Storm' – has died. Danish music has lost its most beautiful voice, and Grith Okholm's two children have lost their beloved mother. She was only forty-one. Grith Okholm's daughter, Sanne Okholm Jensen, confirmed to this newspaper that her mother died after a traffic accident in which two cars collided. The accident happened at 2.30 a.m. last night.

Grith died on the spot and without pain. The car was driven by Grith Okholm's husband Allan Jensen, who is presently in the intensive care unit at Rigshospitalet where he is hovering between life and death. The driver of the other car has a broken leg, but otherwise escaped unscathed from the crash.

According to the police it was Allan Jensen who caused the accident when he suddenly changed lanes. The other car had no way of avoiding the collision.

'I don't know what happened. Dad is often a bit absent-minded. He must have nodded off,' Sanne Okholm Jensen, who is visibly upset, tells our reporter.

Grith Okholm and her husband were on their way home from a reception following the launch of her latest album, the stunning *Quiet Days*. There is, however, nothing to suggest that Allan Jensen was under the influence of either alcohol or drugs.

'Dad would never drive if he had had a drink. He's extremely conscientious. He wouldn't do that. He'll just have had an introspective moment and lost concentration briefly,' Sanne Okholm says, as she thinks of her dad who is struggling to survive. The police consider it possible that Allan Jensen may have fallen asleep at the wheel and that this is what led to the tragic accident. Despite her young age Grith Okholm has been part of the Danish music scene for twenty-five years. She is the bestselling artist in Denmark and enjoys great recognition here,

Archive picture

as well as in Norway and Sweden. She will be very much missed by her children and all of us who have loved her bright and cheerful songs.

After they've gone

Sis is angry with herself for allowing people to make her give statements while Dad is dying. So after that we don't speak to the Press. We're going to be ordinary people from now on, and ordinary people are of no interest to the Press.

'Niko, it's just you and me from now on.'

'What do you mean?'

'All we have is each other,' she whispers, while holding my hands so hard it hurts.

I do know that. Why is she saying that?

'What I mean, sweetie, is that we don't need to talk to anyone else, so if anyone speaks to you, you mustn't answer. I'm here for you, and that's all you need.'

She makes me sort of scared.

It's important to Sis that we get to be just the two of us, but unfortunately it's not up to us. Among other things there's a picture spread in *See & Hear*, including a couple of photos of Sis on the beach, wearing a bikini that has ridden up between her buttocks. They've been given the pictures by an old boyfriend of hers – not Tue but some loser she went out with for a very short time. It's an odd choice. They write an article about our grief, and then they say, 'Look, isn't the grieving daughter gorgeous when she's hardly got any clothes on?' Everyone thinks she looks like Mum, and it makes her even more stressed out than she is already.

They don't try to make me glamorous. They know I'm a lost cause. They speak to my Danish teacher, the one I'll beat up two years later.

'He keeps himself to himself, and a lot of people think he is odd, but not me. He's special, that's all.'

Sis is furious. She yells at him for more than half an hour.

'No, you shut up! Listen to me! I don't give a damn whether you did it for the best. You don't speak about my brother, do you hear me? [*Silence.*] Do you hear me?' and then she slams down the phone. He treats me differently after that, but not in a good way.

All the attention we get means that we can't find our feet.

Strangest of all is the reaction of people on the street. A week after my parents have died, a group of little girls come up to me on the street and ask for my autograph, because I'm supposed to be famous. I'm utterly flabbergasted and tell them to fuck off, and then I hurry away. Old ladies ask me if my sister's going to release her own album soon, because they're really looking forward to it. They hope she'll continue in Mum's style, all bright and cheerful and Danish. They too get a 'fuck you.' Grown men give me advice me on how to cope with my rage against my father, a rage that isn't there. They never get a 'fuck you', because it staggers me every time.

I also meet people who actually knew my dad. I'm standing in the supermarket, looking for frozen pizzas when I notice a fat woman on her way over. She's timid, worried about making a mistake.

'Sorry to bother you.'

I nod and look for an escape route, but listen when she says, 'I knew your father.'

'You did?'

'Yes, I worked with him at the Royal Mail. I just wanted to say that I am sorry that he isn't here any more. He was always polite and helpful. Never forget that, no matter what they write about him, don't forget that.'

I start crying, because of those few kindly words. She puts her arms around me gently, and I sink into her gratefully. She stands there with her arms around me for twenty minutes. It's the first time since my parents' death that I don't have a stomach ache.

Granny and Grandad

They turn up out of nowhere. Mum and Dad are dead and were buried more than a month ago when the doorbell rings. I open the door. Outside are an oldish man and woman who look oddly familiar, even though I've never seen them before. There's just something about them that makes me nervous. They seem so stern.

'Nikolaj?'

'Yes.'

'Hello, I'm your grandfather. This is your grandmother.'

My blood turns to ice.

Mum wrote to them a couple of times. She gets a single letter back. It is a very short letter.

Dear Grith Okholm,

We find your letters confusing. You write to us as if we were your family, but clearly we're not.

We once had a daughter, but she died at a very young age. She was only sixteen. Naturally we have seen you on TV and said, golly doesn't she look like our little girl, but only because of your looks, nothing more. For that

24

reason we would like you to not write to us again. You
remind us of the terrible loss of a much loved daughter.

Sincerely,
Leif Okholm

Now they're at our door, and I don't know what to do. Sis isn't home, but she'll be back soon.

'Can we come in? It's nippy today.'

I know they can't, but I say yes all the same. Sis is going to scold me, but they're family and I've got precious little of that.

We're sitting in the sitting room. I've made coffee and put out some biscuits, and there we are.

'Why have you come?' I wonder.

'To see how our grandchild is doing,' says Grandad.

'Who? Me?'

'Yes, who else would it be?'

'There's two of us.'

'Two of who?'

'Me and Sis.'

'Yes, but it's you we've come for.'

That makes me happy. I smile at them. They have my attention now; I am listening, but Grandad doesn't say another word before I hear the door. It's a matter of seconds before she's in the sitting room. I turn to her. Her face tells me she's scared.

'This is Granny and Grandad.'

'I know who they are. What are you doing here?'

The words just tumble out.

'We are visiting our grandchild. He's lost his parents, and we thought he needed his grandparents.'

'Oh, you thought so, did you? You just piss off right now.'

'I think you ought to speak nicely to us.'

'Oh, you do, do you? Piss off.'

'We can leave, but we will be back. We're a family and Nikolaj needs his family right now.'

'You're not our bloody family. Piss off!' she yells angrily.

Grandad gets up slowly, holding Sis's gaze.

'Come then, Mother, we're leaving. Take care of yourself, Nikolaj. We'll be seeing you soon, I'm sure.'

'No, you bloody won't.'

Sis's face has gone completely red. I don't understand why she's so mad.

'You do use some foul language,' Grandad says.

'It's my house. I'll damn well speak any way I choose.'

They leave. Granny, who hasn't said anything yet, suddenly grabs Sis's arm and whispers, 'I'm so sorry.' Sis looks at her, confused, then shakes her off.

I look after them longingly. I turn to Sis with an annoyed look, and then she slaps me: SMACK! I stiffen, I have no idea of how to handle it, and then I retreat, sullenly, to my room. That's the first time my sister cries after my parents' death. It just pours out of her. I turn on my stereo and crank up the volume so that I can't hear her.

*

26

It's more than a week before they get in touch with us again. In the meantime there's been an article in the paper about how they've put aside old grudges, because their grandchild needs them.

"It has been very difficult for him, and we are doing everything we can to protect him. There are some things yet to be resolved, but then he will be moving here," Nikolaj's grandfather, Leif Okholm says.'

I actually do daydream of moving to Jutland to live with them, because I imagine my unease would disappear if I were surrounded by people from the west coast. It would be mild and calm, and nothing would threaten me. Granny and Grandad would give me a solid foundation that would make me a strong young man. I would bring Sis, of course, and we'd all be happy.

Grandad and Granny have teamed up with a lawyer in Copenhagen they got in touch with through the Evangelical Society. He visits my sister and explains to her that she is too young and therefore unfit to look after me.

'Says who? You can't decide that.'

'No, but Social Services can.'

The social worker in charge of my case has taken a liking to Sis. But he just doesn't think that a twenty-year-old girl should have responsibility for a thirteen-year-old boy. Sis has been relatively calm up until now, because there has been no alternative, but then Grandad and Granny turn up, and she gets scared.

The lawyer explains to her that it would be better for me to move to Tarm, where I can have a safe home with healthy boundaries. She, for her part, tells the lawyer that I'm not going anywhere. I'm her little brother, and she is all the family I have.

'Do you think you can handle a teenage lad? They need a firm hand.'

'Like the hand Grandad used to browbeat Mum?'

The lawyer doesn't know what Sis is talking about, so he says, 'Yes, exactly like your Grandad and Granny were firm on your Mum. She probably wouldn't have been as successful if they hadn't been.'

Sis snorts, 'You really are a tosser, aren't you?'

The lawyer sighs, annoyed. Here he is, trying to be polite and sensible, and she insults him, so he threatens her. If she accepts that I must move to Jutland, then she can come and see me, and I can come and see her. But if they must fight for me in court, then she'll lose all contact with me. She can't visit, call or write to me.

Sis looks at him coolly and says, 'I can afford lawyers ten times better than you. I can afford people who will dig up all sorts of dirt on Grandad and Granny. But you know what? It isn't going to go that far. You're an idiot. You've warned me and the second you leave, I'm going to call up some really big, hairy bikers, and they will seriously hurt you if you try to take Nikolaj from me. Now, you are going to leave.'

Sis doesn't call any hairy bikers, because she doesn't know any.

Big, hairy bikers

The next day Grandad calls Sis. He taunts, humiliates and threatens her. I see it, and I hear it. She tries to hang up several times,

28

but the phone seems glued to her hand. She is shaking all over. Grandad scares her.

'Sis, they won't send me away if I don't want to go. They can't.' But Sis isn't too sure about that. She buries her head in her hands and sits without saying anything for a while. Then she gets up with great determination.

'I'm going out. I don't quite know when I'll be back.'

'Where are you going?'

'I'm going to keep my promise.'

Sis goes from one rundown pub to the next. She keeps going until she sees a table full of really big hairy blokes with really scary-looking tattoos. She orders a pint, takes a sip and looks over at their table. They are very big, and my sister is only five foot and seven stone. One of the blokes gets up to go to the toilet, and she immediately takes his seat. The others gawp at this little, luminescent beauty who's sitting herself down at their table with an apologetic smile. She doesn't say anything, she just sits there. The fourth bloke comes back from the toilet.

'Sorry, but you're in my seat.'

'I know. Do you want me to scooch over? We can just sit close together.'

She scooches over, and he sits down, rather surprised. No-one says anything for while, then my sister decides to get on with it.

'Can I tell you something? My parents died in a car crash a month ago. You probably know my mum. Grith Okholm. You know the one who sang "Storm" and "What the Heart Holds". Do you know her?'

They all nod, and she starts crying, partly because there's something to cry about and partly because she's scared. Suddenly, she notices a comforting arm being put around her shoulders. It's the fourth bloke, the one who went to the loo who is putting his arm around her. He's not used to being gentle, but he does his best. She looks up at him and says, 'Thanks.'

'All I've got left now is my brother. If I didn't have him, I don't know what I'd do. He's seven years younger than me, and he's never had an easy time of it. But I've done my best to protect him. I'm just not very strong right now, and I need to be. They're going to take him away from me.'

She senses how the arm around her shoulder tenses up, and she feels the atmosphere around the table reaching boiling point.

'My Grandad wants to take him to Jutland. He never wanted to see us while Mum was alive, because we weren't good enough for him. Now he demands my little brother, but my little brother damn well isn't moving to Jutland to live with a man who whipped my mother bloody just because she fell in love with my dad.'

The arm is really tight around her shoulders now.

'I just don't know what to do. I'm usually quite ballsy, but he frightens me. I'm really scared. He says I'm filth, and I can't give as good as I get.'

Now the comforting arm is actually hurting her. She looks up and at their faces.

'I need help.'

Grandad is surprised when four motorbikes drive into his drive-

30

way one March morning. He says, 'What do you want?', and then he doesn't say anything else for the next half an hour.

He doesn't give up straight away, even though Sis has scared him. He calls us, hangs up if Sis picks up the phone and if I pick up, he makes me promise him that Sis isn't around before he'll speak to me. He's not doing well, I can hear that and I ask, 'What's the matter, Grandad? Why are you wheezing like that?' He tells me – furiously – that my sister set a group of bikers on him. He has two broken ribs. Is that really the sort of person I want responsible for my wellbeing? Oh yes, absolutely! I am proud that Sis would do that for me. Grandad tries to twist my arm. If I want to, I can ask to be removed from Sis's care and come live with them instead. I actually consider it, because I know that Sis will be there for me no matter what. I can let her down, and she will take me back as soon as I apologize. I probably won't even have to apologize. Not to put too fine a point on it, I am considering it, but I pick Sis, because Sis is Sis, and my grandparents are my grandparents. I call them and write to them several times, but once Grandad understands that he has lost, he wastes no more time on me. It hurts to be discarded just like that, which is why I dream vengeful dreams. But I would never have thought that I would one day be an accessory in Grandad's death.

For two months Sis goes out with the fourth bloke. She's not in love, but she is grateful. She feels that she owes him, so she gives him her love for two months.

I am no longer harmless

I have my battles with the world. I don't feel good, but I get by, particularly because Sis has no project besides me. She works at the supermarket twenty-five hours a week, but only to keep herself busy while I'm at school. It's important to Sis that we are as ordinary as we can be, and working at Føtex is as ordinary as it gets.

We settle in to being enough for each other and, for a couple of years, we are, but then, suddenly, I don't want to play along any more. It's not enough to only have Sis love me. I want to be loved by other people as well, so I dream about other people every night. That's where my infatuations start. It's always girls with whom I stand no chance. Miriam is the ultimate infatuation, and – for that very reason – the ultimate failure. Miriam convinces me that I will never have anyone except Sis, and that I must be a terrible human being if only my sister can love me. It makes me furious with myself, but also with all the people who won't love me. Would it be so awful to give me just a little bit of TLC?

I expect Sis to resign from her job after my suicide attempt in order to keep an eye on me, but she doesn't. She takes a couple of weeks off – while I'm suspended from school – but then she returns to Føtex, and even starts working full time. I feel like she's distancing herself from me. She says, 'I might like to start doing stuff.'

'Doing what?'

'Stuff. Rowing, perhaps. Wouldn't you like to do something?'

'Like what?'

'I don't know, sweetie. What would you like? I think you ought to see people besides me.'

'I don't want to be with people besides you.' But she keeps making weird suggestions. I could take up handball, tennis, judo, playing the guitar, and the more she pushes me, the more I feel that she doesn't care for me any more. I am hit by the stomach ache to end all stomach aches.

I don't speak to her about it, but it's obvious that she loves me less now than she did before, and I don't understand why. I miss her being scared of losing me. I want her to fight for me. I need to scare Sis into loving me again.

A scrawny lad

One Thursday night I am standing on a street corner in the centre of town when I spot a group of four guys beating up a scrawny lad. It catches my attention, and I walk over there slowly. He's struggling to keep them off, but they keep getting closer. There's an empty pint glass on the ground. I pick it up and walk a bit nearer. Wow. They're bashing him up, and he's on his back. He gets kicked a couple of times, but somehow he gets up again. He's tough, but they're bigger, and there's more of them, and he's is going to get such a beating.

I move even closer, and by now I'm only a couple of metres away. None of them pay any attention to me. They're all focused – one on surviving, the four others on bashing his head in. I've found what I'm looking for. I whack the pint glass into the biggest bloke's face. The glass splinters, and he collapses with a scream. His hands are covering his face, and blood is seeping out between his fingers. His friends stare dumbfounded at me, and I hit the one closest to me with all I've got. He keels over and slams his head on the pavement. I'm proud and surprised, as I think to myself, 'Golly, I'm good at this.' The last two look straight at me, and just then one of them has the scrawny guy hanging on to him. It's a strange spectacle, because he doesn't punch or kick, he bites. He hangs on to his assailant's cheek, and then he bites off a proper chunk of it. I get all warm inside, and I know I've made the right decision when I see him spit out a great big chunk of cheek. The last of the four guys runs as fast as he can. He leaves his friends bleeding and screaming. I don't do anything. I just wait. The lad looks at me, all surprised, and then he says, his mouth full of another bloke's blood, 'We'd best make a run for it.'

That's how I meet Jeppe. He's my first and, now, my oldest friend. Jeppe is my age, but he looks like he's two or three years younger. He's potty about me, because I saved him and he does-n't know why. I'm there for him, that's all he needs to know. I hang out with Jeppe, have a couple of pints and wait for something to happen. Nothing happens on the first night. Or, as it happens, the next. Or on the one after that. We just wander about town and talk; Jeppe talks and I listen. Jeppe talks non-stop. He talks about everything: cars, football, his plans for the future. Jeppe wants to be a nurse, which is funny because he's the little fucker that all the big fuckers are afraid of.

Once we bump into the guy who ran. He's sitting in the Kongens Have gardens with his girlfriend (and no-one's sitting close to them). Jeppe pulls me over to them and he stands right in front of the guy.

'Hiya, remember us?'

The guy looks up, obviously frightened, which gets Jeppe all keyed up.

'Not here. Not in front of my girlfriend.'

I decide to sit down next to the girlfriend. She's trembling with fear. Jeppe makes a couple of small hops on the spot. It's the adrenaline that makes him jump.

'How are your mates?' Jeppe asks.

'Won't you let my girlfriend go?'

She tries to get up. I grab hold of her arm and – kindly, but firmly – make her sit down again.

'I asked you a question. How are your mates?'

'Been better.'

'That so?' says Jeppe, mockingly.

'Yes.'

I look at Jeppe, highly amused.

'I hear the big hulk is blind now.'

I didn't know that, but it stands to reason that if you throw a glass into a man's eye, that the eye is going to get damaged.

'Yes, he's blind in one eye.'

I feel like taking part in the conversation.

'What's your name?'

For some reason this scares him.

'Claus.'

'And your girlfriend?'

'Lise.'

'Hello, Claus and Lise. How long have you two been going out?'

They don't say anything, so Jeppe kicks Claus's foot lightly.

'We asked you a question.'

'Seven months,' Claus says quickly.

'Now I am going to ask Lise a question, and I want you to be very quiet, Claus.'

Jeppe's all fired up now. He's got no idea what I am up to, but he can see that they're scared.

'Do you love Claus?'

Lise says that she does.

'Is he good to you?'

Lise says that he is.

'So you would hate it if something were to happen to him, wouldn't you?'

Lise says that she would.

'Then why were you trying to leave just now?'

Lise says that she was scared.

'We won't hurt you. Close your eyes.'

Lise asks why.

'You love your boyfriend and then of course you must be with him, but I am going to hit Claus now, and I don't think you should see it.'

I get up. She doesn't shut her eyes. Jeppe is skipping up and down.

'Close your eyes.'

36

Lise says that we mustn't hurt him.

'I promise I'll only hit him once, but you have to close your eyes.'

Lise shakes her head. Claus takes her hand.

'Close your eyes, babe.'

Lise shuts her eyes, and I hit him straightaway. SMACK! It's not my best punch, because I'm standing up and he's sitting down, but he smarts all right. I turn around and leave. Jeppe comes skipping after me. I look back at them discreetly.

Lise has her arms around Claus and is comforting him.

As far as Jeppe is concerned it's always a good night if it's just the two of us talking and play-fighting. We can be walking down the street, and suddenly he'll jump me, knock me over, get on top of me and taunt me – just for the fun of it – until I topple him. I always end up on top, because he doesn't even try to resist me. That's why he's terribly disappointed when we accidentally bump into his older brother Anders, or – as I call him – Satan. That's what he wants to be called, so I oblige. It would be rude not to.

It turns out that I have a reputation for being an up-and-coming young psychopath. It helps that I am Grith Okholm's son. It makes me sexy.

There's no brotherly love lost between Jeppe and Satan; on the contrary, Jeppe is afraid of him. Jeppe fights to hold on to me, but Satan has decided that I'm his, which means that Jeppe hasn't got a chance. In the end he has had enough of Satan, and stays away, but by then he has served his purpose, so thanks a lot, Jeppe. The following year, which I spend with Satan, really scares Sis.

My first time

It's the day before my seventeenth birthday and I am no longer a virgin. Now I've done it. It was all right. It was just odd doing it with someone who was more than ten years older than me. She's lying naked on the bed, even though there are other people sleeping in here. I sneak into the sitting room. Everything has been smashed to pieces, and the room reeks of beer, smoke and vomit. I'm glad I don't live here. Satan's ex does. She's somewhere in Sweden, on the run because Satan beat her. Satan has a key to her flat. She doesn't know that. She's supposed to be nice, reading theatre studies or some such thing, but it's her own fault for going out with Satan. Now the only thing that's being trashed is the flat, and she should be grateful for it. Anyone who deals with Satan gets their comeuppance. That goes for me too. I deserve to feel crummy.

I'm getting out of here. I just need to find my shoes. It's my birthday tomorrow and I want to be home by then, so Sis can sing to me. She's called me twenty times in the last couple of days to make sure I'm still alive. I'll be coming home with a broken finger. It's a good thing that, because it comes with a story of a fist against a face, and those are the best sort of stories because they scare Sis.

Shit! Satan has woken up. He gestures at me to come over. Needless to say, he has the sofa to himself.

'You going?'

'Yes.'

'Great party.'

38

'Yes.'

He sits up, coughs and reaches for a two-litre bottle of Coke on the table. I've seen the cigarette butts floating in it, but I don't tell him that. He takes a hefty swig, and then – as he spits out a cigarette butt – he says, 'Did you fuck Ditte?'

I assume he's talking about the one in the bed, so I nod.

'How was she?'

'What do you mean?'

'Worth giving her a go?'

'She was all right,' I lie.

She was too drunk to understand what was going on, so there wasn't much cooperation. I bend down and look under the sofa.

'You never know with the old ones. Sometimes they won't let you do fuck-all. What are you looking for?'

'I can't find my shoes.'

'You threw them out of the window yesterday,' he says, cheerfully.

'Did I? Why?'

'You threw them at a dog. It was hilarious. It howled when you hit it.'

Satan gets up and heads towards the bedroom.

'When will we see you again?' he asks.

'I don't know.'

'See you when I see you then,' and I nod at him as he goes to join Ditte.

My shoes are gone, so I walk home barefoot. I am ashamed of being out of control. Once I attack a nine- or ten-year-old Turkish boy. He looks provocatively at me, the way nine- or ten-year-old Turkish boys often do, and I lash out at him. He falls down, and before he even hits the ground I've kicked him in the face. It's a little boy! It's a matter of luck that I don't end up killing someone, but I do what I do, based on some very lucid deliberations about what it is that I want to achieve. Sis must worry about *me* and about nothing else.

Brian Birkemose Andersen

I wear Sis out for a year and a half. Skin, nerves, flesh, everything is worn to shreds. She yells and screams, pleads and begs, but it doesn't change anything. I can see her worry; I can hear it; I can feel it; I can smell it; and I feel loved like never before. I repress the fact that my sister can't sleep for fear, because I bask in her terror. I'm gone for long periods of time, for days on end without getting in touch. She doesn't know where I am; I'm just gone. She has no idea whether I'm all right, or whether I'm somewhere all alone, bleeding to death, and then I turn up again, frequently sporting new bruises and always bearing gruesome tales. She tries to hold on to me, speaks to me with sisterly love, but I steel myself against it. One morning she wakes me up. I've come home drunk and fallen into bed. She's sitting on the edge of the bed, and I look at her sleepily.

'What is it?'

She's stroking my back gently.

'You're bleeding.'

I don't think it's anything too serious, and all I say is, 'So?'

'You have a really big gash on your back,' she says and touches it carefully. I squirm with pain.

'How did you get it?'

'Get what?'

'The gash.'

She touches it again, and I writhe.

'Would you please not do that?' and I turn over and look at her. She looks worn out. There are dark circles under her eyes, and there's no strength in her voice.

'How did you get it?'

I look her in the eyes and say, 'I don't know. I was drunk. We got into a fight.'

She nods, gravely.

'Nikolaj, you're going to kill yourself if you keep this up.'

'No, I'm not,' I say and pull the duvet over my head. She stays put on the edge of the bed for half an hour, and I stay under the duvet. When she finally leaves, I get up. I examine the gash in the bathroom mirror. It looks nasty, but I can't let her see that I'm scared. I can't remember being cut. I vaguely remember Satan jumping on some bloke's face, but not that someone cut me. I inspect my jacket. It's torn, but I put it on all the same and try to sneak out without Sis noticing. It's no use: she latches on to me.

'Please stay at home with me, sweetie.'

She holds on to my arm quite tightly, but with an almighty tug I escape her grip. I leave Sis and go to Satan's, where I thrash poor sods and feel sick to my stomach.

I know she hasn't a prayer, because she would never ask anyone else for help, but then one day comes the shocker. It's a couple of weeks before my eighteenth birthday and Sis says she has something to tell me. I expect another homily on how I'm wrecking my life, but that's not it. She has sold the house. It's a huge house in flashy Frederiksberg with a huge garden. Much too big for us, but we've always lived there, which is why it shocks me.

'I've bought three flats with the money. Two are them are investments, the third is for you. You pick one.'

I don't know what to say as I ponder the mathematics of the situation.

'If two of them are let, and I move into the third, then where are you going to live?'

This is where it gets unpleasant.

'I'm moving in with Brian.'

'Brian who?'

'Brian Birkemose Andersen.'

'I don't know who Brian Birkemose Andersen is,' I say, annoyed.

'He's my boyfriend.'

'You haven't got a boyfriend.'

Sis smiles.

'I've got Brian.'

And that's how it is.

Sis makes it abundantly clear that we won't be seeing each other for a long time. Her new boyfriend says that she has to think about herself if she's not to wipe herself out entirely. Sis is so worn down that she agrees with him, particularly because he makes her feel safe. Now's my time to plead, but it's no good. She needs to have a long break from me, and have Brian look after her and help her get her strength up. There's nothing I can do to change that, and for that reason I pick the flat that's furthest away – a two bedroom place in upmarket Hellerup. It's a cop-out. For eighteen months I've done a whole load of things I shouldn't have, but there was a reason for my doing them. Now there isn't a reason to any longer. I have to get out now, so I hole myself up in the flat in Hellerup.

I go out every day, but only because I'm forcing myself to stick to a strict schedule. I shop at Netto's, buy whatever I need and pop by Blockbuster on Strandvejen. I never shop for more than a day at a time, because if I did I most likely wouldn't leave the flat. I've got the fastest Internet connection, the biggest TV package, a massive television, and I order music, books, games and films online every day, so I'm pretty much self-sufficient. I haven't had a single ongoing physical contact for more than a year, with the exception of one person, Sis's thirty-seven-year-old optician and now boyfriend Brian Birkemose Andersen. Brian is an ugly man, because he looks like a pudgy gnome, but he's a good sort, and Sis needs a good sort.

She phones me every day at exactly 7 p.m., and I dutifully pick up the phone every time. I don't say much – apart from whining – because nothing much happens in my life. Often we just sit holding the phone, knowing that we're listening to each other's breath. I sit for so many hours in silence and yet engrossed in conversation. Of course, I hope that every conversation will end with an invitation, but no. She keeps in touch, but keeps her distance. Brian is her temporary substitute.

Every Thursday my doorbell rings, and there's Brian. I remember the first time I heard the bell. I open the door as surprised as can be, and there's a very ugly man standing on my doormat.

'Hello, Nikolaj.'

'Who are you?'

'My name's Brian. I'm your sister's boyfriend.'

'You are taking the piss.'

'No.'

'But you look like shit.'

'Oh well, um, right. How are you?'

I understand precisely fuck-all.

Brian comes by every Thursday to make sure I look all right. He's my sister's eyes and ears, and at first all he does is look. He rings the doorbell. I open. He asks how I'm doing. I say I'm okay. He says 'Good' and leaves. I can sort of accept that. I don't like him, but I know why he pops by, and he doesn't meddle more than he has to. But the more he and Sis become an item, the more he feels that he must take an interest in her disturbed little brother. Nowadays a conversation is required. He invites himself in, sits himself down and talks to me. I can't count the number of times I ask Sis to make him shut up, but she says that if I want a proper relationship with her again, I must get on with Brian. I need to talk to other people. Other people, perhaps, but not Brian. He doesn't really care. He does it for Sis. I am merely her disturbed little brother.

One day I have had it. He tells me about Sis and him going to the zoo, and he gets up to show me how the elephants danced for them. While he dances like an elephant in my kitchen, I strike at him. I aim for the nose – that's always a good one – but he fools me. He looks harmless, big and clumsy, and I underestimate him. He sees the punch, easily evades it and comes up close, and then he hugs me so tight I can't move. He holds me close, soaring above the floor, while I thrash about like a fish on the shore. He just stands like that until I relax. He lets go of me, and I consider jumping him again, but I daren't. He's fast, and he's strong, like the elephant he resembles.

'Well now, I'd best be off. See you in a week, Nikolaj.'

He doesn't tell Sis, which pisses me off all the more. He considers me of so little importance that he doesn't even have to tell. That's why I devise a means of getting even. When he rings my doorbell the following week, I open the door, pick up the bucket and throw the contents at him. He doesn't have time to move, and he's covered from head to toe in my vomit. He looks himself up and down. He's almost sick, making a couple of spastic movements. He looks at me sadly, then turns and leaves. I think I have won, but at 7 p.m. on the following night the phone doesn't ring. Nor does it on the night after that, nor for all of the following week. The knot in my stomach explodes, and I drink until I'm dazed to handle the pain. On the Thursday after that my doorbell rings, and I open the door, like a good boy, to Brian.

The invite

I haven't seen Sis for fifteen months. It's a long time, and I weep with joy the night she invites me over for dinner.

I get a taxi to drive me to 10 Peder Skrams Gade. It's on the fourth floor and with each step up the stairs, I shake even more. I try to control myself, but I realize it's a lost cause. I stand hesitantly outside the door, ringing the bell. Brian opens. I expected Sis to rip the door open and throw herself into my arms, but instead I get Brian, who shakes hands. I'm surprised by how stilted and awkward it seems. He shows me into the sitting room. There's Sis. She's every bit as nervous as I am, and on top of that she's fat in a strange way, not really fat and yet sort of big. She gets up and falls into my arms, as much as she can with her belly sticking out. There we are then, bawling away.

'You've grown so skinny, Niko.'

'I'm not skinny. You've grown fat.'

She gives me a playful slap.

'I'm not fat, you prat. I'm pregnant,' and I faint.

I wake up in the middle of the night. I'm lying in their bed. Sis is sitting next to me, holding my hand. She's only partly awake.

'You're really pregnant?'

She makes herself wake up and looks at me tenderly.

'You okay?'

'You're pregnant?' I ask, sceptically.

'Yes, six months gone. Aren't you happy?'

I don't say anything, because I don't know what to say. What a mess. She asks me again.

'Yes, of course I am,' I say.

It's a lie, but it's what she wants to hear. She lies down next to me, holding me. I find her hand. We're so close I can feel her breath. When she exhales, there's a gentle breeze caressing my back.

'I've missed you. You do know that, don't you?' Sis says.

'I know.'

'But now we're together again, and you're about to have a nephew. That means that everything is finally going to be okay.'

She caresses my chest gently.

'It's a boy?'

'Mmm.'

'Let's hope he doesn't look like Brian, then.'

She doesn't say anything.

'You do realize he's butt ugly?'

'He's kind to me.'

'I should bloody well hope so, because he is one ugly bugger.'

'That's enough,' Sis says, and gives me another affectionate smack.

'He is.'

We lie together in silence for a while. It's nice.

*

I visit them frequently, but it doesn't feel right. I'm the guest who visits. Brian has more right to be there than I do. Her big tummy has more right to be there than I do. Sis loves it when I'm there, but that's just not enough. She's doing so well, she is able to cope with more than just me. It hurts every time I leave, simply because I have to leave.

One day I pop by, and she's not there. After a year of utter isolation it doesn't take very much before fear overwhelms me. A locked door will do the trick. It's happened once before when I sat down and waited. It was an hour or so before she appeared, snorting and panting, carrying a shopping bag. She could see that I had cried, even though I tried to hide it, and it made her feel sad and miserable. This time, too, I sit down, waiting and crying, with a god-awful stomach ache. An hour passes, then another, and another, until the whole afternoon is gone. It's on the top floor, which means that no-one sees me. I am convinced Sis has fled from me, but of course she hasn't. As it happens she is in the middle of a long, complicated labour. Brian calls me at home repeatedly, but I don't pick up because I'm not there. I don't have a mobile, because I'm hardly mobile myself. Sis refuses to give birth until I know. I should preferably be there, because the labour itself is making her superstitious. If something new comes into the world, then something old must leave it, and she's worried it might be me. In the end she sends Brian. He objects, but it's no good. He breaks all kinds of traffic regulations to get to my flat, rings the doorbell, but I don't answer. He breaks down the door. It splinters. He drives down to Blockbuster, no luck. Where the hell can I be?

And then it hits him. He drives to 10 Peder Skrams Gade as fast as he can, darts up the stairs, and there I am. I'm a sorry sight. I see Brian as through a haze. He picks me up, carries me down the stairs, puts me on the back seat, and then we're off to the hospital. I am left in a waiting room with a blanket over me. Brian walks briskly to Sis's room. Nothing much has happened since he left, because Sis refuses. When he comes in, Sis looks at him with a hope that's ready to burst.

'He's just outside, resting under a blanket. He was sitting outside our door.'

Within half an hour I have a nephew. He's called Allan after my dad. I don't have a close relationship with him. I don't intend to have one. Not because I don't want to, but because I can't.

When Allan arrives, they're suddenly a family. Before they were just a couple, and Sis and I were the family. Now they're mum, dad and child. I try to swallow my agony in silence, but Sis notices. She constantly asks me how I'm doing, but there's a little bawler who needs her love even more than I do.

'Isn't he the sweetest?' she says as we lean over his cot.

'Allan?'

'Yes, Allan. Your nephew. Isn't he just adorable?'

She picks him up, rocking him proudly back and forth, then holds him out for me to take, but I don't want to.

'Go on, Niko, hold him.'

I shake my head. She tries to force him into my arms, but I dodge the attempt, and he starts to cry. Sis holds him close, and when he is finally calm again, she turns on me.

49

'What the fuck is the matter with you?'

She's never asked me that before. I can't take it.

One day I pick up the phone and call her to say goodbye.

Goodbye

ME: Hello, it's me.

SIS: Hello you. When are you coming over?

ME: I think I might stay in today.

SIS: Are you ill?

ME: No, I'm fine.

SIS: You've seemed a bit unwell lately.

ME: I'm not ill.

SIS: You've got even skinnier.

ME: So?

SIS: You have. How much do you weigh?

ME: I don't know.

SIS: I'd bet you're less than ten stone, and you're taller than six foot, you know.

ME: I weigh more than that.

SIS: How much more?

ME: I don't know. I haven't been on a pair of bathroom scales for years.

SIS: Then you don't actually know how much you weigh.

ME: (*Silent.*)

SIS: You really must start eating more. You never used to be this skinny.

ME: (*Silent.*)

SIS: Hello? Niko?

ME: I hear you.

SIS: Yes, but do you? Are you actually listening to what I'm saying?

ME: Yes, but it doesn't really matter, does it?

SIS: You need to look after yourself. That's why you fall ill, you know.

ME: I'm not ill.

SIS: Then why aren't you coming over?

ME: Because.

SIS: That's not an answer. You're not five years old, are you? Why aren't you coming?

ME: Because I don't want to.

SIS: Well, I want you to. I actually really want you to.

ME: Stop it, will you? I'm not coming. It's my own bloody business.

SIS: Of course it is. I'm not saying it isn't.

ME: (*Silent.*)

SIS: (*Silent.*)

ME: How's Allan?

SIS: He's fine.

ME : Good. How's Brian?

SIS : He's fine too. You know, you saw them two days ago. It's not like a great deal has happened since then.

ME : Are you happy?

SIS : Why do you ask?

ME : I just want to know. Are you?

SIS : Sure, I'm happy.

ME : I mean, are you really happy?

SIS : I feel a lot better than I have in a long time.

ME : Yes, but are you happy?

SIS : I've become a mum.

ME : Sis, just tell me. Please.

SIS : Sweetie, what do you want me to say? My heart aches when I speak to you. No, I'm not happy. How can I be happy when you're not?

ME : I know. That's why I'm doing it.

SIS : Doing what? What are you doing?

ME : I love you very much, Sis.

SIS : What is it you are doing, sweetie?

ME : I've been such a bastard to you. You've always been so good to me, and I've been the greatest arsehole in the entire world.

SIS : You're not an arsehole.

ME : Yes I am. I'm evil.

SIS : Don't say that. Don't you ever say that.

ME : I am. I'm glad you've got Brian and Allan.

SIS : I've got you too.

ME : No, you haven't. You haven't got the time or room for me.

SIS : Nikolaj, you're not doing something stupid are you?

ME : It's not stupid.

SIS : You haven't done something stupid yet, have you?

ME : You can't be happy while I'm still around. I'm doing it
for your sake.

SIS : WHAT HAVE YOU DONE?

ME : Bye, Sis.

Suicide attempt No. 2

I hang up and sit down, waiting to die. Five minutes later I'm still sitting with my eyes wide open. Paracetamol is a shit painkiller. I feel like I ought to stay put, even though I'm bored. I try to, but in the end it's too much. I watch *Beverly Hills 90210* and notice a drowsiness come over me ever so slowly. Maybe it's death. I focus on the drowsiness, but my concentration is interrupted by a frantic pounding on the door. It's Sis, of course. She's not supposed to be here until it's too late, but here she is after all. She's been quick. Christ Almighty, what a racket she makes. I try to block out the noise, but it's impossible to focus on dying when Sis is pounding on the door like that. The neighbour has come out now. Sis begs him to do something. My neighbour is a nice guy. We always say hello when we meet. He tries to break open the door, but after Brian smashed my door to pieces I got myself a really sturdy door, so he fails. He bruises his shoulder, that's all. The pain makes him swear, but while Sis is yelling and crying he can't just give up.

'The door's solid. It hurts.'

He's nice, but a bit of a wimp. It's not classy to die while watching *90210*, so I get up to turn it off and that's when the pills hit me. I fall down with a serious stomach ache.

'What was that?'

'What?'

'I heard a noise.'

'From inside the flat? That's a good thing, isn't it? Then he isn't dead.'

'I want to get to my brother right now!' sobs my glorious sister.

I'm lying on the floor. I can't breathe, and I shit myself. It's far more unpleasant than I'd planned. More people arrive on the stairs. Again there's a pounding and a bashing on my door, but there's a lot more power behind it now. My eyelids slide shut, but I force them open with a final exertion of will as I hear the door breaking open. Just before I lose consciousness I see Sis's face contracted in terror. It's going to be a good death after all.

But I don't die. On the contrary, I get my hopes up again, because Sis makes a decision which tells me how important I am to her. While she struggles to save me, my little nephew is home alone. Sis has forgotten all about him, because right now I'm the only thing that matters to her. For four hours he cries, and then his dad comes home to an unlocked flat with an abandoned baby who just cries and cries. He picks up his son, holds him against his chest until both father and son relax.

When Sis comes home, her boyfriend is white-hot with anger. Since he has finally got Allan to sleep Brian doesn't yell at Sis, but he is aggressive without raising his voice. Sis tries to explain, but Brian doesn't care. She simply cannot leave a six-month-old baby home alone. Sis sinks into the easy chair and allows Brian to yell at her softly. She doesn't defend herself. That makes him even more furious. Why doesn't she plead for forgiveness? Why doesn't she promise it won't ever happen again? She can't, that's why. Sis is sorry for what she's done to her little boy, but her sweetie was about to take his life.

Just the two of us

Major trouble is afoot between Sis and Brian. A single wrong word about me, and Sis will scream at Brian until tears spray from her eyes. She'll sit in another room, bawl and wait for Brian to apologize, but Brian refuses to apologize, because I am nothing but a little turd. Neither of them is prepared to yield.

I'm no longer allowed in their flat. Brian doesn't want to be bothered by me, so Sis and I go out for meals, nip into the National Museum to look at art, or go to the cinema. Slowly Sis starts to associate life at home with hardship and strife. Suddenly, I am her refuge. It's a lovely time, and we get every bit as close as we were just after Mum and Dad died. The knot in my stomach is still there, but it doesn't poke and tear at me. It only gives me the occasional twinge to remind me that I can't feel too safe. Her worry has become warm, calm and sad, which makes me feel happy and all juiced up. She so wants me to get a real life with a girlfriend and friends, but I'm happy as long as I've got her.

We're sitting in Sticks 'n' Sushi on Strandvejen when she tells me that she's started sharing her worries with Jesus.

'You talk to Jesus?'

'Yes. I say a prayer every night.'

'Why?'

I try to catch a *nigiri* with my chopsticks, but I'm useless with chopsticks, so I pick it up with my fingers and dip it in the soy sauce. Sis chews very slowly, so she won't have to say anything. She's embarrassed. When she finally finishes chewing, she says, 'Mum did it.'

'Mum was from Jutland. You never used to believe in God.'

'No, and I still don't. I just like the things Jesus says.'

'What's that?'

Sis puts another fish in her mouth and chews slowly. I wait for her to finish. She considers the question carefully.

'It's about love, about comfort and forgiveness, and he listens to everything I say.'

'You can talk to me about everything too.'

Sis shakes her head.

'No, sweetie, I really can't. I can't talk to you about you, and you are all I think about. And you know how Brian feels about you. So who does that leave me to talk to?'

I don't get it. Sis isn't the type who needs to believe in anything.

'It's just weird, that's all.'

'So you say. All he has to do is listen, and give me someone to talk to. That's all I need,' she says, but of course she needs more than that.

Silje

I fall in love for the first time since Miriam. I meet her at my regular haunt, Sankt Peder. I frequently go on a bender alone, sit down at Sankt Peder's and stay put till they close; then I slink home with a feeling of being just like everyone else. She's sitting at a table with a dark-haired tomboy and a slight bloke. They're talking about me. Not in a bad way, though. They're just curious. Suddenly the slight bloke is standing in front of me.

'Hi, I'm Jakob. I'm sitting with this beautiful blonde girl who thinks you look nice. How would you like to come and sit with us?'

It takes me aback, and I blurt out, 'I suppose that'd be all right.' I sit down next to the blonde girl. Her name is Silje. She gives me a shy smile. The two others sit on the other side of the table. On autopilot, Jakob asks what I do for a living.

'Nothing. I don't do anything.'

'You're unemployed?'

'No.'

'Studying?'

'No, I just don't do anything,' I repeat.

'Then how do you make ends meet?' he asks, surprised.

'I'm rich.'

Now the dark-haired girl asks me. Her name is Camilla.

'Rich how? Did you make your own money?'

'No, my parents did.'

'You're living on your parents' money? Isn't that a bit sad?

I don't even get a contribution for my train fare home.'

I shrug, indifferently. She's not the one who thinks I look nice, so I don't really care what she thinks of me.

'They're okay with your doing nothing, are they?'

'I don't know.'

'What do they do?'

'They're dead.'

And with that the table falls silent. I have no idea if I'm doing the right thing, but I say, 'They died in a car crash when I was thirteen.'

They're still not saying anything.

'And my mum left quite a pretty penny.'

'Your mum?' Silje says.

'Yes, my mum. She was a pop singer. My dad was a postman.'

Silje mumbles, 'Your mum was a pop singer, and she died in a car crash?'

'Yes, my dad fell asleep at the wheel.'

'Not Grith Okholm? Is your mum Grith Okholm?'

I hear the thrill of anticipation in her voice.

'Yes, that's my mum.'

They fall silent again. They look excitedly at each other, and then Silje says timidly, 'I'm the lead singer. Jakob's the bass player, and Camilla's the guitarist in Grith Okholm Jam.'

The rest of the evening Silje talks about the unperceived depth in Mum's songs and about tunes that have a beauty no other Dane has come close to attaining. She laughs a lot, even touches me occasionally and smiles, while looking affectionately at me. I'm not used to that kind of attention from beautiful girls and it makes me strangely flustered. I stammer and say all the wrong things, followed by a nervous giggle; but the more flustered I get, the more she touches me. I'm fit to burst.

After a while the other two leave. They say their goodbyes, not even trying to get Silje to come with them, happily leaving her with me. It has to be said that I must seem anything but dangerous as I stammer and blush.

At 2 a.m. Sankt Peder closes for the night, and it's time to say goodnight to Silje. We give each other a hug and face each other awkwardly.

'I've had a really lovely time. It's been great talking to you,' Silje says.

'Me too. It's been fun,' and then we don't say anything for what seems like absolutely ages. We just stand there looking at each other in anticipation, but then Silje says, 'Don't you want to see me again?'

I manage to say, 'Yes, that'd be great.'

She smiles.

'Well, good. Have you got a pen?'

I have a rummage through my pockets and pull out a pen.

'My number's 22416936. Did you get that? 22416936.'

'Got it,' I say, and show her the number written on my hand.

'You'll call me?'

'Yes.'

'When?'

I'm taken aback and mumble, 'I don't know. Do I have to tell you now?'

'Will you call me tomorrow?'

'I don't know.'

'I think you should call me tomorrow.'

'Okay, I'll call you tomorrow then.'

'Good. I'll look forward to it,' she says, then she kisses me quickly on the lips.

The next day I'm actually physically sick with apprehension. I'm convinced she doesn't really want me to call her. Late in the evening I press the first four numbers, then hang up. I lie down, sad and disappointed, and try to make myself sleep. At one minute past midnight the phone rings.

'Hello.'

'Hi. I thought you were going to call me.'

It's a few seconds before I recognize Silje's voice.

'Yes,' I mumble, embarrassed.

'Good. I'm going to hang up now, and then you phone me.'

'What?'

'I'm hanging up, and then you're going to phone me.'

'Why?'

'Because that's what we agreed,' and then she hangs up.

I look at the phone with confusion, but finally manage to dial her number.

'Hello, it's Silje.'

'It's Nikolaj.'

'My, you're calling late,' she says, teasingly.

'Yes, well, that's because…

'You don't have to apologize. Did you have a good day?'

'I've had a great day.'

'What have you been up to?'

'Nothing much.'

'Then why didn't you call me sooner?'

'I'm sorry.'

'Don't apologize. We're talking now, aren't we? I just want to know.'

'I was too nervous. I was sick.'

Silence.

'You were? That's so sweet.'

And that's how I become Silje's boyfriend.

During all of the time I go out with Silje, I keep a lookout for the monster under the bed, but no boo is heard. If the knot in my stomach wasn't there I might relax, trust her and myself, but the knot is there! It tells me that everything can fall to pieces, and that things will likely go wrong in a painful way.

It's difficult for me to get used to being with her. I have to take an interest in things, including her band, but I don't think it's cool that she sings in Grith Okholm Jam. It's too incestuous, and I tell her as much. She thinks it's disgusting of me to use such a word, but she accepts that I'm not going to see her perform, even though it means a lot to her. She'd like me to share the experience with her, but I don't want to. She also insists that we don't get stuck on the sofa. She forces me to spend time with her friends. She studies music at uni, and I'm dragged along every time Camilla picks up a guitar. Camilla doesn't trust me. There's something not quite right about me, but as long as I make Silje happy she'll tolerate me. She actually threatens me. She says, 'Nikolaj, if you ever hurt Silje, I'll get you. I'll make you regret it. I promise.' It's a feeble threat, because of course I'll regret it, but Camilla scares me a little bit nonetheless.

What I find particularly strange is the touching. My muscles contract when Silje touches me too much. I push her away and start massaging my calf. It's usually my left calf which cramps up – very strange that, because my calf plays no central part in the cuddling. Silje has never petted my calf.

During the very early stages of our relationship we're not all that physical. One day when we're sitting on the sofa, kissing, I put my hand between her legs. She holds her breath in anticipation. My hand is just lying there; I'm not sure what to do with it, so I just let it slide back and forth. I feel like a prat, but suddenly I'm a prat with no trousers on. I barely catch on before she has got my cock out, whipped off her own trousers and got on top of me. Her cunt is clutching my cock, and I'm not thinking about holding back, I'm not thinking about performing, I'm just on the receiving end. I come inside her, and I apologize for my performance straight away.

'I've come. Sorry,' I say, sheepishly.

'Yes, I know. I mean, I could see, hear and feel that. Don't apologize.'

I'm still inside her. She's sitting on top of me, fondling me. I'm still wearing my shirt, but she's unbuttoning it now and strips it off me. She throws it on the floor and lets her hand run through the hair on my chest. She kisses me all over my face and down my neck. Then she whispers, 'We're taking it nice and slow, Niko, and you're going to get lots of opportunities to make me scream like a madwoman.'

She speaks with a sweetness that calms my nerves.

Now she's kissing my nose.

'You're weird, but I love you.'

It's the first time either of us says it. She starts rocking gently back and forth while she continues to talk.

'It means a lot to me that that you risked doing this. It's so fucking sexy – it's not just about endurance.'

By now my cock has started growing again. I'm still not doing anything, as she ever so gently rocks back and forth, telling me how lovely it is to be with me. I don't say anything; I listen, enjoying the sensation of being inside her. She chatters away. Most of it I get, but not everything, because the feeling of having her is loud inside my head. I don't make her scream the second time we shag either, but at least I don't have to apologize again.

I love you

She bends down to get the good saucepan out, and I want to take her doggy-style as she stands there, flaunting her arse. I keep quiet. She's proud of her chilli, and I shouldn't interrupt her. It's been several weeks since she said she loved me. She's said it a couple of times since then as well. I've said thank you. I know she's waiting for me to say it to her, and the words are ready in my mouth. I go into the kitchen. She turns around and smiles at me, just a quick smile telling me that I'm lucky, and then she focuses her attention on the chilli. I walk over and hold her from behind. We're standing still like that for a minute or so.

'Niko, you're going to have to let me go, or the chilli will burn.'

'Silje Kjær, I love you so fucking much.'

It's only a few words, but it's huge. I sense that from the effect they have, because I take her on the worktop, and she doesn't care that the chilli burns, and the good saucepan is ruined. I feel punch-drunk with love, but most of all I feel scared, because it can't last. Fuck happiness if it isn't strong enough to give me peace of mind.

Sis and Silje

For more than six months Sis knows nothing about Silje. She can sense something has happened, but I won't tell her what it is, nor how huge it is – and it really is huge. It's easy enough to keep them apart, because Sis and I plan ahead every week, so I always know when we'll be seeing each other, and Silje knows that I need time on my own. I've told her that I'm seeing Sis, but that I do it more out of a sense of obligation than because I want to. Why do I need them apart? Because they belong to me, not to each other. I don't want to share.

*

Silje drags me along to a party in Camilla's flatshare in Prins-essegade and, as usual, I seek out a quiet corner, sit down unobtrusively, and wait politely for when we might be able to leave. Silje is out there, proving to herself that she is a sociable human being, even though her boyfriend is an antisocial chap. Every once in a while she pops by, kisses me, snuggles up a bit, and then is back out there. Once she comes dancing up to me with a big smile on her face.

'I've come to say hello.'

'You've come to say hello?'

She kisses me.

'Yes, from one of Camilla's cousins' colleagues, Brian.'

'Brian's here?'

'No, he just left, but he said to say hello.'

I go pale.

'Did you talk to him?'

'Yes.'

'What about?'

She doesn't understand my fear. How could she? She doesn't know what she has ruined.

'About us. Niko, what's the matter?'

She tries to pet me, but I push her hand away.

'What did you tell him?'

'Nothing.'

She tries to pet me again, but I grab her hand and hold on to it.

'You must have said something.'

'Not really. I just said that we've been going out for seven months. I was just making conversation, Niko. Who is he?'

What am I supposed to say? That he's a good sort who unfortunately is my sister's boyfriend? I let go of her hand and get up.

'I'm going home.'

'Niko, don't,' but she goes home with me. Camilla tries to persuade her to stay, but Silje just shakes her head and says, 'No, I can't let Niko go home alone when he feels like this.' Camilla is pissed off.

The next morning while I'm in the shower I hear the doorbell ringing, and I know that my two worlds are about to collide. I dry myself off slowly, put on my underpants and a T-shirt, take a deep breath, and go out to meet them.

Silje is confused, and Sis is delirious with joy. Today is their day, not mine. They only have eyes for each other. I have a girlfriend; I have let someone into my life, and it takes such a weight off my sister that she's almost high. She stays for two interminable hours. Two hours of which I can't remember a single word that was said. I just remember the basic atmosphere. She keeps touching Silje, as if to make sure she's really there. It looks strangely off, almost sexual. She seems in love, gaga over Silje, in that state where you just need to touch the object of your affection. She laughs, giggles. At one point she kisses Silje fervently. Not as lovers kiss, but the way I have seen devout people kiss the cross, and that's what Silje is: a symbol for my sister to put her faith in. Silje tries to keep up, but she doesn't understand where this enormous reaction is coming from, and she gets no help from me, although her entire body is pleading for it. I say nothing. I simply stare, despairing, into thin air. Allan is invited to a birthday party at one of his friend's from the crèche. If he wasn't, Sis would never have left. Before she leaves, she holds me for a good ten minutes, filled with more hope than ever before.

'Everything's going to be all right now.'

Damn me if she doesn't believe it, too! When I hear Sis running down the stairs happily, I turn to Silje. She is frowning, looking bewildered.

'She's nothing like I expected.'

'No, she probably isn't.'

'It doesn't seem like you don't get along.'

I take a few steps away from her, turn my back to her, and say as calmly as possible, 'Doesn't it?'

She follows me.

'No, it doesn't, Niko. Actually, she seems to really love you a lot.'

'Hmm.'

'Don't hmm me, Niko, and do turn around and look at me when I'm speaking to you.'

I turn around, looking at her anxiously.

'We've been going out for seven months, and for seven months you've told me that the only thing you share with your sister is your surname, but that's not true, is it?'

'No.'

'Because the two of you are really quite close.'

'Yes,' I admit.

'Why did you lie about it?'

'I don't know.'

'How often do you see your sister?'

I hesitate.

'Twice a week.'

'Every week? Why have you kept her a secret?'

'I don't know. Please stop asking me, won't you?'

'You're weird.'

'Right.'

'You are.'

'I was weird before this happened.'

'Yes, but you're even weirder now.'

We say no more about it. Silje is insufferable to be around for several days after, but Sis is now a part of Silje's life, and vice versa.

After that a lot of things change. I don't have to hide anything any longer, and that ought to be a good thing, but it's not. Inside me the knot tears and gnaws at me. It hurts like crazy, but still I try to accept that everything has been changed. Then Silje starts to annoy me a bit, and then a bit increasingly becomes a bit more. It isn't her fault. She's as lovely as ever, but she wrecks my carefully planned life by loving me.

Sis's tactics are clever. She knows that I'm not likely to just hand Silje over, and that's why Sis takes a shortcut. We meet up as usual. She – of course – talks about Silje, but for the longest time it's no more than enthusiastic chatter, until one day she says, 'Why don't you bring Silje along next time? It'd be nice if we could all do something together.'

'She wouldn't like it. She's a very private person,' I mutter.

'She would like it. I'm sure of it. She's not shy.'

'She really is.'

'No, she really isn't,' my sister says, all geared up for battle.

'She's my girlfriend. You've met her once.'

'Niko, I've met her many times.'

She's been out for meals with Silje; Silje has been to their flat, has said hello to Allan and Brian; they talk on the phone regularly about everything, especially about me. Sis has adopted Silje, and vice versa. They're using each other, and they're using each other vis-à-vis me. It's Sis who has asked Silje not to tell me, because she worries about my reaction, worries that I might get in the way of things. I feel betrayed, and I run away without another word. Sis calls after me, but I don't care. I know I'm behaving like a ten year old, but sometimes I really am just ten. I come home to the flat. Silje is there already. She has her own key now. We might move in together soon.

'Hey, babe.'

I don't say anything. I just go straight to the bedroom and lock the door angrily. Silje comes to the door and tries to reach me. I am deaf, but I'm not so deaf that I can't hear the phone ringing. It's difficult to make out the conversation, but there's no doubt it's Sis calling, and it's only ten minutes before Silje's voice isn't the only one trying to reach me. I have to concede defeat. I open the door, looking at them in anticipation. Then Sis's hand moves up Silje's back. She gives her a gentle push towards me, and Silje falls lovingly into my arms. It's a shite push, because so many things would have been different if Silje had taken a step back instead.

I go along with pretending to be happy, because the forces willing me to pretend are too powerful for me to refuse. I am now part of a couple, just like Sis is part of a couple, and couples meet. Their flat is no longer out of bounds, although Brian still looks at me askance. He still looks at me with profound scepticism, but Silje's smile makes him relax. At one point he takes me aside.

'I don't know how you've pulled this off, but you've managed to get yourself a really lovely girlfriend. Don't mess it up.'

'Likewise.'

Which is an idiotic reply, because Brian is nothing like me.

Things are so good, they can only go wrong. Sis and Brian think it's great that she pays tribute to Mum, and now I am being made to take an interest. Not long after I'm standing at a concert with my sister and brother-in-law gawping at my girlfriend, who looks and sounds like my mum, and I feel sick. I refuse to touch her for more than a week after the concert. The relationship is increasingly less on my terms, and I can tell that my will and ability to love is disappearing bit by bit. I would so like to hold on to that will and ability.

I'm not blind to the irony of it. The worse I feel, the better Sis feels, and the ironic thing is that she feels better because she thinks I feel better. My fear that Sis will stop loving me takes up more and more space. One day Sis won't be bothered with me, because other things are better and more important. I manage to keep the knot at bay, but in order to do so I need them to not put added pressure on me. I need Sis not to say, 'We're going off to Thailand for a month. We've never been on holiday together, and now we're going. What about you two? Shouldn't you and Silje go on a trip somewhere?'

I want to scream, 'How can you think everything is all right, everything is normal? Don't you get that I'm in agony?' but I don't. I try to accept it, because of course I have moved on. I happen to have a girlfriend who loves me, but I also have a truly horrendous stomach ache. I let them go without saying anything. The first week is difficult, and I snap at Silje. The second week is more difficult, and she begins to see that I'm dangerous. She's never been afraid of me, because I've never given her reason to. I do now, and she – clever girl – keeps her distance. The third week is just too much, and that's when I do it. My entire body is tense, and the air is so thick that I have to bite it to bits. I start crying, and Silje instinctively holds me.

'Will you please let go of me?'

'Niko, don't.'

'Let go of me!'

She doesn't let go of me; she wants to protect me. I grab hold of her arms and wrench them off me.

'Nikolaj, that hurts!'

My fist flies off on its own. I hit her hard in the stomach, and she falls over in abject despair. She can't breathe, so she can't scream for help. I think, 'What the fuck are you doing? Stop it, you tosser!' but instead of helping her I sit down astride her and let the punches rain down on her. I start to apologize every time I hit her,

71

and inside my head I scream, 'Won't you stop? Please! You're hurting her, and I'll never forgive you. Stop. Won't you, please?', but it's no good.

When my fist finally stops, she's lying bloody and unconscious on the sitting-room floor. I lie down next to her, kissing her tenderly over and over and over. We lie close together one last time. I fall asleep with a strange feeling of calm in the knowledge that these are the last hours I will ever be holding her. She wakes up screaming. She almost can't see a thing, because her eyes are really swollen, but she's aware that I'm holding her. I have to let go of her, and I pull away into the room, away from her because I haven't got the words to make it better. She stumbles blindly around, looking for the door, finding it and tumbling down the stairs and out on to the street.

Through the open window I can hear her call, 'Help me! Someone please help me!'

I'm covered in Silje's blood, and my knuckles are sore. Outside, on the street, there's yelling and shouting, and not long after the police and an ambulance arrive. I await my punishment, but they're not coming up for me. There go the police. I don't understand. Why aren't they coming, truncheons at the ready? Why aren't they coming up to dispense brutal police violence? There ought to be truncheons pounding my back, boots stomping on my face.

Hours pass, and then the phone rings. I putter listlessly over to pick it up. The line buzzes and hums, but Brian's voice is clearly audible.

'I'm going to kill you, you little turd.'

It ought to scare me, because I can hear he is in earnest, but instead it makes me smile. He wants to kill me, and I'm grateful.

Silje never tells the police that I did it. It was random violence on the street, no witnesses, and she didn't see who it was, but she does call my sister in Thailand.

'Hello?'

'Silje, is that you?' Sis says, confused, because Silje is speaking through her nose in a really odd way.

Silje starts crying on the phone, and Sis panics.

'It's Niko, isn't it? He hasn't done something, has he?'

I have, but not the thing Sis is worried that I might have done. Silje gives her every single detail: broken nose, broken teeth, concussion, twenty-four stitches. My sister collapses on the bed, and she shuts her eyes, hoping that everything will be all right when she opens them again, but it isn't. She rushes off to the airport and pays a lot of money to get on the first plane to Stockholm, and from there to Copenhagen. Brian is at the pool with Allan, and when he comes up to the hotel room – all wet with a chirpy, little boy – there's a note, but no Sis.

I'm so so so so sorry, but I've gone home.
Niko has done something stupid.
I'm sorry, Brian, I'm so sorry. I had to.
He's beaten up Silje. Sorry.
Love you!!!
Sanne

There Brian is, in Thailand, with moist eyes, a crumpled note in his hand, and an inconsolable little boy screaming for his mummy. But she's alone and distraught, stuck on a plane filled with strangers who seem blind to her pain.

I am a disgusting human being.

Sis falls apart

Sis doesn't come over to mine. Worn and tired, she goes to Silje's. She knocks on her door, expecting the worst, but is nowhere near prepared for what's to come. It's not Silje who opens the door, but Camilla, steaming with rage, who says, 'What do you want?'

'I want to see Silje.'

'Do you realize what your little brother has done?'

She says, 'Yes, that's why I'm here.'

She tries to slip past Camilla and into the flat, but Camilla gets in the way. Sis pushes on, and Camilla gives her a ruthless shove. Sis is not going to be let in. She tumbles backwards, and she almost falls down the stairs, but she doesn't leave. She has to see Silje, and Camilla can't scare her off.

'I have to see her!'

Camilla doesn't move.

'Camilla, let her in, it's all right.'

That gives Sis a hope that things might not be so very bad after all, because it does sound like Silje, and not like someone who's been killed and maimed. Camilla stares furiously at Sis, and Silje has to say it again, 'Camilla, let her in.' Camilla is obviously irked, but she stands aside, and Sis steps gingerly into the flat. There's Silje with a face that has been mangled beyond recognition. Sis has decided that she must be brave and show that she can be a support to Silje, so that she'll forgive me one day, and we'll all be happy. But Sis stares at the face which used to hold all her hopes and which now represents only a taunt, a ha-ha you didn't actually believe, did you? She turns around silently and hurries out.

Brian comes home as fast as he can, but coming home from Thailand takes time. For more than twenty-four hours Sis is alone in their flat. She gets out Suede. She always listens to Suede when she's depressed. She puts it on repeat and starts skipping about the sitting room. She skips about for hours until her legs won't carry her any longer, then she curls up in a ball on the floor. She's still lying like that when Brian comes in.

He picks her up carefully; he's worried she might break. He puts her on the bed and turns off Suede. He hates Suede. She hasn't slept for forty-eight hours, but she can't fall asleep. She stares vacantly at the ceiling. Brian smoothes her hair, speaking to her in comforting tones, but she seems distant and lost.

Allan is at Brian's parents'. Brian is always thinking ahead. He sits at Sis's bedside for the longest time, but he needs to get his own back, so he calls up a friend to come and look after Sis. I can tell by the way the doorbell rings that it's Brian. My doorbell is aggressive. I've been expecting him, and I open the door with glee. I expect him to hit me straight away, but the punch doesn't come and we are looking at each other with bewilderment.

'I can't be arsed to hurt you.'

He can't say that.

'You promised.'

'Apparently, I'm a liar,' and then he turns around and leaves.

He must have seen a look of expectancy on my face, and it's made him unclench his fist. He won't hit me, because every punch would pummel my guilt out of me, and my guilt must be retained undiminished.

I'm driving myself round the bend

The longer it has been, the harder it gets. I think she's selfish not to call, and I tell my stomach to shush. Be mad at me, be angry, be disappointed, be furious, be something. I don't know that Sis is feeling shite. I just know that she's back, but she doesn't get in touch.

I make up my mind that Sis has to see my agony in order to come back to me. When she sees how much I'm suffering, there'll be no stopping her. It's dark, because it's half-past three in the morning in Hellerup. When the taxi arrives, I argue a bit with the cabby. I stink to high heaven, because I haven't had a shower in a week, and I still have traces of Silje's blood on me. It's only when I fish a 1,000 kroner note out of my pocket that he agrees to drive me to Peder Skrams Gade. They don't think I know it, but I do: the combination to the front door, as well as where they hide the key to their flat. There's a hollow knob on the banister, and that's where the key is. I lock myself into the flat, go to the kitchen and find the sharpest knife there is. I take a deep breath and cut, first my left wrist and then my right. I cut deeply, but not lengthways. I have no actual desire to die. I just have to bleed enough to scare things to rights. I open the door to their bedroom and switch on the lights. They squint at me and look confused.

'Sis, Sis. Help me,' I say, holding out my bloodied hands.

Sis just looks despairingly at me and mutters, 'Oh no.' That's all I get from her. Something's very wrong. Brian looks at me with confusion, then wraps a couple of jumpers round my wrists. He turns to Sis.

'I'll take him to the hospital. I'll be back soon. Don't go anywhere.'

Even with blood dripping onto the floor I wonder why he barks it out like an order. Where would she go in the middle of the night? And then I'm in the car with Brian. He's a good sort, I'll say that for him. We don't speak a word to each other. Suddenly he stops the car, gets out, goes to my side, opens the door and drags me out of my seat. WALLOP! WALLOP! WALLOP! He hesitates for a bit, then flings me back into the car – now my face is also bleeding – and drives me to the hospital, where he dumps me unceremoniously. He hurries back home, but on the way home he senses a terrible coldness, and he knows that Sis isn't there any longer. He cries so hard that he almost drives himself off the road.

Suicide

My sister commits suicide. She drowns herself in Nyhavn, and that's all I'm going to say about that.

This is how I hear the news

I come home to an empty flat and sore wrists, and then I wait for Sis, because she has to react to it one way or another. I wait, and I wait, with the feeling of the knot travelling up into my throat. After three days I call Sis, but no-one picks up. Of course, no-one does. My wounds are a great big waste, and I feel stupid. After a week or so, I think about popping round to theirs, but my last visit has made it impossible. I must have an invite, and while I haven't got that, I must stay away. That's the rule, and I shouldn't break it again unless I want to risk being banned for life.

I need to get out, so I walk the streets aimlessly. I go to a kiosk to buy a packet of blue King's, and that's where I start gasping for breath. On the counter is the news, and my sister's coffin is on the front page. The small, Turkish gentleman behind the counter is worried about me. He thinks I'm choking on something, and he darts over to me and starts pounding my back. After a couple of bashes the air rushes back, and then,

'AAAAAAAAAAAAAAAAAAAAAAAAAAAAAAAAAAAAAAAAAAAAAA
AAAAAAAAAAAAAAAAAAAAAAAAAAAAAAAAAAAAAAAAAAAAAA
AAAAAAAAAAAAAAAAAAAAAAAAAAAAAAAAAAAAAAAAAAAAAA
AAAAAAAAAAAAAAAAAAAAAAAAAAAAAAAAAAAAAAAAAAAAAA
AAAAAAAAAAAAAAAAAAAAAAAAAAAAAAAAAAAAAAAAAAAAAA
AAAAAAAAAAAAAAAAAAAAAAAAAAAAAAAAAAAAAAAAAAAAAA
AAAAAAAAAAAAAAAAAAAAAAAAAAAAAAAAAAAAAAAAAAAAAA
AAAAAAAAAAAAAAAAAAAAAAAAAAAAAAAAAAAAAAAAAAAAAA
AAAAAAAAAAAAAAAAAAAAAAAAAAAAAAAAAAAAAAAAAAAAAA

AAAAAAAAAAAAAAAAAAAAAAAAAAAAAAAAAAAAAAAAAAAAAAAAA
AAAAAAAAAAAAAAAAAAAAAAAAAAAAAAAAAAAAAAAAAAAAAAAA
AAAAAAAAAAAAAAAAHHHHHHHHHHHHHHHHHHHHHHHHHH
HHHHHHHHHHHHHHHHHHHHHHHHHHHHHHHHHHHHHHHHHH
HHHHHHHHHHHHHHHHHHHHHHHHHHHHHHHHHHHHHHHHHH
HHHHHHHHHHHHHHHHHHHHHHHHHHHHHHHHHHHHHHHHHH
HHHHHHHHHHHHHHHHHHHHHHHHHHHHHHHHHHHHHHHHHH
HHHHHHHHHHHHHHHHHHHHHHHHHHHHHHHHHHHHHHHHHH
HHHHHHHHHHHHHHHHHHHHHHHHHHHHHHHHHHHHHHHHHH
HHHHHHHHHHHHHHHHHHHHHHHHHHHHHHHHHHHHHHHHHH
IIIIIIIIIIIIIIIIIHHHHHHHHHHHHHHHHHHHHHHHHHHHHH
HHHHHHHHHHHHHHHHHHHHHHHHHHHHHHHHHHHHHHHHHH
HHHHHHHHHHHHHHHHHHHHHHHHHHHHHHHHHHHHHHHHHH
HHHHHHHHHHHHHTHAT'SMYSISTERTHAT'SMYSISTERTHAT'S
MYSISTERSISSISSISNONONONONONONONOTHAT'SMYSISTERYOU
CAN'TSTUPIDFUCKTHAT'SMYSISTERWHATAMIGOINGTODONOW
SISYOUCAN'TYOUSTUPIDARSESTAYSTAYSTAYILOVEYOUFUCKFUCK
SHECAN'TDOTHISSHECAN'TFUCKINGARSEHOLESHECAN'TTHAT'S
MYSISTERTHAT'SMYSISTERFUCKFUCKFUCKFUCKFUCKTHAT'S
MYSISTERTHAT'SMYSISTERTHAT'SMYSISTERTHAT'SMYSISTER
THAT'SMYSISTERTHAT'SMYSISTERTHAT'SMYSISTERTHAT'SMY
SISTERTHAT'SMYSISTERTHAT'SMYSISTERTHAT'SMYSISTER!'

When I stop screaming every single newspaper is torn to shreds.

The small Turkish gentleman is holding me and saying, 'There, there, my friend.'

He smoothes down my hair and takes the last bit of newspaper out of my hand.

79

She's dead. The cold sweat is pouring off me, and I am shaking all over.

'Have you got anyone to help you?'

No, not any more.

After Sis's death

This is when the knot really starts growing. It fills my head and my body. There's nothing but agonising pain for weeks. The knot is tearing down everything to make room for itself. Walls, rooftops, floors, everything is being smashed to pieces in the loudest possible way. Suddenly the noise and the pain stop, because what's the point of giving me a stomach ache when I no longer function? All is silent, the demolition is over, the knot is everywhere, and I am no longer me. I am the knot. It's the knot that knows what needs doing. I shop, I wash my top and tail, and hoover every day. I live in an emotion-free zone where everything is a routine designed to keep me going rather than alive, and as long as I don't take any chances, I stay afloat. If I had more strength, I would have greater ambitions, but right now all that matters is keeping myself going. It's been more than six months of which I remember nothing, because nothing happens. I have no events to attach my memory to.

After Sis's death I am now the sole proprietor of Mum's songs, plus twenty-six flats in Copenhagen; and if I were a well man, I could be living a fantastic life.

Uncle John

After six months of doing nothing, I do something unusual. I visit my parents' grave in the Assistens Kirkegård. Sis and I used to go there on their birthdays. Sis would talk of everything and anything, and about the way we were treated by other people. It was always Sis who did the talking. I just looked on in wonder as she had long conversations with a headstone, but when she left, she was always happy and unburdened. I want to be unburdened too. I have a hard time finding their grave. Assistens is a big cemetery, and it's been a while since I was last there. I actually walk past it a couple of times. There's already a sad-looking man of about seventy or so standing by the grave, and that makes me think that it can't be my parents' grave. I have a wander around and return to the grave. I walk over and just to make sure I look at the stone.

'Did you know my parents?' I ask, surprised because he's weeping.

'Nikolaj, my boy, it's been such a long time.'

He pats me sort of hard on the cheek, twice. Crikey!!

'Uncle John?'

'Yes. What?'

'Nothing.'

He looks old. He is just a tad younger than Dad, so he can't be more than fifty-five, but he looks much older, at least ten years. /We're standing silently next to each other. It's awkward. It doesn't get any less awkward when John starts talking, because he suddenly grabs my hand and says, 'Allan, I've had a rough time of it these many years.'

I assume he's talking to the grave, so I pretend nothing's going on.

'Allan, have you gone off into a trance?' and he gives my hand a squeeze.

'My name is Nikolaj.'

'Yes, he's a good boy. You don't mind that I call myself their uncle, do you?'

'Uncle John, I'm Nikolaj.'

'No, Allan. It does matter. It matters to me, because I think of your family as my family.'

'Allan is my dad. I'm his son.'

I try to get him to let go of my hand, but he won't. He holds on tightly.

'Don't say that. People need other people. I need you to be my friend.'

I am silent, but the hairs on my arms stand on end. It's very uncomfortable in a very insistent manner. He falls silent, lets go and I pull my hand back.

He looks at me and says, 'I miss your dad, even though I don't think he misses me.'

It takes me a moment before I understand that he's back.

'I don't think he misses me either, if that's any consolation to you.'

'Piffle. He loved you both, and you in particular. Do you think they're all right?'

'They're dead.'

'Yes, but are they all right?'

'No, they're dead.'

'But are they all right?'

'Look, I have no idea what you're on about.'

He looks at me with disappointment, but it doesn't actually bother me much. I want him to leave and give me some peace. I came here to be unburdened, not to be bothered by some loony, but he isn't going. On the contrary, he looks at me as if he's curious.

'How's your sister?'

I have to take a deep breath here.

'She's dead too.'

'Then you're all alone?'

I feel a stomach ache coming on, which surprises me, because I haven't had a stomach ache for six months. I nod.

'I knew that – you look exactly like me.'

That shocks me quite a bit, because he looks completely broken, and I turn to him and say, 'What are you on about? I don't look anything like you. I'm okay,' but for the first time I notice Uncle John's eyes. They have the same sad look as the ones I've seen staring back at me from the mirror every morning for six months. I turn around right then and there and leave.

When I get home, I cry, and I don't stop for a week, except for intervals of yelling and screaming. I don't mean the things I yell about Sis. I just have to let it out, true or not. My stomach ache is back. I am feeling stuff again, but that doesn't make me feel any better.

Every day when I look in the mirror, I see Uncle John more clearly than I did the day before, and it's not because I let myself go to pieces. I still wash my top and tail, even when the pain is most acute, but it's John's eyes that are looking back at me. I don't understand how John has snuck in behind my eyes, and I try to find the latch in my forehead. One day I ask him, 'How did you get into me?' Of course, he doesn't answer, but I continue my interrogation for more than half an hour. I haven't said much for so long, and talking feels good. I want to have someone know how I feel, and for it to matter. Strangers are just strangers. It must be someone who knows who I am. I think about calling, but I'm not brave enough; I almost write an e-mail, but haven't got the energy for it, so in the end I get out pen and paper and then I write Silje a letter.

The letter for Silje

Hello Silje,

I don't deserve that you read this, but it has to be said. I never got what you saw in me. It seemed ridiculous that someone like you could care about someone like me, but you made me happy. I made myself unhappy. I did, a long time before I hit you, because I'm a prat. If you regret not filing a report against me, then this is my confession: I, Nikolaj Okholm Jensen, wrecked the best thing in my life. I hit Silje Kjær over and over, until she lay bleeding and unconscious

84

in my sitting room. She was my girlfriend. I destroyed her,
and I destroyed myself. I don't expect forgiveness; I'm not
even begging for it. I just want you to know that in spite of
what I did, I love you, and I always will. You can't requite it.
You mustn't, because I don't deserve that you do. My sister is
dead. I don't know if you've heard. You probably have. She
committed suicide, but really it was me who did it. In just
under a month I attacked you and killed Sis. I wish I could
say I'm better than that, but I'm not. I have done vile things
that you don't know about. Once I kicked a ten-year-old boy
in the head. I regret it all today, but I don't seem able to do
anything, except things I later regret bitterly. I'm a bad
person, and it controls me. I know it. You just made me
think that I could be something else. You know that I have
attempted suicide twice. That's 2½ times now, and that's
what pushed my sister into the water. That, and what I did
to you. I'm alone now, and you'd think that I'd want to
finish the job. Take my life, but this time – without Sis to
save me – it's all over and done with. The thing is, I haven't.
It's too easy and too disrespectful to Sis. Instead I pace about
inside myself. I'm on my way to getting lost, hopelessly lost,
and before I do, I just want to say this. I'm sorry.

Love,
Nikolaj

I don't expect an answer, but after just under a week a letter from
Silje soars through my letter box. All it says is:

Nikolaj, you can't ever contact me again.
Silje

Why doesn't she just ignore me?

Sanne's little brother?

I start to take long walks and return home with two shopping bags filled with junk. Half of it I throw out as soon as I get in, because it's a useless – though often expensive – load of rubbish I've bought, simply for the sake of doing something with myself. I can buy expensive things with all the money I've got. I start to stare angrily at people on my shopping sprees. I stare at all you people who have each other. You with the girlfriend. You with the friends. You with the parents. I'm not doing anything, but in my mind I'm kicking you all off your feet. No-one comes over to ask me if I'm okay, because I frighten people.

There's this girl who's kissing her boyfriend. He pops into the FONA music store for a minute, and I decide that I hate her more than anyone else that day, because she looks like Sis without being Sis. She gets the evil eye, and she doesn't care for it. I've almost scared her off when her boyfriend comes out. She turns to him and, nestling against him, she whispers something into his ear while she looks at me. They discuss it for a bit. He wants to confront me. She doesn't want him to. He wins. He comes over. For some reason I instinctively like him. He seems like a nice person. There's ten metres between us, and while he is crossing those ten metres, my anger abates. When he's standing in front of me, I smile at him. He asks me, 'Excuse me, is there some sort of problem?'

I don't know what to say to that – I've got truckloads of problems – so I just smile at him.

'You're scaring my girlfriend.'

'Yes.'

'Is that all you've got to say?'

'Is there anything else you'd like me to say?'

'Now look,' and he stops and stares at me in a weird, now-it's-your-turn sort of way, and I realize that he wants me to say my name. He just wants my first name, but I'm out of practice with the whole saying hello business, so I say, 'Nikolaj Okholm Jensen.'

'Now look, Nikolaj…' and then he stops.

He looks at me with visible bewilderment.

'Nikolaj?'

'Yes.'

'Sanne's little brother?'

For the first time I look him in the eyes. Until then I've stared fixatedly at a spot just below them. His girlfriend is standing a stone's throw away and is looking at us with worry. Wasn't he just supposed to march over and show her he was protecting her?

'Who are you?' I ask him.

'Tue. I went out with your sister years ago,' and with those words my anger returns.

I stay calm, but say pre-emptively, 'Go away.'

'Do you need anything?'

I clench my fist.

'Go away, Tue.'

Either he doesn't appreciate the gravity of the situation, or he's ignoring it. His girlfriend comes closer, looking worried. The more she worries, the more she resembles Sis. Maybe it's because I know it's Tue, and because I see what I want to see: a happy, much loved Sis who has a doting and gentle boyfriend who protects her.

'I read about your sister. I'm sorry. I know how much you loved her.'

I barge ahead, roaring loudly, ramming my head into his stomach, winding him and knocking him over. It must have hurt a lot, but his girlfriend throws herself down on top of him. I'm surprised she doesn't try to pull me away, rather than protect Tue, but it makes me let go of him, and I run off. She deserves that. He deserves that. They love each other, enough to bleed, and that's not merely something to respect, that's something to be honoured. I leave quickly, and Tue has only had his honour bruised a little.

I scurry home and switch on the television, hoping it'll help me to cool down, but there's a portrait of Mum on, and out of sheer shock I don't change the channel quite soon enough.

'*Tarm and Grith Okholm would seem at first glance to be utterly incompatible. Tarm is a tiny place, epitomising the sleepy quiet of Jutland; yet a star lived here, a veritable supernova such as would light up the skies wherever she went. Most people actually believe that Grith was a Copenhagener born and bred, but she was as far from being a Copenhagener as you can be in this small country, and those of us who love her music can hear the truth. There is a*

calm and a decency in her music typical of Jutland', says the pre-
senter in his distinct Jutland lilt. *'If you are ever in these parts, you
should pop by Tarm. If for no other reason than for the love these
people bear Grith. This is where her greatest fans are to be found'.*

Breaking and entering

It's half past three in the morning. I know because I look at the
clock when I hear the sound of footsteps in my flat. I get out of
bed warily and have a rummage for something that will do some
damage. I decide on the ashtray I've nicked from Sankt Peder. It
fits nicely in my hand, and it's sturdy, made of good, heavy stuff.
He is as noisy as if he were at home. I tiptoe out of the bedroom,
and I just get a glimpse of him as he goes into the bathroom. He
looks tough, long-haired, bearded, big and strong, and he oozes
confidence. I need to be careful here; I couldn't take him on in a
fair fight, but people who break into my flat shouldn't expect to get
a fair fight. I tiptoe to the bathroom, stand beside the door,
hidden, ready for him to come out. He's washing his hands now,
and leaves the bathroom as carefree as could be. I swing the ashtray at his head, and my aim is perfect: KAPOW! in the back of his
head. He stays upright, but grabs his head in pain. I should hit him
again straight away when he doesn't collapse, but I'm astonished
that he can stay standing after a blow like that. It's the perfect
blow with a very sturdy ashtray. He turns to me, his eyes flaming,
and, desperate now, I swing the ashtray again. This time I don't hit
him: he catches my arm mid-swing, and I'm convinced I'm done

for. There's a strength in his arms that I've never encountered before, not even in Brian.

'You're hitting me?'

His eyes are flashing, and his voice rumbles like thunder.

'You're in my flat,' I say, pathetically.

'Let go of the ashtray.'

He loosens his grip and my arms hurts so badly I dare not do anything but what he tells me. I let it go. It falls to the floor and breaks.

'Sit down.'

I sit down obediently on the sofa. He's bleeding just a little. He touches the wound carefully and looks at the blood on his fingers.

'Do you hit everyone who tries to help you?'

'You're in my flat.'

'Did you hear me?'

I shake my head.

'I've come to help you, Nikolaj.'

I don't know who he is. I've not seen him before, so why is he talking to me like that?

'Do I know you? Who are you?'

He smiles at me, then opens his arms wide and says, 'I am Jesus Christ, and I've come to make you a better man.'

I'm looking discreetly for another weapon, but the only thing I can reach from my vantage point is a cushion. He waits for my reaction, but when I remain silent he says, 'You don't believe me, do you?'

I keep still.

'Do you?'

I don't say anything.

'Why is that so hard to believe?'

I continue to stay still.

'Is it because you don't think you deserve my help?'

I'm still silent.

'I'm here to make you a better man. Do you understand?'

I shake my head.

He's frustrated now.

'What don't you understand? I, Jesus Christ, have come to make you a better man.'

For the first time I notice that he's wearing sandals, which only confirms my suspicion that he must be mad.

'Why me?'

'Don't you need help?'

'So do a lot of people. People who believe in Jesus and stuff.'

He nods, seriously

'That's true, but did they have a sister who used to pray for them several times a day?'

'You know Sis?' I ask, timidly.

'Yes, Nikolaj, I do. She used to pray for you many times a day, every single day. You see, she believed you could be more than you are now. She believed that you don't have to hurt others. That you don't have to be violent and mean. That you could improve yourself and have a good life. Do you believe that?'

I shake my head and say, 'I'm just not very good at it.'

I don't believe that he is Jesus, but he knows Sis, and that changes everything. It means that I listen to him. He doesn't even look like Jesus, certainly not that chap on the cross. He's much too big and tough.

'Do you think your life will get better if you become a better man?'

I hesitate, but not because I don't know the answer. I hesitate because the answer is so obvious.

'Yes, of course I do.'

'Well, why don't you become a better man then?'

I can't answer that.

'I need to take a wee, you know.'

I get up from the sofa and move past him cautiously and go to the bathroom. I don't need a wee, but I do need to get my head round this, so I sit on the loo and try to relax. I stay there for ten minutes, then splash some water on my face. When I return, he's standing with my photo album. He's taking out a picture of Silje.

'Is that your ex-girlfriend?'

I nod.

'Silje, the one you thrashed completely?'

I almost can't breathe.

'How do you know?'

'Your sister told me. She's beautiful. You must beat yourself up about that,' he says, looking at the picture.

He leafs through the album.

'You've got a lot of pictures of your sister. I hope you miss her.'

'Please don't look at that,' I say, and reach for the album, but he won't let me have it.

He continues to turn the leaves, sitting in my easy chair and studying the pictures. I stand floundering on the floor. He closes the album, putting it on the sofa table. I hurry over to pick it up and put it back on the shelf, because I don't want to stand too close to him.

'Do you believe I'm Jesus Christ?'

'No, of course I don't.'

'Then who do you think I am?'

I say warily, 'Some nutter who knew my sister.'

He smiles and says, 'Some nutter? I'm not a nutter.'

Silence.

'Are you willing to do what I tell you?'

I take a deep breath, and think, 'Fuck it, what's the harm?' and so I say, 'Yes, because I need help.'

I baffle him.

'Even though you think I'm a nutter?'

'Yes.'

'You're willing to trust a nutter?'

'I'm willing to trust you.'

'Sit down, Nikolaj, and relax. There's nothing to be afraid of.'

I sit on the sofa, but as far from him as I can. He just moves the chair closer and leans towards me.

'We need some drastic measures to help you on your way.'

'Yes,' I say, not even knowing what he means by drastic.

'You've got far too many bad memories of Copenhagen. You need to get out of here.'

I nod. Of course I do.

'Where do you know people who can be there for you, Nikolaj?'

'I don't know anyone who doesn't live in Copenhagen.'

'No-one at all?'

I shake my head, but of course there is that one noted exception, and I mutter, 'My grandparents live in Jutland, in Tarm, but they're really not there for me.'

He smiles.

'Don't you know anyone else from Tarm?'

'Mum and Dad were from Tarm, but that's hardly helpful when they're both dead.'

'Yes, it is.'

And that's when it dawns on me. He's sending me to Tarm. That's too drastic by far. I stare at him in shock.

'I'm bloody well not going to Tarm. What are you, a nutter or something?'

He laughs.

'Yes, you keep telling me I am. Are you willing to do as I say?'

I've promised to, so I tell him yes even though it annoys me.

'Good. When the month is up, you're moving to Tarm.'

I have a hard time seeing how that will make my life easier, on the contrary.

'What am I going to do in Tarm?'

'That's up to you. Trust me. You've got much better options there than anywhere else.'

Sodding Tarm, but I must. Jesus has decreed it. He holds out his hand, and I take it warily. As soon as flesh touches flesh, I feel the knot in my stomach loosening. For the first time there's not just discomfort and pain, and I smile.

'See you,' he says, and leaves.

Once again I'm alone in my flat. What the hell was that? I manage to get off the sofa, pick up the ashtray and throw it in the bin. I can't help laughing at how I hit Jesus over the head with an ashtray – KAPOW! – but I'm glad I didn't laugh in front of him. He is formidable. I expect God's son has to be. Thor is probably formidable as well. I go back to bed, but I can't fall asleep, because my thoughts are flying every which way in my head. They're good thoughts, though. They're Jesus telling me that he's come into my life so that I may become a better man.

The next morning I wonder if it's just a dream, or whether I've finally become Uncle John, but the ashtray in the bin and a sore wrist tell me it's real. It doesn't feel like a dream, and I am moving to Tarm.

Part Two

NATO

The journey to Tarm

I'm sitting in the train to Tarm. Today is 1 June. It's been three weeks since Jesus' visit. I've been busy. Only a few days after the visit I met my estate agent. He doesn't understand what it is I'm asking for when I say that I'd like a house in Tarm.

'Isn't that practically in Germany? I know bugger-all about property in Jutland. Do you mean to start investing over there as well?'

'No, I'm moving there. It's where my parents were from.'

He himself is originally from northern Jutland, but has lived over here for twenty years. He hates Jutland as fervently as only emigrated Jutlanders can hate it.

'Why would you do that? Jutland is boring.'

'I've got to. Jesus told me to.'

That shuts him up.

'What about your flat?'

'You're going to put it up for sale'

*

A week later I'm informed that I have bought a 600 square foot house with a 2,000 square foot garden. I only see the house in the pictures my property agent took while in Tarm, but at first glance it looks all right, outside and in. It's a nice, red-brick house on Poppelvej in a family-friendly area, and I only pay 1.2 million kroner for it, while my flat in Hellerup is put on the market at an asking price of 2.7. At first I'm a bit hacked off that the house is only 1.2, because I want a decent place to live, but he assures me that nothing's wrong with the house. It's just that everything is cheaper in Jutland.

Strange as it may seem, I feel quite good about moving to Tarm now that I'm getting used to the idea, because for the longest time nothing has happened in my life. At least something's happening now. Once again the train comes to a halt next to a herd of cows. I never knew there were so many cows in Jutland!

When I change trains in Esbjerg, there's an old lady with a crossword puzzle. It takes me a couple of seconds to work out who she is. It's Granny, and my stomach growls angrily. I sit down a small distance from her. She hasn't seen me, or else she doesn't recognize me. I can't help staring grumpily. I've got every right to, but she's busy with her crosswords, and she doesn't notice my glare even though it's glued to her.

I've thought a lot about Granny and Grandad lately, because Tarm equals my grandparents, and very little else. I've decided to try to steer clear of them. They're there; I'm there, but that's it. I'm likely to bump into them, but I'm not going to go looking for them. After about twenty minutes – by the time we reach Varde – I start to think that it's remarkable that she never looks up at the other passengers. During the half-hour journey from Varde to Tarm, she doesn't look up once, not even when people walk just past her. Then the speakers announce that we are due to arrive at Tarm in a few minutes. I've got butterflies, and I forget about Granny. Blimey, Tarm is a small place. It's not that I'm disappointed. I'm just making the observation.

Granny leaves the train at the other end of the carriage. At first I want to leave without saying anything, but I can't help myself. Something forces me to get right in front of her and make her stop short. She's standing still, looking at the ground, but out here she can't hide behind her crossword puzzle. I'm in her face. I'm deliberating what to say, but I can't think of anything, not even 'Hello, Granny.' Suddenly she reaches for my hand. Fuck, fuck, fuck! What's she doing? Frightened, I recoil and, turning my back on her, hurry away.

She reached out for me!

The route from the station to my new home

As the station's in the northern part of the town and Poppelvej is in the south, I get a good look at the high street, which makes up most of Tarm. I'm hungry after my long train journey – four and half hours it's taken me to get here – and I make a stop at Las Vegas. Las Vegas is the largest greasy spoon in Tarm. It has a bigger menu and more slot machines than the other, smaller greasy spoon, Westside. I order half a deep-fried chicken and some chips. People look at me. I eat undisturbed, but there are two blokes in particular – a smaller and larger one, my own age – who continue to stare. When I've got outside with the last chips I make my way up the high street. I take my time, stopping whenever there's something to stop for. It takes me a long time to get to Poppelvej. I come across a stream, which later turns out to be a wide rivulet, and I have to sit down for fifteen minutes or so and just enjoy it. Juttish college girls, healthy as bells, are passing by and, feeling strangely alive, I have a good look at them. I pop round to the corner shop to see their selection of films. It's not bad at all. I allow myself to examine each stone and every street sign. I'm slowly inching closer and closer to my new home.

My new home

I'm standing a bit hesitantly outside 22 Poppelvej, because I'm almost afraid of unlocking the door. The house is exactly as I imagined it. The next-door neighbour – a plump, little lady whom I later discover is called Karen – looks at me as I stand outside the front door fumbling with the keys. I manage to let myself in, and, as it's a very empty house, everything is suddenly quiet. I have a queer sensation in my stomach. For once it's not pain, because I'm not afraid; I'm excited.

There are five rooms, a large sitting room, a large hall, a large kitchen plus a tool shed and garage, where someone's left an old, brown racing bike. I have no idea what I'm going to do with all the space; I couldn't even fill up my old two-bedroom flat. I spend several days just being here, puttering barefoot about the garden, lying down in every room to work out which one is nicest to lie in, but I haven't got a favourite. On the contrary, I feel comfortable in every room.

I threw away all my stuff before coming here; I wanted to start out with as clean a slate as possible. Kirkens Korshær came and collected some rather expensive furniture, about five hundred films, a couple of thousand CDs, and a shitload of other things, including most of my clothes. All I've got with me is a sports bag filled with my most indispensable possessions, among other things my photo album. It goes without saying that I have to go and shop for furniture to make my house a home.

At Falke Furniture (the only furniture store in Tarm) they are astounded by my shopping frenzy

'You've already bought a bed, you know,' the shop assistant tells me, politely.

I nod and point at two sofa beds.

Later on when I pay, the shop assistant giggles.

'Your name is Okholm, is it?'

I get nervous, but fortunately he thinks it's a coincidence.

'I don't know if you know, but Grith Okholm is actually from Tarm.'

I exhale with relief and say, 'The singer Grith Okholm? Surely she was from Copenhagen.'

The shop assistant shakes his head energetically.

'No, on our city gates it says "TARM – Birthplace of Grith Okholm". Didn't you see that?'

'I came by train. So she lived here?'

'She was born here.'

'She must have played a lot of gigs here then,' I say, knowing full well that she never sang in Tarm.

'No, she never actually gave a concert in Tarm...' The shop assistant suddenly sounds as if he's got a cold.

'That's odd.'

'Yes, we think so too.'

I thank him for his help and for the chat. It's only five hundred metres or so to one of the city gates. It's a clumsy white abomination, and I walk up to it. Blimey, it really does say that!

It had to happen

A week is spent shopping for clothes (for the first time in my life I now own several polo shirts), furniture, kitchen utensils, a television, and shifting things around and moving them into place. Once that's all done, I have a finished home. There are beds in four of the rooms (two of them sofa beds) in case I want to sleep in a different room, and almost all of my furniture is beige. My home is nice and tidy, just as I imagine every other house in Tarm.

Jesus hasn't told me what I'm to do here, which makes me afraid of doing the wrong thing. I spend a lot of time in front of the television, and when I go out, I leave the town and walk around woods and fields, or roam the streets without entering the shops. Of course, I shop for food, but I shop using single syllable words and pay with cash. No-one knows that I'm my mother's son. On my letterbox it says Nikolaj Jensen.

I've been in Tarm for three weeks when I am crossing a cornfield to get to a patch of wood that I haven't been in yet. Suddenly, I see Grandad come running after me. I freeze. He comes up to me, giving me two biffs on the noddle with his knuckles, 'Hello there, anybody home? You've just ruined a cornfield.'

I gawp at him in confusion. He's standing a hand's breadth from me and talking about crops; that's seriously odd. I don't know why, but it seems the most natural reaction. I give him two biffs on the noddle with my knuckles too, not saying anything, but letting those two biffs do the talking. He is surprised and takes a few steps back.

'What do you think you're doing?'

'You hit me, I hit you. You leave me be, and I'll leave you be.'

My voice breaks, and I'm no way near as tough as I'd like to be.

'Then respect other people's property!'

I wait for it, but nothing more seems to be coming, and I realize that he is yelling at me because I'm trampling someone's crops and not because of who I am. I say, 'Don't you recognize me? Hasn't Granny told you I've come to town? It's me, Nikolaj.'

Grandad goes pale, and takes another couple of steps back. He's embarrassed, and searching for words, but he only manages to say, 'You must respect other people's property.'

'Yes, you've said that. Isn't there anything else you'd like to say?'

'Some man spent time and effort sowing and minding this field, and then you come along and trample it. That's vandalism.'

'It's not even your field?'

I just can't be arsed to fight about other people's trampled corn, and I turn around and continue across the cornfield, demonstratively trampling the corn as I go. When I've put about a hundred metres between us, he yells at me, 'I'm keeping my eye on you! You'd best behave, Nikolaj!' I can't believe I was ever afraid of that old man.

Biscuits, television, a house in the country, and nothing bad to threaten me. My lifestyle is not that remote from what it was in Copenhagen. But back there it was sad and lonely. Here it's cool to watch television and do nothing all day. My stomach is calm. The knot's asleep.

Bike and Kink

I eat at Las Vegas regularly. I don't have all my suppers there, but most of them. I'm not the only one who eats a lot of fried foods. The two blokes (Bike and Kink), who looked persistently at me on my first day in Tarm, do too. They're metalworkers down at HS Kedler. Kink looks like a metalworker, big and bulky. Bike, on the other hand, is improbable as a metalworker, small and slight. They leave me alone for the first couple of weeks, even though they're dying to approach me, but Bike especially moves closer and closer, and one day he sits himself down at my table. He assesses my reaction. Am I annoyed? But I'm not. I'm far too curious. I'd like to know why it is I'm so fascinating to them.

'You're that Copenhagener, aren't you?'

I smile. So that's why.

'I suppose so,' I say, and put out my hand. 'Nikolaj.'

He takes it immediately, shaking it, delightedly.

'Bike, or Jonas, but everyone calls me Bike. Can I ask you why you've moved here? I might have understood if you came from Herning, but leaving Copenhagen for Tarm?'

'I felt like some peace and quiet,' I say.

'Oh. Can't you have peace and quiet in Copenhagen?'

'I couldn't.'

Kink eavesdrops from over by the slot machine, while Bike looks at my left hand. My index finger is sort of stiff, because I once broke it in a fight and didn't have it looked at till it was too late. He lifts his right hand and points with his index finger which he then bends all the way back.

'Blimey, I think we're lovers,' he says, laughing. 'Yours is stiff, so that must be the male.'

I grin.

'Got any other injuries, have you?'

'A few.'

Kink comes over. His hand is full of coins he's just won. He puts them down on the table and shakes my hand.

'Hiya. Kink, as in Kinked Cock. It's got to be cool.'

'Nikolaj. What's got to be cool?'

'Being from Copenhagen. That's where it all happens. You set cars on fire and fight in the streets.'

'Not all the time, we don't.'

'We never do. You know what happens here? Bugger all, that's what,' he says, annoyed, and sits down.

'You two have some funny names.'

That makes them proud.

'Yes, we're bloody funny, we are,' Bike says with a big, beaming smile.

His eyes shine with enthusiasm, and he looks at me hungrily.

'You were saying something just now,' Kink says.

'Yes, about my injuries. My front teeth are not my front teeth; my upper lip has been split twice; I've broken three fingers; I've got a small scar on my chin; I have a scar on my shoulder; I've broken two toes; I've got a scar on my right thigh, and a really big scar on my back; I've split my eardrum, broken two ribs, and split my left eyebrow three times. I think that's about it.'

There's a bemused grin on both their faces.

'How did you get all those injuries?'

'I don't want to say.'

'What about your hands? You didn't mention them,' Kink says, pointing at the scars on my wrists.

I hold my breath (this is why I rarely wear T-shirts).

'It almost looks like you've tried to commit suicide.'

I try to come up with a plausible explanation, but I can't, so all I do is grin sheepishly and mutter, 'No, that's not why. I can't really remember how I got them.'

'Were you drunk?' Kink asks.

I nod, and Bike laughs.

'That's typical. I can't remember how I broke my index finger either.'

They try to get me to talk more, but I'm very cautious about what I say. Not having much luck, they start sharing their own stories.

There is a mad story involving Super Glue, little toy soldiers and the sleeping Kink's willy. When Kink had passed out after a night of drinking, Bike pulled off his trousers and got out his little plastic soldiers and some Super Glue, and then he got to work, staging battle scenes on Kink's cock.

'The best bit was when he got a stiffy. Suddenly one lot of soldiers was going uphill.'

'It must have hurt like mad when you tried to take them off.'

Kink gets off the chair in a determined way and pulls his cock out, here in the middle of the greasy spoon. It's the most kinked cock I have ever seen, and it's covered in tiny scars.

'I just tore them off, but fuck me, did they stick. My willy bled like mad. The worst ones were the ones he'd glued onto the bell-end,' he tells me enthusiastically.

I'm flabbergasted to say the least, gawping at his cock, but then I laugh and that makes them laugh too. An elderly couple walks past outside and, seeing us, look scandalized. Kink quickly puts his cock away.

There are also boring stories about village fairs, like the time when the Tarm men's handball team was in the second division and beat GOG Svendborg in the finals. They've been put back down to the Jutland series, because neighbouring Skjern steals all their best players. I hear the anger in their voices, but I don't understand why. Who bloody cares about handball?

And then there are the violent stories. It surprises me, but it actually doesn't scare me, because there's something affectionate about them.

'He keeps on throwing peanuts, but then I headbutt Kink.'

'Yes, and then I give him a good smack. His front teeth are dangling afterwards, and he starts talking about cops and prisons,' Kink laughs.

'But then I grab hold of him and explain that if he's throwing peanuts at the girls, he's asking for it.'

I think about sharing a couple of stories of my own, but decide not to, because that would scare them. My brand of violence is violent. Over here they don't kick little boys in the head.

We start eating together at Las Vegas; not every day, but a couple of times a week. I enjoy being around them. Sometimes they talk a lot, other days we just sit quietly together and eat. They invite me to come out for a drink with them quite often, but I always say no. I want to, but I'm not brave enough.

A plump little lady

Someone's ringing my doorbell very persistently. Outside is my next-door neighbour, the plump little lady.

'Hello, my name is Karen. I live at Number 19.'

'Oh, hello.'

'You know we've talked about how it's really frightful that we haven't made you feel more welcome here at Poppelvej, so I've baked you a cake,' she says, and hands me a baking tin.

As I reach out to accept it, she slips past me and into the house. It's cheeky, but it's also disarming, and I think, 'What the hell, why not?'

'Yes well, we have talked about what sort of a character you might be.'

'Have you?'

'You've had us quite puzzled. We thought a young family would be moving in. This is the nappy valley around here. Then it turns out it's a young man without any children, moving here all the way from Copenhagen.'

She's opening all the doors, peeping into all the rooms. It's taking cheekiness to the max, but I don't mind, because I want her to see how nice my home is.

'You've got four bedrooms?'

'Yes, in case I have visitors.'

'Oh, so it's a hospitable home. That's nice. The more the merrier. My, you have made this a homey place,' she says with a warm smile.

'Thank you.'

'This is some nice furniture. Did you get it at Falke?'

'Yes, I did.'

'That's good stuff.'

She sits on my sofa and looks at me inquisitively, waiting for something. I'm still walking about with the baking tin in my hand, and feeling a bit blown off course, but in a nice way.

'Would you like a cup of coffee?'

'Yes please, and maybe a slice of cake to go with it,' she says with a smile. She has a pleasant smile.

There I am with Karen, drinking coffee and eating chocolate cake. She's married to Kaj. They have two daughters. One's my age, the other's a couple of years younger. I've just turned twenty-five. Both girls have moved to Århus, and Karen is now alone all day.

'It can be a bit dull, but then you just think of something. Don't you? I've noticed that you're home alone during the day.'

'Yes, you think of something,' I say, even though I deliberately don't do anything.

They've lived here all of their lives, and all of their friends live on Poppelvej – and what about me?

'What about me?'

'You haven't been given the house by the council, have you?' she asks, suspiciously.

'No. Why would the council buy me a house?'

'They give all sorts of things to the unemployed.'

'I'm not unemployed,' I say, peevishly.

Karen looks at me with confusion.

'But you don't have a job.'

'I don't need a job.'

Her face lights up.

112

'Dear me, are you rich?'

'I don't want to talk about that.'

'Dearie me, this is so exciting. You're not a gangster or something like that, are you?'

'What?'

She cuts another slice of cake and hands it to me. By now I'm on my fourth slice, because she keeps feeding me.

'You hear so much about gangsters and bikers who enter witness protection programmes – like that Dan Lynge character. You're not involved in all that, are you?'

'No, of course I'm not.'

She smiles with relief.

'We're just wondering why you've moved all the way over here to Tarm.'

'Who are we?' I ask, feeling confused.

'Everyone I talk to. What was your name again?'

'Nikolaj.'

'It's a bit more than Nikolaj, isn't it?'

I take a good-sized bite of the cake and say, 'Yes.'

'Is it Okholm as well?'

I hesitate, but then I nod, and she gives a little twitch of delight.

'Dear me. Oh dear, oh dear. So your mum's our Grith Okholm?'

'Yes, my mum's the singer Grith Okholm, born and raised in Tarm.'

'Really, you must be the most interesting person we've ever had living on this street, and we once had someone who was in the SAS and he knew that chap off the survival programmes on telly.

Why have you moved here? Is it because of your mum?' she asks.

'No, I just felt like it.'

'Golly, this is exciting. It's almost like your mum's moved here.'

'She hasn't. It's just me.' But one look at Karen's face tells me that there isn't such a thing as just me any longer.

I don't ask Karen not to tell anyone, because I know there's no point. Within twenty-four hours everyone in Tarm knows I've come to town, including Nadja Jessen from the *Skjern-Tarm Daily*. She calls and asks if I'd be interested in letting her do a piece on me. I say yes, because if it has to be said, it might as well be said as loudly as possible.

The return of the prodigal son

By Nadja Jessen
nj@skjern-tarm-dagblad.dk

Nikolaj Okholm, son of Grith Okholm, has thrown himself in at the deep end. He's moved from Copenhagen to Tarm in an attempt to get to know himself and his famous mother a bit better.

Nikolaj Okholm has been through a lot in his young life, and when you meet him, you both see it and feel it. He has an air about him which says 'I've had a hard time, I've lived hard, but I won't let it get me down.' His famous mother died in a car crash when he was thirteen, and just over six months ago his older sister Sanne Okholm committed suicide. 'It's been difficult more than once,' Nikolaj says. He's cool, calm and collected but very sad. When his parents died, his older sister looked after him. 'I wouldn't be here today if it wasn't for her. She has saved my life, and she carried me on her shoulders all of her life. In the end I became too heavy for her, and that killed her.' Nikolaj thinks about his family every day. It's difficult being alone, and for a long time he was pessimistic and didn't think he would pull through. He holed himself up and sat all alone, feeling sorry for himself, but now he's embarked on a new chapter. A chapter which is all about returning home and finding himself. An optimistic chapter, taking place in Tarm, where his mother was born.

A criminal past

'My sister did her very best to keep me on track, but I was a live wire,' Nikolaj says with absolute candour. He's ashamed of many of the things he's done. 'For a while I hung out with scum, and it's a miracle that I've not been killed or arrested. Every weekend you'd find us right in the middle of a massive fight. We'd have a go over the smallest thing, and I pity the people who were around,' Nikolaj says. You can hear the regret in his voice, but what's done is done, and every day he has to live with the mistakes he made then. It's been hard because his mistakes have hurt a lot of other people, especially his sister. Nikolaj always refers to her by the pet name Sis, like a little boy, though there's nothing little about him.

He misses his big sister more than anyone else. He says so with his words, but more than anything he says so with his eyes, which become woefully sad every time he mentions her.

She believed in him

When his parents died, he was suddenly alone with his older sister, who had just turned twenty. Being responsible for a thirteen-year-old boy was quite a challenge for a young woman, but his sister never had a moment's doubt that she would take care of him. 'She felt responsible for me my entire life.' She was his guardian angel to whom he could go for comfort when he had been bullied at school or when he felt lonely, and she was always there for him. That's precisely why she never doubted her responsibility after their parents' death. 'Of course we were both badly shaken, but I was probably the worst off, because I'm not as strong as Sis. So she carried me, but I got heavier and heavier the more stuff I got mixed up with. For a while we didn't meet, because it was too hard on her. For more than a year we were only in touch on the phone, and then she had Allan. That's my nephew. He's named after my dad. That gave her some extra energy, and we started meeting again. We were close until her death,' Nikolaj says sadly. He had long since abandoned his criminal career. Largely because of his sister's faith in him. Everyone else gave up on him and said he was past rescue, but not his sister. She believed he was a good person who just found it hard to find his place in life. It was that faith in him that led Nikolaj away from the violence and the crime, and things had started to look brighter when his sister suddenly committed suicide by drowning herself. He is convinced that he drove his sister to commit suicide. 'Of course I am to blame. I never gave her a moment's peace, and in the end she couldn't take it any more.' His sister's death is the cross Nikolaj bears. For six months he

Nikolaj is finding his stride and his smile again after all the hardships.
Photograph: Anders Lollike

was depressed and had a hard time moving on, but he found comfort in Christ. He hadn't previously considered himself devout, but lately the words of Jesus have been his pillar of strength. 'He has helped me and made me make something of my life.' In the future, the words of Jesus will be a guideline in Nikolaj's life. 'I probably won't do everything he tells me, but I'll certainly pay attention. I'd be afraid not to,' Nikolaj says with a smile.

A pilgrimage to Jutland

He has now moved back to Tarm, the town where his mother was born. All of his life he has been trying to work out where he fits in. He doesn't know if it's in West Jutland, but he does know that if you don't know your roots, then you'll never have a sound foundation. 'I think I'm getting to know myself better. If you don't know your parents' background, then how can you understand yourself? That must be why I've moved here,' is Nikolaj's thought-provoking message. He readily admits that he himself is uncertain why he chose to come to Tarm, but now he's here. He hopes that he will prove a valuable addition to Tarm for many years to come. Welcome home, Nikolaj Okholm.

This is how people take it up

People turn around and look at me on the street, pointing me out to each other. At first I am extremely self-conscious, because I can't do a thing without everyone noticing. People come up to me in the supermarket, peering down into my shopping trolley and saying, 'Oh, someone's getting porridge oats.' How am I supposed to respond to that? At one point I'm picking my nose and an elderly lady tells me that my mother never picked her nose, and I exclaim, 'Now that's just not true!' It takes me a while to get used to the attention, but it's amazing how quickly I start to think that it's pretty great. I am special, without even having to try to be special. There are a lot of people who knew Mum, played with her or went to school with her, and they all want to share their experiences with me. I listen politely as they pet me the same way Sis petted Silje, almost devotedly. Karen tells me the whole town is talking about me. They all agree that I may have been a thug once, but that was back in Copenhagen. These days I'm a good lad. I don't behave as if I were famous, but as if I'm an ordinary person. They like that in Tarm.

'Nik & Jay played at the festival last year, and they behaved like they were something special. They got smacked about a bit – that'll teach them to behave – but you're nothing like that,' Karen says.

She's right. I'm nothing like Nik & Jay.

Grandad calls me just once. I almost hang up, but I let him speak. He spends twenty minutes explaining to me that it wasn't him who abandoned me back then, but me who abandoned him. He opened his home to me, but I would rather stay in Copenhagen with my sister, who obviously didn't have the moral fibre to cope with me. If I've had a bad time of it, then it isn't his doing; it's my own.

All I say is, 'Hmm.'

'But Nikolaj, it's not too late.'

'What's not too late?'

'I can still help you if you'll let me.'

This is where I cut him off: 'Would you just shut your mouth?'

Grandad mutters, 'Don't you speak to me in that way. I'm your grandfather.'

'I'll speak to you in whatever way I like. How are you going to help me? You're a leech. I know exactly what people are saying about you. Sod it. It's you who needs me, not the other way round.'

He's silent.

'People think you're pathetic.'

He hangs up, and I feel strong.

According to Karen, people in Tarm hate Grandad, because he wouldn't help them get Mum to play a gig there. They begged him to get in touch with Mum, but he made it abundantly clear that he would have nothing to do with her. That's why no-one will talk to him, not even people from the Evangelical Society. There are even rumours that he's the reason Mum stayed away. I tell Karen that the rumours are true.

'Are they? What did he do to her?' Karen asks.

'I don't want to say.'

'It's nothing to do with paedophilia, is it?'

'I don't want to say.'

A couple of days after the article comes out I stop by Las Vegas. Bike comes up to me right away.

'You really must come out for a pint with us now.'

'When?'

'On Friday.'

'Sounds good,' I say, happy to be going out drinking with the lads.

'Great. Nikolaj, it's fucking incredible, you know, about your mum.'

Friday night I head down to The 60. It's been a long time since I was last in a pub. Kink and Bike are already pissed-up. We said we'd meet at ten and I suppose I arrive at twenty past, but they've been sitting in the exact same spot since they got off from work, just getting pints and shots. When I come through the door, Kink shrieks jubilantly, 'Ahhhhhhhhhhhhhhhh!' pointing feverishly at me all the while. Bike staggers up and says in a loud, proud voice, 'Didn't I say we knew him?'

They all turn around and look at me, and then there's a roar of jubilation from the entire room. It's a bit annoying at first, but after a while my vanity kicks in and I allow them to rub up against me. I play cards and darts, and I chat with the local hairdresser. Pretty girl, a bit older than me and tarty in a rural sort of way. Her name is Anita, but Kink and Bike call her Open All Hours. It takes me a while to understand why, but in the end I get it with a bit of help from her.

I'm taking a wee, and suddenly I'm aware of someone else's hand on my cock. Fortunately it's Anita, and not Bike. I'm not sure what to do, but as I haven't finished weeing I decide to carry on. The hand attempts to goad my cock into action, but all she manages to do is get wee on her hands. When I've finished weeing, she wraps herself around me. She's stripped off her trousers, and I still have my limp cock out. Now she's facing me.

Her arse is dangerously close to being sat in the urinal. It's too absurd to be a turn-on. Anita's pretty, and she's rubbing my cock against her cunt, but this is the men's room, and she's just said 'Fuck me' in a voice booming with beer. She's very drunk, and she loses her balance, lets go of my cock and lands with her arse in the urinal. I don't think she realizes where's she's sitting, because she stays there, legs wide open, looking suggestively at me. The door opens, and Bike comes in. He needs to have a wee. I look at him, utterly gobsmacked. He laughs delightedly, and Anita repeats 'Fuck me' in a voice that echoes with the regrets of tomorrow. Bike comes over and stands next to me, gets his cock out and pisses. The jet of piss lands a mere inch from Anita and sprays her in wee. Finally she catches on to where she is sitting. She jumps up screaming and tries to wipe off the wee, then runs howling out of the men's room. I tuck in my cock and look at the trousers and knickers that are lying on the floor, and realize that Anita has run off with her arse bare.

'Now Anita's bid you welcome in Tarm,' Bike says, laughing. 'It's all cock, cock, cock.'

The door opens on the final 'cock', and Anita returns sheepishly for her trousers. The entire pub is cheering and laughing at her. Several people follow her with their mobile cameras to photograph her naked bottom. She's not feeling so hot. Bike picks up her trousers, but instead of handing them to her, he throws them to me. The idea is for Anita to have to jump about trying to get her trousers back, while we all laugh and take humiliating photos, but I don't want to be part of that and I give her back her trousers.

She puts them on straight away. People are disappointed, because we were all having such fun, but Anita is grateful.

I don't stay there very long after that. One more pint, then I say goodnight to Bike and Kink. They try to talk me into coming with them to Skjern, but I say no. It was fun, but I only want a little bit of it, no more than I can handle.

I feel good. 'Good' is a word that covers everything in my life right now. I talk to people on Poppelvej, especially Karen, because she makes me feel calm. It's reassuring to know that if I feel any anger rising up unbidden, I can just nip round and say hello to her. Maybe I should feel guilty about my complacency, but I've always felt bad, and now suddenly I'm feeling good; and I'm very careful not to indulge in all of that coulda-woulda-shoulda-malarkey. I don't want to think about it. Too much has happened. My parents shouldn't have died. Sis shouldn't be dead. Silje should be with me. I shouldn't have fucked up so badly. It's too much, and so I try not to think about it, because things are better now. Even my worst day in Tarm is better than my best day in Copenhagen.

Marianne and Mathias

The doorbell rings and I open the door, hoping it'll be yet another cake – Karen has a talent for baking cakes – but it's not. It's Jehovah's Witnesses. They've noticed my saying in the article that I've started listening to Jesus, but that I still am a bit hesitant in my devotion to him. Wouldn't I like to hear about him, and about how he can save my soul? One of them is a bloke whose hair has been slicked back with a wet comb, and if he'd been alone, I would have just shut the door; but the other one is a gorgeous redhead girl who reminds me of Miriam. And so I let them in. He is nothing short of ecstatic to be inside. They sit at my kitchen table and start pulling leaflets and brochures out of their bag. I position myself a couple of metres away, leaning against the worktop and folding my arms.

'Do you know about Jehovah's Witnesses?' the bloke asks.

'Not much. I'm sorry, but what did you say your names were?'

'Did we forget to introduce ourselves? I'm so sorry. I'm Mathias, and this is Marianne.'

So it's not Miriam. I didn't think it would be, but it doesn't change the fact that I can't help looking at her tits. They are very fine tits. Of course, she notices me staring at them, and she stoops to make it harder to get a good look.

'Maybe we should start by telling you a bit about ourselves, and what Jehovah's Witnesses stand for. Jehovah's Witnesses means God's Witnesses. The name implies that we give testimony about God, and what he stands for. Jehovah is the name of the almighty God, just like your name is Nikolaj, and our names are Mathias and Marianne.'

He continues to talk about God, and why Jehovah's Witnesses are amazing, but I'm not listening. I'm looking at Marianne's tits. I can't help it. I've never seen a better pair. At one point I catch her eyes; she doesn't look away. On the contrary, she makes me look away. She's stronger than you'd think. Mathias doesn't notice anything; he is totally preoccupied with all the big words he's using. I try to listen in again for a bit.

'Jehovah has a plan for us humans. Of course, you know about Adam and Eve, and you know what happened. They sinned because they broke God's law, and that's why man lost Paradise – but not for ever. Evil must be got rid of before Paradise can be returned, and Armageddon will see to that.'

He looks heavenward with such delight it's as if my ceiling were the way itself.

'Only those who serve God will survive Armageddon. For a thousand years those who serve God will toil to make earth a Paradise with Jesus as their king, and the surviving humans will live for ever. Wouldn't you like a happy life without suffering, violence and death? It would become reality if you accept the word of Jehovah.'

His face is completely red now, and he makes a small, rhetorical pause, catching my eyes as he does so.

'Do you want to be a man who in all his doings strives to follow God's will and God's word? Do you want to be a man who helps others to do God's will? Do you?'

He waits for my answer.

'I really don't believe in God,' I mutter timidly.

That takes them both aback. They look at me with confusion, and Mathias says hopefully: 'But it said in the article that you listen to Jesus.'

'Yes, Jesus helps me.'

'How can you listen to Jesus if you don't believe in him?' Marianne asks confused.

'I believe in the Jesus, who showed up in my flat, but he's not the son of God.'

'Sure, Jesus is the son of God.'

I smile.

'Yes, yours maybe, but mine isn't.'

'You can't believe in Jesus without believing in God,' he says and points at me, in my own kitchen.

'That's up to me, isn't it?'

'No, that's not how it works.'

'It does in my home.'

Mathias puts his hands to his face and rubs it. He is weary and frustrated. Marianne gawps at me with some curiosity. Mathias gets a hold of himself, and says, 'But if you follow God's will –' and I interrupt him.

'I can't be bothered to talk any more about God.'

'God says.'

'Didn't you hear what I just said? This is my house. You are my guests. It's been interesting, but now it's getting awkward, and I can't be bothered with any more God stuff.'

'Then what do you want to talk about?' Marianne asks, gently.

I look deep into her eyes.

'You.'

She blushes, but she also smiles in a flattered way.

Mathias's face goes quite pale. He gets up angrily, slams his hand down on the kitchen table and hisses, 'We're leaving, if you can't behave.'

'Okay, I'll walk you out.'

Mathias stands dumbstruck in my kitchen, and Marianne sniggers discreetly.

Just before I shut the door, I ask Marianne if she's related to someone called Miriam who is also a Jehovah's Witness?

'I've a cousin called Miriam,' she says, surprised.

'From Copenhagen?'

'Yes.'

'I think I went to school with her.'

And then she remembers that her cousin told her the story about the pervert boy with the famous mother many years ago.

'Good God, that's right,' she says with a mixture of a laugh and a shock.

It's back

I wonder whether to sleep or watch telly, but I'm a bit too awake after all the stories about Judgement Day and God's Great Plan, so in the end the telly wins. I never spend less than five or six hours in front of the television. What else am I to do? I've got a mission which is to become a better man without having a stomach ache. I've managed so far. I used to watch a lot of telly when I was a self-loathing, violent fuck-head, but now I enjoy it. There's a distinct difference. These days I'm a harmless man without stomach aches. Jesus can't say fairer than that.

I fetch a beer, grab a packet of biscuits and sit myself comfortably in the easy chair and switch on the television. It's one

American sitcom after another. Suddenly, I notice a rumbling in my stomach. It's a quiet rumbling, so I don't really think about it. Maybe I've had too many biscuits. I put them down and concentrate on *Frasier*. There's another rumble, but I ignore it because I feel good. Then my knot explodes in anger. It's not going to put up with being ignored. It's back, rested and violent, and I'm about to get a good thrashing. I fall off the chair with a scream. It fucking hurts. I snort and pant. I try to get up to shake it off, but I can't. I only get up on my knees and then I vomit in cascades. I start whining miserably as I look at my own sick. I roll a couple of metres away from my own vomit and bump into a pair of sandals.

'Help me...'

Jesus bends down and smoothes the hair away from my forehead.

'Nikolaj, did you really think it would be this easy?'

I have no idea what he's talking about, but my pain is fading, and I can breathe again. I stay on the floor, panting, while Jesus steps over my sick and turns off the television.

The sun is shining. It's mid-August. We've gone out for a walk in the wood and fields where I can breathe freely. I'm on my guard, because he seems disappointed in me, and I don't understand why. Right now I'm in shock, but I'm convinced that I'm living a good life. Jesus bends down and picks dandelions. If I weren't so worried, I'd find it funny that such a beefy bloke is picking flowers. As he sits there, with his back to me, he asks, 'How are you finding Tarm?'

127

'I like it. It's a nice town.'

'Have you enjoyed being here?'

Then he gets up again with a fistful of dandelions.

'Yes, I have. It's been nice.'

'You've got fat,' he says, and walks on.

I follow him, looking down at my stomach and saying, 'I suppose. A bit.'

Since coming to Tarm, I've put on almost two stone, and it's all sitting slap in the centre on my stomach; but I was scrawny before, so I'm not too fussed.

'So you're content, living in Tarm, are you? Everything's as it should be?'

Something's not right, because he says that with no feeling in his voice.

'Don't be fooled by what just happened. It's really only happened once,' I say hastily.

'Why did it happen?'

I hope this is the last gasp, a final grim assault before the knot goes for good, but I can't be certain, so I say, 'No idea.'

'Right. Nikolaj, did you come here to have a good time?'

'Not just for that, but I've changed a lot. I'm harmless. That's got to be better than before.'

'It's not enough,' he says quietly.

There's an annoying silence for several minutes, during which neither of us speaks. We can't even hear cars, only wind and, every so often, a cow mooing. It's torture, because I know there's more to come, and I'm getting fed up. Finally, he breaks the silence.

'You are who you are, and you've done what you've done. You can't ignore that.'

'Oh. Says who?'

'Says I!'

I stop and look at him with surprise. Who does he think he is? I am doing all right. I've never done all right before. I might not be happy, but doing all right is enough for me. I don't hurt all of the time. If I'm only hurting every three months, then I'm content.

'I've got my house. I've got neighbours I talk to. I'm admired. That's not nothing to me. That's huge,' I say decisively.

'You're not allowed to be content yet.'

'I'm where I'm supposed to be.'

I get angry and step away from him, walking over to a horse and patting it, while he waits patiently. In the end he walks up to the horse and holds out his dandelion leaves. It abandons me and trots over to him, where it munches away. I have to turn and face him.

'I'm a better man now. I'm happy.'

'No, you're not, but you don't know that yet.'

'I'm content with what I've got. That's what happiness is all about.'

My stomach starts rumbling belligerently. It warns me that pain is coming if I don't do something right now. The horse trots away from us.

'I need you to rise above the joy of being content. It's not enough,' Jesus tells me firmly.

'It is to me.'

'No, not any longer. If you hide, you drown.'

My face is distorted by a terrible stomach ache. It's not fair. He's

129

supposed to protect me, not torment me. It makes me fucking furious, and I yell at the top of my voice, while poking him hard in the chest, 'FUCK YOU! YOU'RE A NUTTER, SO JUST SHUT YOUR FAT FACE! YOU KNOW NOTHING!'

He grabs my finger, then shakes his head in such a provoking way. I yank back my hand and walk home to Poppelvej. It's a two- or three-mile walk home, but I stubbornly keep quiet. We don't speak a word to each other. Right before we get back, he manages to strike a clean blow at me when he says, 'How often have you thought about Sis?'

I have deliberately pushed her out of my mind, so I've done very little of that, almost none at all.

'How often have you thought about Silje?'

That's even less, even though I frequently have nightmares about it.

'What about Brian and Allan? Have you considered the fact that you've ruined their lives?'

'Shut up!'

'How often have you cried about Sis?'

'I'm going to give you such a beating if you don't stop!' I spit at him.

'You couldn't even if you wanted to.'

He's right. He's too strong. We're home now, so I walk off.

'What are you doing?'

'Taking a piss. Do you want to come, or does the Messiah think I can handle that on my own?'

*

130

Once again I'm hiding in the bathroom to calm myself down a bit. He's right, I know that. I don't deserve to feel good so soon. I stare in the mirror and then make a big gob. I spit at my reflected image, right between the eyes. Someone knocks on the door.

'Nikolaj, are you feeling all right? You've been in there half an hour.'

'I'm okay. I'll be out in a second.'

I yank up my jumper and look at my love handles. Two stone in two months. Why has the pain been such a large part of me, if I can just forget it and eat biscuits and get fat? I put on my jumper again and unlock the door. Jesus is standing outside, looking very worried.

'Are you sure you're all right?'

'Of course I'm not. I feel shit.'

Suddenly, without a word of warning Jesus pulls me close. I feel his muscles tighten as he clasps me in his arms. It's strange to be so close to another man, his hard body against my lardy one. I rest my head against his chest. It's my first real hug from a man. I've done that thing you do with the two quick pats on the back, but I've never held another man and continued to hold on to him.

The Plan

This is what Jesus tells me to do:

1. I must look after Jeppe when he comes. He's an old friend, and he needs my help. Of course, I don't

131

understand. Why would he come to see me? Jesus, however, seems sure that he will, and when he does, he'll be my responsibility.

2. I mustn't let Granny die weighed down by guilt. She has felt so guilty, because she did want to help us back then, but Jesus says she wasn't strong enough. She still isn't. I have to help her, because if I give her strength, she'll come to my aid.

3. I must help Brian move on. Right now he's sad and angry. He must love again.

4. I beat up Silje, and now she's afraid, not just of me but of pretty much everything. She mustn't be afraid any more. She asked me not to contact her again, and I don't want to, because it scares me, but Jesus says it's necessary.

5. I must strive to become a person that I can care about and whom others can care about too.

'How am I supposed to do all that?' I ask Jesus.
'You're not going to be doing it alone. You'll be helped by your friends.'
'What friends?' I ask, but he doesn't answer.

Someone's in my garden

I've just got up. It's the day after Jesus' visit, and I'm looking sleepily out of my kitchen window. Someone's in my garden, but I have no idea who, because I can see bugger-all without my contact lenses. I go outside, a bit closer. This person isn't saying anything; he merely stares intently at me. When I'm about ten foot from him, every hair and follicle on my entire body suddenly stands on end. Unfuckingbelievable! It's Jeppe. I'd been warned he was coming. Jesus had said so, but I cannot believe that he's actually standing in my garden, looking hollow-cheeked

'Hiya Niko. I don't know if you remember me,' he says warily.

'Of course I remember you, Jeppe.'

He purses his lips and lifts his hands to his head, then drops his chin to his chest and wails, but there are no tears, just a body in spasms. I know what I ought to do, but it takes me a long time to go over to him. As I let my arm slide around him and pull him towards me, he starts shaking like a worn-out tumble drier. It's all I can do to hold him.

We're standing like that until he pushes me off and, embarrassed, turns his back to me. He gets a hold of himself, sort of. He turns to me with an assumed toughness, which doesn't in any way mask his insecurity.

'What are you doing here?' I ask.

'Visiting you.'

'I guessed that much, but why are you here?'

'Don't you want me to be?'

The dread of my answer is clearly visible in his face.

'It's good to have you. I'd just like to know why you've come?'

It's obvious that I'm tormenting him. I don't mean to. At once he starts skipping on the spot. He's so bloody thin, he's almost transparent.

'I wanted to see you.'

'You track me down after ten years because you want to see me?'

'Yes. Or, no, I didn't track you down. You got in touch with me.'

His enthusiasm tells me that he's serious.

'How's that?'

'You sent the article. The one about you moving to Tarm.'

Suddenly it makes sense. Of course he doesn't turn up out of the blue. He thinks the article is an invitation from me to him. Jesus is clever. He sends Jeppe here, and now he's my responsibility.

'It's good to have you, but I didn't send the article.'

'You didn't?'

He's surprised. He wonders if I'm lying and skips a bit faster.

'No, but it doesn't matter. How long are you staying?'

'I don't know.'

'You can stay as long as you like.'

He seems not to hear me. He looks at me blankly, but then I notice that he's biting his lips again, and his bony shoulders are starting to shake. This happens several times on the first day. I show him the room with the purple sofa bed and say, 'This'll be yours now,' and straight off he starts shaking. He's brought almost nothing, only a small shoulder bag. I don't know what he's expecting, but he has packed for failure. I say, 'Anything that's mine is yours, that goes for my clothes as well,' and there's another fit of shaking. I have to wait patiently every time he gasps for breath, trying in vain to hide his relief.

Because we need each other

The first night I wake up screaming, because he has snuck into my bed. He can't sleep and my snoring calms him. But I don't give a monkey's toss: I'm not sharing a bed with him!

My stomach ache has returned, and now I'm thinking non-stop about what I did to Sis, Silje, Brian, everyone. It haunts me. When these thoughts are at their worst, I go to the bathroom. I'm not always sick, but sometimes I am. When I come out, Jeppe looks at me, but he never says a word. It's strange, that, because he used to speak constantly, and now he's silent, pale and he's almost hiding. I see him looking longingly at me, but he says nothing, and when I ask him about something, he just says 'yes' or 'no'.

That makes it odd, but very easy to share a house with him. On the other hand, he is hardly a tidy person. Every time he's been in a room, everything in it has sought refuge on the floor. I'm not exactly a methodical person myself, but I can't abide other people's mess, and least of all other people's mess in my house. I tell him repeatedly to tidy up. He nods politely, and he does try, but two hours after I've told him, he's forgotten all about it.

Annoyed by this, I go into his room after a couple of days. I take his little bag, empty everything in it out on the floor, kicking

135

at his things, throwing them around a bit to make a real mess. I'm a bit too brutal, but that'll teach him. I wait excitedly for his reaction. When he sees it, he shuts the door quietly. I'm standing outside for five minutes, all geared up for battle, but he doesn't come barging out. I open the door warily. He's sitting silently on the bed, and then he turns a sad face towards me. I've done something stupid, because he's sadder than the mess I've made might account for. He doesn't say anything, just looks sadly back at his things again. I don't know what to do. I'm ashamed of myself.

'It was just because you were making such a mess. You mustn't make such messes, Jeppe.'

He nods very seriously.

'Don't be mad at me, Niko. Please, don't be mad,' and his voice breaks.

'Are you upset?'

He shakes his head, but I can tell he's lying.

'Damn it, Jeppe, we're so stupid. We really have to talk to each other if I'm going to be looking after you.'

'Don't worry about me,' he says, as he starts to pick up his clothes and put them in the bag.

'I have to, or he'll be mad at me.'

He stops tidying.

'Who'll be mad?'

I sit down next to him and say, 'Jesus will.'

I witter away for an hour, telling him the Jesus story and the full prequel to it. The grizzlier the story gets, the more he seems to open out. He swallows every word with delight, and he can't sit still. He gets up and skips while I talk. When I finally stop talking, he says enthusiastically, 'I'll help you.'

'Help me do what?'

'I'll help you become a better man.'

It's only a few days before Jeppe isn't transparent any longer. I'm beginning to understand why Jesus has made Jeppe come here. We're too weak on our own. Jeppe needs me if he's not to disappear completely, and I need Jeppe, because I need other people to motivate me.

We're debating intensely what might be the best way to proceed; that is, where and how to make our first assault. For days on end we hole ourselves up, drink a ton of beer and talk about old times. It's bloody marvellous to be able to talk about old times, but it doesn't get us anywhere. The plan seems scary, because neither of us is used to taking responsibility for anything at all. We veer away every time it seems dangerous. We need help, because otherwise we'll just keep drinking beer and discuss what we might do if we had the guts to do it. We can't just be us. We need NATO (that's what we call our gang) to protect us from doubt and hesitation.

It's not easy to get a gang together when you don't know anyone, but we'll just have to use what we've got. After all, Jesus didn't know his disciples before they became his disciples. They were fishermen and tax collectors. People Jesus met because he happened to walk past a lake. At least I've talked to mine before.

NATO

'Hello, Karen.'

She is on all fours in her front garden, removing the weeds that have crept in between her pretty flowers. She's pleased to see me; both her mouth and her eyes are all smiles.

'Hello, Nikolaj. Haven't seen you about much in the past week.'

'No, I've been busy.'

'Yes, we noticed you've had a friend to stay. Has he gone now?'

'He's going to stay.'

'Well, I think that's great, Nikolaj.'

She gets up, takes off her gardening gloves, and the expression on her faces changes completely. It becomes far more serious.

'What's great?'

'Your courage! People are keeping an eye on you, because you are who you are, and yet you don't allow that to stop you.'

'Stop me from what?'

I have no idea what's she on about.

'Being openly gay. I spoke to Bitten – that's Kaj's sister, you know – yesterday. She was shocked when I said it, but then I said that you did come from an artistic family after all. We've never had a real gay in Poppelvej, although there were some rumours about Erling at number 37. What does your friend do? Is he an artist? He looks dangerous in that mysterious way, you know.'

'He's not an artist or gay. I'm not either.'

'Are you not? And he's not either? He's very thin. Dear me, so embarrassing. I shouldn't have told Bitten then,' she says, throwing her gardening glove at me and laughing sheepishly.

'Not to worry. All I wanted was to hear if I could invite you round for some R&R tomorrow night?'

She claps delightedly.

'You certainly can. We'll look forward to it.'

'We?'

'Me and Kaj. We are really supposed to be going down to play badminton, but we'll just cancel that.'

'It's just you.'

'Just me? Is it only going to be the two of us?'

That makes her a bit nervous. Why am I asking a married woman round for a bit of R&R all on her own?

'No, there'll be others, but it's sort of a secret meeting combined with some R&R.'

'Now, it's not going to be one of those sex orgy things, is it? Because me and Kay tried that once. We won't be doing that again. It was awkward with all those willies. There was this man who touched Kay's willy, and then he wanted to go home straight away, but we couldn't, because I was in the middle of something. We rowed over that for weeks. So no orgy. Kay wouldn't want me to go to one.'

I pick up the gardening glove and hand it to her while I say, 'It's got nothing to do with sex.'

'So you're not trying to seduce me?'

'Lord, no,' I say, feeling a little shocked, although I do immediately picture me and Karen shagging.

139

'Because you do hear about young lads from Copenhagen who fancy older women all the time, you know.'

I really don't know what to say now. We're looking awkwardly at each other, and then we both of us stare stiffly at the ground. The final bit of the conversation is made without any eye contact.

'So, what time should I come?'

'Seven.'

'Okay then, I'll see you tomorrow.'

She sits down again and picks away the weeds from between the flowers.

It's a lot easier inviting the next two, even though I haven't seen them since Jeppe came to town. I pop in at Las Vegas and stand before them awkwardly.

'Come round mine tomorrow around seven, yeah?'

'Sure.'

'22 Poppelvej.'

'We do bloody know that.'

After that it gets a bit harder. I've arranged to have a haircut. Because I've got a receding hairline, I shave my head every three weeks. In other words, there's nothing to cut, but I'm sitting there at Trendy Look, and Anita is staring bewildered at the top of my head. There isn't anyone else in the salon. Trendy Look isn't doing so well. There are two other, far more popular salons in Tarm – New Look and Salon Chris – and there isn't all that much hair to be cut in Tarm. Anita has just let her two employees go. Now it's just her and a mostly empty salon.

'I'm not sure there's a lot I can do.'

She runs her hand over the quarter-inch stubble on top of my head.

'I know. I just came because I wanted to chat to you. I was wondering if you'd like to come round to mine tomorrow night at seven for some R&R.'

Her hand is still running over the crown of my head, but her movements are more affectionate now.

'You booked a time with me to ask me on a date. But we don't know each other.'

'I do know you a little bit, and I'd really like to see you tomorrow.'

'That's sweet. I'd love to.'

She doesn't appear to be uncomfortable about our little men's room romance. In fact, it's a lot easier than I'd expected. I suppose I ought to explain to her that it isn't a date, but I can't be bothered right now. She's coming tomorrow, and we'll deal with it then.

I ring Marianne's doorbell. She's my age, but she isn't married and she lives alone in a small house on Vardevej. I thought they married young so they could have sex? Of course, she isn't expecting me to visit her, but if they can ring my bell, then I can ring theirs.

'Hello.'

'Hiya.'

'I'd like to invite you and Mathias to a small get-together at my house tomorrow night.'

She looks at me as if profoundly puzzled and, inevitably, I gawp

141

at her tits again. She forces herself to smile politely, while folding her arms protectively over her chest.

'I think I can answer for Mathias and say thanks but no thanks. We don't want to.'

'Oh. Why not?'

'We're very different.'

'That's no reason not to come.'

'But we don't want to. Mathias was very angry last time.'

'I'd really like it if you'd come.'

'But we're not going to. Goodbye, Nikolaj,' and then she shuts the door.

I ring the bell straight away. She doesn't answer at once, but I keep pressing it. In the end she gives up and opens the door again.

'Why don't you stop? We're not coming. Mathias doesn't like you. He thinks we should steer well clear of you.'

'Oh. What do you think?'

'We're not coming,' she maintains stubbornly.

'My place tomorrow at seven.'

'We're not coming,' she repeats.

'It's about making me a better man.'

I catch a glimmer of interest in her eyes.

'We're still not coming.'

'I need you.'

'What do you mean, you need us?'

'Just that. Tomorrow at seven. I need you to be there.'

I turn around and leave. She follows me with her eyes until I'm out of sight.

Need them! Who wouldn't like to be indispensable? And I hadn't even planned it. It just came to me.

NATO meets for the first time

Karen shows up half an hour before everyone else. She's been so excited all day, and by now she simply can't stay at home any longer. Jeppe sits still and tries to work her out. Is he supposed to feel threatened? It's one of the reasons why he's no good with people. He's constantly on his guard. She walks over to him with a big, beaming smile.

'Hello,' she says, holding her hand out.

'Hello.'

Not even a big, beaming smile and an outstretched hand make him lower his guard.

'Nikolaj says you're neither gay nor an artist. Then why are you looking so glum all the time?'

I've warned him about Karen, but he didn't believe me, because Karen needs to be experienced first hand. She sits down next to him. Jeppe is nervous.

'I don't know. Maybe I'm just glum.'

'We're all of us glum, but that's no reason to be going about moping, is it?'

Jeppe is rocking back and forth on his chair. He wants to get up and skip on the spot, but he knows that seems odd when people don't yet know him, so he makes himself stay on the chair.

'So, what do you do?'

'What do you mean?'

He tries to sit still, because he thinks she's referring to the fact that he's thrashing about. He looks at me for help, but I'm enjoying myself, and I don't want to stop her.

'Are you rich too?'

'No, I'm not rich. I'm anything but rich.'

'Then what do you do?'

As Jeppe's eyes go blank, I had better step in and help him out.

'You know, Karen, I've known Jeppe for almost ten years. He's my oldest friend.'

'You are?' she shrieks.

Karen looks at Jeppe with delight. He's not an artist, but being my oldest friend is just as interesting. Jeppe is still afraid of her.

'He's come here to help me with the hardest thing I've ever had to do in my entire life.'

Jeppe sits up straight and, finding a better balance, stops sliding quite so much back and forth in the chair. Karen immediately becomes maddeningly curious, and she turns to face me. Jeppe is visibly relieved.

'What is the hardest thing you've ever done in your entire life?'

'The thing we're about to embark on.'

'What is it?'

'I'll tell you when the others get here. I'm saying nothing until then.'

For the next fifteen minutes she paces the floor restlessly, and when the doorbell rings she dashes over to open the door. I like her cheekiness, but it would have been obnoxious and utterly insufferable in absolutely anyone else. She just does it with a disarming sincerity.

They are just about equally taken aback. Karen looks at her hairdresser with disappointment, and she gets an equally disappointed look in return. Anita is wearing a little black dress, and she's pretty when she's not sitting with her arse in a urinal. Jeppe pulls himself together and says hello, but it doesn't help her relax. He's just another person in the sitting room who's not supposed to be there. She's at a loss as she looks from Jeppe to Karen to me. I pull Anita aside gently and whisper, 'I'm so pleased you've come.'

'What are they doing here?'

'It's not a date. I'm sorry if you thought it was.'

'But, I'm not wearing any knickers.'

She blushes because she just blurted it out.

'It'll be all right. We won't tell anyone.'

Bike and Kink are fifteen minutes late. They decide – demonstratively – not to say hello to Jeppe when I introduce him as my oldest friend. Kink is about to shake his hand, but Bike indicates elegantly that he finds it unnecessary. For some reason Bike thinks Jeppe is all wrong. Throughout the entire evening the two of them glare at each other with ill-concealed hostility. Bike glares; Jeppe merely reciprocates.

It's a quarter to eight, and it would seem that Mathias and Marianne are not going to come. It annoys me, but I can't have everything.

145

We crack on. It's a warm evening in August, and I open the windows wide. As I've decided to be honest, I treat them to the story of my life. It's the third time in not too long that I've told it. This time I include each and every grizzly detail, because I want them to know what they're getting involved in. There are constant little squeaks of 'Oh dear', 'Dear me no', 'Poor you.' When I get to the part about beating up Silje, they go especially pale. Kink gets up, points at me angrily and says, 'Someone should give you such a beating. You can't hit girls, dammit!' Kink is a big fellow, but fortunately Bike grabs hold of him. They go out into the hall and Bike tries to talk him down, while the rest of us remain seated in the sitting room, feeling a bit uneasy.

'He bloody beat her up!'

'I was there. I heard too. Go on. Get back in there.'

Silence.

'It's Niko. Last night you said he was the dog's bollocks.'

'Yes I did, but that was before I knew he beat girls.'

'One girl, not girls. There's a reason he has all those scars,' Bike says.

'I can't be arsed to go back in there. Plus, it'd be awkward now,' and we hear footsteps. Then my front door is opened and shut, as Bike says, 'Kink, dammit.' I look out in the hall. They're gone. I'm not sure if I should continue with just Anita and Karen here, but after thirty seconds the doorbell rings. I open the door to Bike and Kink. He nods at me and says, 'I'm sorry, Niko, it just really pissed me off.'

I'm standing awkwardly in front of Kink and mutter, 'I understand. No need to apologize.'

We continue.

Strange as it may seem, Karen only interrupts me when I say that I didn't attend Sis's funeral.

'You weren't there at your sister's funeral?'

'No. Like I said, I didn't know about it.'

'But you've been there?'

I shake my head.

'Nikolaj, it's your sister. You've got to say goodbye. You do know where she's buried, don't you?'

'Yes, of course I know. She's buried quite close to the pond in Vestre Kirkegård.'

'You really have to say goodbye to her. She deserves that,' and then she shuts up, because I'm getting upset.

Time and time again they are shocked, but they're not scared of me, because all the dangerous stuff is all in the past, and the present is all about making me a better man. I finish by telling them that I want them to be my NATO, helping me to become a better man.

'Any questions?'

Four hands shoot into the air.

'What exactly is it you want from us?' Anita asks, confused.

I understand her confusion.

'I want you to help me, because I can't do it on my own.'

'Are you asking us to be your friends?'

I have to think about it before I can answer. 'Friend' is a very big word, which makes me hesitate, but in the end I say, 'Yes, I suppose I am.'

I hope Jesus is right.

'I'll be your friend,' Anita says without any hesitation.

'Thanks. But I mean friends that I'll be asking for rather a lot,' I hurriedly interject.

'Nikolaj, people do ask their friends for a lot. That's what friends are for,' Karen says, looking at me tenderly.

'It is?'

How would I know?

'Yes, it is. Jeppe, why is Nikolaj your friend?'

He hasn't said a word until now, hasn't made a sound, hasn't moved a muscle, and the sudden attention makes him completely flustered. They're all waiting excitedly for his answer. I am too.

'Because he is.'

It's not good enough, and he senses that straight away. He stammers warily, but surprisingly firmly, 'Because he saved me. That makes him amazing in my eyes, and I'd do anything for him.'

Now it's my turn to be flustered. That's no way to speak about me. I'm an arsehole. Karen smiles at Jeppe.

'That was a good answer. You see, Nikolaj, when you're asking us to be your friends, you're really asking us to be there for you the way you were there for Jeppe.'

The Q&A continues late into the night. Jesus, of course, attracts quite a few questions.

'Are you sure he's real?'

'That he's Jesus? No, I'm pretty sure he's not Jesus.'

'No, that's not what I mean. Are you sure he's real? I mean, that he's really there?' Bike asks the question they're all thinking. I smile tolerantly at them.

'Are you asking me if I'm a nutter?'

'No, but when you're stressed out, you might perhaps be imagining things.'

'I've felt him, physically. He gave me such a powerful hug, the flab on my tummy squelched round and settled on my back.'

They're not convinced, but still Karen says, 'If you say he's real, then of course he is. Isn't he?'

They all nod enthusiastically. They accept that I am speaking to him, and if I want to talk about it, they'll listen, but it has to come from me.

It's three o'clock in the morning when they leave. We've talked about my grandparents, Sis, Silje, Brian, my life in general, and I can't think of anything else that I need to tell them. We agree that they will leave now, go home and have a good think about things, and then we'll meet again in a couple of days, but I'm convinced that NATO is a reality, because they leave with an air of excitement. Even Kink has come around.

It's been a long night, but a good one. Jeppe has gone to bed, but I need a bit of fresh air, some wind in my ears and grass between my toes. I go out into the garden. Everything is silent, until I hear snoring. Blast you, Jeppe! Then I realize it's a quiet, girly snore, not the thundering snorts Jeppe produces. Below the open window I can just make out someone curled up. Curious, I walk over and squat down. Even in the dark she has amazing tits. I rouse her gently, and she wakes up with a frightened jolt. She looks at me with fear, but then she realizes that she is sitting under my window in my garden. She's the one who has some explaining to do, not me, but she doesn't say anything.

'Have you been sitting here all night?'

She's scared. Not of me but of the situation. Her breathing becomes heavier and heavier. I get up and hold out my hand to her. As the evening was a success, I'm currently full of confidence.

'Upsy-daisy.'

She hesitates, but I let my hand float in front of her nose until she grabs it, then I pull her up. There's a bit too much strength in my pull. We bump into each other, and for two seconds we are standing very close together. It's far more intimate than intended. Now she's afraid of both the situation and of me, so I take a hurried step back.

'Let's sit down on that bench over there.'

Once again she hesitates.

'I won't do anything. I promise.'

'I think I'd better leave.'

'You can't eavesdrop, then just leave.'

She doesn't try to deny it, and even in the dark I can tell she's embarrassed.

'Have you been there all night?'

'Since eight o'clock.'

'And you heard everything?'

'Yes, everything since eight o'clock.'

'Then why didn't you come in? You knew you were invited.'
'I don't know.'
'Let's sit down on the bench, what do you say?'
She's still hesitating.
'I'd like to talk to you.'
'I don't think it's such a good idea.'
'Us talking?'
'Me staying.'
I groan.
'Come on. I'm not asking you to snog me, am I?'
Stupid! She says it again, 'No, I'd better leave.'
This time she does. There's no goodbye. She just turns around and leaves. My life is fucking weird. At three in the morning I find the prettiest Jehovah's Witness in all of Tarm sitting in my garden.

The last members join the alliance

Jeppe is cranky, because I wake him up too early. We're on the lookout for Marianne. Jeppe doesn't understand why. He thinks we're enough people as we are, especially as Karen won't leave him alone and Bike stares at him with open hostility.

We've been round to her house, but she wasn't there. Luckily, her neighbour was home and she told us that Marianne works at Mathias's accountancy firm next to the supermarket. We hurry over, step inside and look at three dull people – Mathias, Marianne and an elderly woman – behind three dull desks. Mathias gets up and comes over to us.

'How can I help?'

'We're here to speak to Marianne.'

'If it's got anything to do with our little chat, then you can speak to me too,' Mathias says.

'No, it's got nothing to do with that. I'm still not devout. Sorry about that,' and I move towards Marianne.

Mathias steps in front of me and puts a hand on my chest.

'May I know what this is about?'

Marianne signals to me to say nothing by shaking her head slightly.

'It's private.'

'I see, but this is a workplace. What's it about?' Mathias says suspiciously.

'It's private,' I say emphatically.

'Then I'm going to have to ask you to leave.'

'It won't take very long.'

I try to take a step towards Marianne. Mathias won't allow it. He gives me a shove and says with some hostility, 'No, this is a workplace.'

I try to take another step towards Marianne, and Mathias shoves me again. By now Jeppe has had it. He jumps out and hisses, 'For fuck's sake, we just want to talk to her!'

Mathias doesn't seem to understand that he ought to be afraid. All he says is, 'Yes, well, you can't.' He tries to shove Jeppe too, but Jeppe grabs hold of him and yanks him to the floor, and with spittle spraying from his mouth, he says, 'Why was she in our garden last night?'

I should have let Jeppe sleep it off, and I pull him away as quickly as I can. Mathias, who is frightened, stays on the floor. I bend down to help him up, but he's intimidated and inches away from me. Marianne and the old lady, now both alert, have got up and are standing behind their desks, but they don't do anything. Jeppe scares them. Mathias looks at Marianne with something like bafflement.

'Were you in their garden last night?'

'No, of course not,' she says.

Jeppe isn't having any of this.

'Yes, you bloody were! You were eavesdropping all night.'

'Jeppe!'

'She's such a lying cow!'

'Jeppe, shut up, will you?'

Mathias ought to be glad I'm here. For crying out loud, why doesn't he stand up? It looks really daft, him lying there.

'What are they talking about, Marianne? Have you let us down again?'

'I have no idea what it is they're talking about.'

'I don't believe you.'

The old woman walks over to Mathias and helps him get up. They stay well away from us, creating a wall between us and Marianne.

'What have you done?' he asks Marianne, who tries to avoid his accusing glare.

'I haven't done anything.'

'Marianne! You must tell us the truth if you want to be forgiven.'

153

There's an uncomfortable atmosphere. I'm starting to regret having barged in and got her into trouble.

'I certainly hope you haven't let me down again.'

'I haven't,' she says, but she's lying, and Mathias knows it.

She sits down, despondently. She's close to tears. Mathias turns to us with a phoney smile.

'Marianne doesn't have time to speak to you. We're very busy at the moment.'

Jeppe roars and walks towards them angrily. They jump aside, looking frightened. He's almost a foot shorter than Mathias, but they recognize danger when they see it. Jeppe grabs Marianne by the wrist, yanking her out of the chair, then drags her out of the office. I'm left standing there, confused. Then I nod at them and leave. Outside Jeppe is holding on to Marianne. She is crying, trying to go back inside, but he won't let her.

'Let's go home.'

Jeppe gives me an affirmative nod, then drags the reluctant Marianne all the way back to Poppelvej. If she's in for a penny, she's in for a pound.

Once we get home, she paces the rooms in a state of befuddlement. She doesn't try to run, but she doesn't say anything either. I decide to be patient, and after ten minutes of pacing up and down she forces herself to be sort of calm. She puffs herself up, looks us over and smacks first Jeppe and then me resoundingly.

SLOP! SLOP!

I turn to stop Jeppe from attacking her, but he has no intention

154

of doing so. He's absolutely quiet, and accepts the blow.

'Have you completely lost your minds?' she yells.

Neither of us says anything.

'You can't just barge into my workplace and yank me out of there!'

We're still not saying anything. We're looking at her rather sheepishly, because we do know that we've crossed a line.

'Do you have any idea how long I've struggled to get them to trust me again?'

'They're just arses, the lot of them,' Jeppe says quietly.

I agree with him.

'No, *you* lot are just arses.'

As she says the word, she becomes suddenly quiet.

She can leave if she wants to, but she sits down, and there we all sit until she decides to speak. It's a long time before she says anything, and it doesn't happen until after the police have been to see us.

The doorbell rings, and I open the door. Outside is a police car, parked in a way the neighbours can't possibly miss.

'Nikolaj Okholm?'

'Yes.'

'May we come in?'

'Of course.'

One of them is a young, slim officer; the other's slightly older with a bit of a paunch. Mathias has reported us for kidnapping and assault. Both Marianne and Jeppe are visibly discomfited when the officers step into the room.

155

'Are you Marianne Pedersen?' the older officer asks.

'Yes,' Marianne says nervously.

'Are you all right?'

'Yes, why wouldn't I be?'

'We were told you were being held here against your will.'

This is when she decides in favour of us and against Mathias.

'Who said that?'

'Your colleague, Mathias Brandt. He said Nikolaj Okholm and a friend hurled you out of your workplace against your will.'

'I quit today. He's just mad about that.'

'So you're saying he's lying? You do realize that you're saying he has filed a false report, and that that is a criminal offence? Are you sure he's lying?'

She nods in a manner so natural it's almost brutal.

'He's just ticked off. You won't punish him, will you?'

'You're here of your own free will, and it's not because you're afraid of something?'

She shakes her head, but they're not convinced. He turns to Jeppe.

'Mathias told us that he had been assaulted as well by a friend of Nikolaj Okholm, someone called Jeppe. Is that you?'

'I haven't done anything,' he blurts out much too quickly. The words tumble out.

They hold his gaze, and Jeppe nervously has to look away.

'I had a row with Mathias. We yelled at each other, but Jeppe didn't interfere,' Marianne says.

She seems worried that something will happen to us. We look

at her, puzzled. Only ten minutes ago she was hitting us.

'That's strange, because both your colleagues say that you were dragged out of the office by Jeppe, and that he threw Mathias to the floor.'

Suddenly, Karen is standing in my sitting room. She hasn't rung the doorbell or knocked; she's just there.

'Hello Jens, what are you doing here?'

The older officer turns towards her.

'Hello Karen, I suppose I could ask you the same thing.'

'Yes, you can indeed. I saw the car outside and thought I'd pop in and say hello and see what was afoot. Has Nikolaj been riding his bicycle without lights on?'

She smiles at the officer, but he doesn't smile back. He says, 'No, it's much more serious. The two young gentlemen here are accused of assault and kidnapping.'

'Jeppe and Nikolaj? They're the most peaceable lads you'd find anywhere. They wouldn't hurt a fly.'

'Now, you do know that it's up to me to decide whether this thing sticks or not? It's not up to you.'

'Are you saying you don't trust me?'

'No, I'm not saying that. Of course I trust you.'

'Because Kaj and I would take that very much to heart, you know.'

'Karen, that's not what I'm saying!'

'Are you saying I've got criminal friends? That makes you either a criminal or not my friend. Are you my friend?'

'Of course I am. You know how fond I am of you and Kaj.'

'Well then, if that's so, then you must be a criminal, because otherwise it doesn't add up, does it Jens?'

'It does.'

'No, it doesn't. When I say they're perfectly harmless, then they are.'

'Now I've only just read an article where Nikolaj says he was once violent.'

Something wild gets into Karen's eyes.

'You stop right now. You're crossing the line, and you ought to be ashamed of yourself. The entire town knows what a good boy he is these days, and you weren't too well-behaved yourself when you were a lad. I remember several scuffles when Kaj had to come and save you,' Karen says.

We are all of us – the young officer included – completely dumbfounded. He sniggers, and Jens turns around and gives him an angry glare.

'If it wasn't for Kaj and me, you wouldn't even be a policeman today; you'd have gone down for assault. Isn't that right?'

He doesn't say anything.

'Now, you two apologize for the inconvenience and nip right off.'

'We can't do that.'

'Jens!'

Karen is very upset now.

'Yes, but we just can't.'

'Are you the one who's been kidnapped?' she asks Marianne.

'So they tell me.'

158

'Have you been kidnapped?'

'No.'

'Good, then that's settled. Why didn't you ask her that straight away?'

'We did,' Jens says testily.

'Then why haven't you gone again instead of bothering the poor people? She said no.'

When the officers have left, and Karen has said her goodbyes, she comes back into the sitting room.

'You're not here against your will, are you?'

Marianne shakes her head, and I mutter something about there having perhaps been a spot of bother.

'Jens and Kaj have been friends since they were boys. Kaj is a couple of years older than Jens, and Jens has almost been a younger brother to him. You needn't worry; when I say you're all right, then you're all right. If he tries anything funny, you just let me know and then Kaj will set him to rights.'

This is the first time I realize that Karen is capable of tact. She looks at Marianne and says kindly, 'Would you like to be alone with Nikolaj?'

'Yes. Please.'

'Come on, Jeppe, we'll leave them alone.'

'What do you mean?'

'You're coming with me.'

'Why?' he asks anxiously.

'Because they need some privacy, and I need some help around the garden. You can mow the lawn while they have a chat.'

He looks at me for help; surely the word 'alone' means him and me, but I signal that he is to go with her. He leaves us to spend time with a lawnmower and Karen, who tells him that he is too thin by far and ought to eat more.

There we are then. There's an oppressive silence until Marianne mutters, 'I just wanted to know why you had said you needed us.'

'Why didn't you come in? You were invited.'

'I didn't want to without knowing what it was all about.'

That's fair enough. I'd be sceptical too if someone like me came asking for my help.

'Well, now you know. Are you in?'

I consider the evening such a success that she can't possibly have reservations, but she does.

'I don't trust you.'

'Why not? The others do.'

'What do you mean why? You kicked a little boy in the head, beat up your girlfriend and drove your sister to suicide. The others think you're lovely because your mother is Grith Okholm. That's a very poor reason to trust you.'

I see her point, but that doesn't necessarily mean I agree with her.

'I've changed.'

'You kidnapped me.'

'No, Jeppe did that,' I say huffily.

'It was you and Jeppe.'

'If you're not in, then why are you here? Why didn't you tell the police the truth just now?'

'I haven't said I'm not in. I'm just saying that I'm not comfortable with this.'

'Are you in?' I ask.

'I'm not saying that either.'

'Then what are you saying?'

'I don't know,' she says and looks at me expectantly.

What does she want from me? And then I smile delightedly, because I realize that she'll end up giving in. She can protest all she wants, but she made the decision much earlier. It doesn't add up otherwise. If she felt so bad about me, why would she lie to the police? Why hasn't she left? She's waiting for an invitation.

'I'd really like you to be a part of this. How can I convince you?' She chooses her words very carefully.

'You must listen to me. When I say no, then it's a no, or I'm out.'

'The others can't be bothered to join Jehovah's Witnesses, so don't go trying to convert them or anything like that.'

She gives me a look that tells me I'm an idiot. I may as well get used to that look, because whenever I say anything stupid Marianne never tries to hide her contempt. She doesn't even have to say I'm an idiot, but she usually does anyway.

'Don't be daft. I'm not even a member myself any longer.'

'Since when?'

'Since you two stepped into the office.'

'Just because of that?'

There's that look again.

'No, of course not. There are many reasons why not, but they're my reasons and I'm not going to tell. This isn't about who I am. It just can't hurt anyone else.'

I nod seriously. I entirely agree with her on that. It can't hurt anyone else, not ever again.

The first couple of weeks at NATO

We meet for some R&R, to get to know each other and bond. Jeppe and I cook, and I'm surprised to discover he isn't bad at it. Our chilli con carne's not as good as the one Silje makes, but it comes close. I've asked everyone to do a ten-minute presentation, so we can get to know each other.

Karen tells us about Kaj and the girls. Their eldest girl has just gone up to Århus University. She is studying Danish, and Karen tells us, 'She's reading novels all day long, and Kaj thinks that's just silly. It's hardly an education, reading novels.'

Kink tells us he's a former Juttish heavyweight champion.

'That guy I beat in the final went pro the year after. I could have done that too, but then I would have had to practice every day, and I wouldn't be able to go out very much. I would have been bored off my tits.'

Bike tells us about the time he filmed Kink shagging a random, drunken girl he had picked up in Skjern.

'Do you want to see?' He gets out his mobile and shows us Kink's arse moving up and down.

'I can't see a girl anywhere.'

162

'She's underneath the arse.'

Anita tells us about her ex-boyfriend. They almost got married, but unfortunately the ex's four-year-old son didn't like her, and in the end the boyfriend called it off.

'He said I was just lovely, but that I wasn't exactly mummy material.'

Karen is white-hot.

'What a numpty. You most certainly are mummy material, Anita.'

Anita doesn't seem to be quite sure if that's a compliment or not.

Jeppe doesn't think he has anything to say, and Marianne doesn't want to tell us anything, at least not where everyone can hear it. Later that evening Karen and Marianne are speaking confidentially to each other. I overhear bits of their conversation.

'Have they been in touch?'

'Mathias has. He says I'm ruining my life yet again, now and for all eternity. I said I felt lonely and hypocritical. He doesn't understand why. I need this. This is so whacky that it can't help but shake things up a bit.'

When they realize that I'm straining to hear what they're saying, they pull away from me. Neither of them wants to tell me what it was about.

We meet every night during those first two weeks, but we're getting nowhere. We have a great time, but it's not particularly productive. Of course I tell them everything I can about Brian and Silje, but my information has a major flaw in it: I have no idea how they are now.

Karen has a suggestion, which is that a couple of us go on a field trip to Copenhagen to do some research. Kink volunteers straight away, but Bike explains to him that he won't be able to take time off work. They're busy down at HS Kedler. Karen thinks that I ought to be one of the people to go, because I know Brian and Silje, and because I'm from Copenhagen. I shake my head.

'I don't want to. I don't want to go back to Copenhagen.'

'Yes but, Nikolaj, love, you'd only be going for a week.'

I'm close to tears at the mere thought of it. Then Jeppe volunteers. It ends up being Karen and Jeppe who are going. Karen looks forward to her week in Copenhagen, and Jeppe is terrified at the thought of spending a week with Karen.

Jeppe and Karen in Copenhagen

They've been following Brian around all day. Karen has clicked with her camera as Brian drags the screaming Allan to nursery school; as he stands and weeps by Sis's grave; as he visits prossies right after leaving Sis's grave. They wait for him to come out, but he's in there for nearly two hours. When he leaves, Jeppe wants to go after him straight away, but Karen stops him. She walks up and knocks on the door. A suspicious-looking Eastern European woman answers.

'Yes, what do you want?'

Karen looks at her with some bewilderment. Jeppe is standing behind her, looking embarrassed.

'Danish?' Karen asks.

The woman points at Jeppe and repeats, 'Danish?' Jeppe shakes his head emphatically and says, 'No, no, not Danish. Karen, dammit, Danish means ordinary sex.'

'Oh. That's very strange. Do you speak any English?'

Jeppe nods.

'A bit.'

'Ask her if she knows Brian,' she says, and hands Jeppe the camera.

Jeppe shows her a picture of Brian.

'*Do you know this man?*'

The woman looks at Jeppe sceptically. She doesn't say anything, and Karen produces a 500 kroner note, which she gives to the woman.

'*Yes, I know him. He comes here many times.*'

'What's she saying?'

'He comes here a lot.'

'What do they do?'

Jeppe blushes. 'I can't ask her that.'

'Of course you can.'

Jeppe pulls himself together. '*What do you do?*'

She looks at Jeppe as if he might be a bit slow.

'*I am a – you know – prossie.*'

'*No, no, I mean what do you do with Brian?*' Jeppe asks her, looking flustered.

'*We sleep. No sex. Never sex, we only sleep.*'

Jeppe turns to Karen.

'They sleep. They don't have sex.'

Later they're standing outside the Ladybird Nursery School when Brian comes to pick up Allan. He's screaming when he's being picked up too. Once again Jeppe wants to follow them, and once again Karen stops him. Two nursery school teachers come out, and Karen walks over to them straight away. She holds out her hand and says, 'Hello, I'm Karen.' They look at her hand, obviously confused, but they say hello all the same.

'Hanne.'

'Gitte.'

'Do you work here?'

'Yes, I'm the head mistress, and Gitte is a nursery school teacher.'

Karen nods with interest.

'Then you know Brian Birkemose Andersen? Allan's dad?'

They look at Karen suspiciously, but it is difficult to be suspicious where Karen is concerned. They nod.

'What's he like?'

Gitte says, 'He's really crabby.'

Hanne shushes her.

'We really can't discuss Mr Andersen with you.'

'Why not? I know him. I'm worried about him.'

Hanna and Gitte look at each other. Hanne says warily, 'We are too. He seems very sad.'

'And crabby. He's never happy,' Gitte says.

*

166

Karen and Jeppe try to follow Silje around as well, but it turns out to be quite difficult as she stays in her flat most of the time. She only leaves it when Camilla comes to take her out. They argue several times; Camilla seems to be at her wit's end. At one point they're sitting at the Bang & Jensen café. Karen and Jeppe sit at the next table, pretending to be reading the newspapers, while they eavesdrop on Silje and Camilla's private conversation.

'That is just sick!' Camilla says.

'It's not like I'm doing it on purpose, is it?'

'That doesn't make it any less sick to be having sexual dreams about someone who beat you up.'

'I'm not going to tell you about this if that's how you're going to react.'

Karen and Jeppe have a hard time hiding their curiosity.

'Do you really think I want to hear that you've had yet another dream about Nikolaj? Why can't you dream that you chop off his balls instead?'

'As if I wouldn't much rather dream that,' Silje hisses, and Karen can't help looking at her.

Camilla turns on her immediately.

'What are you looking at?'

At one point they're afraid that Camilla has worked out that they're stalking them. She spots Karen and Jeppe later that same day outside the practice room. Jeppe wants to make a run for it, but Karen makes him stay and says in a loud Jutland brogue, 'I don't understand this camera. Has it taken the picture or not?' She winks at Jeppe, who nods enthusiastically, and Camilla is reassured and walks away. They're just a couple of stupid Jut-landers. On Tuesday and Thursday nights the band Grith Okholm Jam practise (I'm shocked to hear they're still playing Mum's songs). Jeppe sneaks a peek through the practice-room window, and sees Silje telling the other band members off for not being focused enough. When Silje isn't looking, Camilla hurriedly tries to appease the band members, who are not hiding their frustration. Jeppe and Karen have seen on Grith Okholm Jam's website that they haven't played for a year. When the band leaves, Karen decides that they are going to follow the bass player, Jakob. He's standing at a bus stop with his bass on his back when Karen pretends to recognize him.

'Excuse me, don't you play in Grith Okholm Jam?'

He's utterly taken aback. He's not used to being recognized.

'Yes, I play the bass.'

Karen smiles. 'I thought so. You really are great. Why aren't you playing any more? You used to be gigging all the time. I must have seen you at least twenty times.'

Jakob mutters, 'Our lead singer doesn't want to play live. She's working through some stuff.'

While Karen and Jeppe are in Copenhagen, I hang out with the others. They stop by more or less every night. We play games and watch films. Anita has a tendency to snuggle up to me when we're watching films, which is a bit disconcerting.

Bike asks me several times whether Jeppe really is my best friend. I nod.

'Isn't he a bit weird?'

'What do you mean?'

Bike mutters, 'I just think he seems weird.'

'He's no weirder than I am.'

'You're not weird. You're just strange.'

When Karen and Jeppe come home

We now have the information we need, and the question then is: what we are going to do with it? I've decided that I want to spend some of my money. It's daft to have money and not benefit from it. Consequently, I tell the members of NATO that I would like to pay them a salary for as long as they help me, because it would give us much greater freedom if they don't have to worry about their work.

'No, Nikolaj, you really mustn't,' Karen says, while the rest of them look at me with ill-concealed curiosity.

'I want to. Now, if you give me your bank account details I can transfer 35,000 kroner a month to each of you.'

Kink and Bike look at one another, delighted, and Kink says, 'I think we should all go to Copenhagen.'

Everyone quickly backs him up, because we can be so much more efficient if we're not in Jutland, when Brian and Silje are both in Copenhagen. I'm the only one to object, and I know that it's only because I'm afraid. I have no defence. I just keep saying, 'Yes, but I don't want to.' They ask me why and I mutter, 'I just don't want to.' They ask if I'm afraid, and I say, 'Yes, of course I am.'

'But we're coming with you. You're not alone any more,' Marianne says.

How can I say no?

Which is why we all go to Copenhagen, except for Karen who stays at home with Kaj, because she can't leave without knowing when she'll be back again. Apart from Karen, none of us have responsibilities in Tarm. Bike and Kink quit their jobs. They can always come back to them: there's a shortage of metal workers in Tarm. Marianne has been laid off by Mathias, and Anita files for bankruptcy for Trendy Look. Nobody goes there any more. Apparently, people prefer to have their hair cut at New Look or Salon Chris. Anita is looking forward to getting away and experiencing something different to cheer her up. No-one, apart from Karen, has a wife/husband/partner/children.

Going to Copenhagen

I'm sitting in the train, staring out of the window in an attempt to ignore my aching stomach. Kink and Bike have fallen asleep. They were on the booze last night in order to say a proper farewell to Tarm, and now one's snoring louder than the other. They almost didn't make the train. Marianne is sitting, reading a book. She's good at keeping herself busy. Jeppe is looking blankly out of another window. Anita, on the other hand, is staring at me. I give her a half-smile. She gets up and comes to sit next to me.

'Can I use you as a pillow?'

She snuggles up to me before I can say anything. I haven't got the energy to resist, so I just put my arm around her; not to encourage her to do anything, but simply because it's more comfortable. Karen has promised to empty my letter box, answer enquiries and look after my beloved 22 Poppelvej while we're away.

Part Three

THE MARRIAGE OF TRUE MINDS

In Copenhagen

I'm standing in the midst of all the commotion of the Central Station, bent over with my hands on my knees, gasping frantically for breath. Marianne is gently stroking my back, and the others, who are looking at me, are visibly worried. I get my breathing under control and stand up, feeling a fool.

'Are you okay?' Bike asks.

I shake my head, but I don't say a word, simply hurrying towards the exit. We flag down a couple of taxis, then go to Rantzausgade. I've got a three-bedroom flat that's empty, because I'm in the process of selling all my flats. Kink tumbles delightedly out of the taxi. He's nuts about the place, Copenhagen, Nørrebro. He turns to us with an air of astonishment.

'There are niggers all over the place.'

'Not so loud.'

'It's filthy too. Just look at that.'

He picks up an empty pizza box and proudly hands it to Bike. Bike accepts it and dumps it straight away.

'It's just lying there. You'd never see that in Tarm.'

Brimming with excitement, Kink runs a hundred metres down the Rantzausgade, past the Eagle Steak House and the pub called Tjili Pop, kicking at the rubbish all the while. He stops, looks around him, and yells, 'Every other person is a wog!' Bike, fortunately, has enough sense to call him back and haul him into the flat before anything untoward happens.

Bike and Kink, Anita and Marianne, Jeppe and I all share rooms, and then we have a communal sitting room. The flat has very minimal furnishings. We don't need much as it's only a temporary base.

They're all waiting for my move, but I've been unmanned by an excruciating, exasperating stomach ache, so all I manage to mutter is, 'I just need to have a think.'

I have a bit of a think for the next three days. I lock myself in my room, sleep around the clock and try – in vain – to string together a bit more than just one or two thoughts.

Talking to Sis

'No, all he does is sleep. Mmm. No. He only gets out of bed to go to the bathroom. I think he's being sick. Mmm. Yes. Three days. Mmm. Mmm. No, Jeppe says he hasn't said a word to him either. Mmm. Mmm. Yes well I know that, Karen. Mmmm. Mmmm. It's just a nuisance for the rest of us. We're waiting for him. Mmm. Mmm. Mmm. Yes, he's afraid but – mmm. Yes? You think so? Mmm. Mmm. Mmm. Mmm. Okay, I'll try that then. Mmm. Mmm. Thanks so much, Karen. Speak to you soon. Mmm. Yes, bye now.'

Marianne hangs up the phone and calls Jeppe, then the two of them disappear for a couple of hours. When they come back, they march into my room and pull off my duvet.

'Up you get. Time for a walk.'

I shake my head, but Jeppe brutally forces me out of bed. I don't feel like going for a walk, but they leave me no choice, and I'm too listless to resist.

We're heading toward Vesterbro. Marianne is pulling me along. I'm trying desperately to keep up, because that way we almost look like a couple. I even let my thumb caress her hand. For a brief moment it makes her stop. She turns to me with a frown, and then, on we go. Jeppe keeps up with us. Marianne catches his eyes several times, and then there's a discreet I'm-ready nod. Bike and Kink are strolling some 50 yards behind us. They make sure we're never out of sight, but that aside they're just strolling along, chatting. Anita didn't want to come. She hates walks.

'Where are we going?'

Marianne doesn't want to say, even though I ask her ten times. We're walking past the Carlsberg breweries, crossing the traffic lights, and then I realize what it is she wants me to do. I try to yank my hand out of hers, but she holds on tightly. I squeeze her hand so hard, she has to let go. I turn to run the other way, but Jeppe grabs me. We tussle for a bit. He's stronger than he looks and pushes me onwards, while I struggle to go the other way. Kink and Bike come running up. Marianne commandeers them, and they grab me as well. I don't stand a chance. When they let go, we're at Vestre Kirkegård. Marianne tries to reassure me.

'You have to, you know.'

'I can't.'

She takes my hand again. It soothes me. She starts walking, and I follow her past headstone after headstone. She walks as if she knows where she's going. Suddenly we've reached Sis, and Marianne whispers, 'We'll just step back and give you some privacy.'

I squat down in front of the stone. The grave is handsome and well looked after. There are freshly cut flowers, and lots of them. I let my fingers run over the headstone. It's uneven and cool. I bend down and hug the stone.

'Sweetie, how lovely you're finally here. I've been so worried about you.'

It's just so marvellous to hear her voice again. I hug her tightly, and she notices that I'm shaking.

'Niko, relax.'

I cling to her.

'I'm sorry I didn't come sooner.'

'Sweetie, relax.'

The stone is burrowing into my arms, as Sis tries to get me to relax.

'You're here now. Relax. Breathe. I'm just happy to see you,' and she pulls me close. I say nothing for a while. I'm just sitting, while Sis and I hold each other. When I've calmed down, she asks, 'How are you?'

I have a think, and then I say, 'I'm good – well, good enough at least.'

'You seem stronger. Fatter but stronger. That's good,' she says gently.

'I know I'm fat. How are you?'

'I'm fine, apart from the fact that my little brother doesn't come to see me. And I didn't say you were fat.'

I loosen my hold on the stone.

'Allan and Brian must come by.'

'Yes, they're here all the time, but they're not you. Brian makes me depressed. He's been going to prossies. Did you know?'

I nod.

'You do? Have you talked to him?' she asks, surprised.

'No, but some of my friends have been keeping an eye on him.'

'That's a really strange thing to do. So you know he's not having sex with them?'

'Yes.'

'Hm. I'd almost rather they were having sex. Why were you keeping an eye on Brian?' Sis wonders.

'Jesus made me.'

'Jesus? He's making you stalk Brian? Are you all right?'

'Yes, don't I seem it?'

'Apart from the fact that you're speaking nonsense. Now that you relax, you seem almost happy,' she says, and seems relieved.

'Happy may be too strong a word, but I'm doing better than I have been for a long time. I've moved to Jutland.'

'Because of the girl with the big tits? Are you going out?'

I turn around and look at Marianne, who smiles at me reassuringly.

'No, there's nothing going on between us.'

'She's pretty.'

'Yes, she is. Very.'

This is where the conversation ends, abruptly. I never get around to telling her why I'm here, because I'm suddenly soaring. I end my embrace of the stone, and I'm soaring over the graves. The others see him as he moves towards me, but they only recognize him when it's too late. Now he's flinging me onto the footpath. I weigh well above 14 stone, yet he's throwing me about with brutal ease. I'm flying ten or twelve feet before I land on the tarmac with a thud. It hurts like hell, and my hands and legs are bruised. I try to get up and away, but there's no time, because Brian's hand is already slamming into my face. I pass out. I'm totally out of it. Fortunately, the gang is there and they reach me before Brian can do any more damage. Kink punches Brian hard on the chest. He's holding back, though, because he doesn't want to hurt Brian. Brian doesn't even notice the blow and slams Kink to the ground. That frightens Bike and Jeppe, but they still try to wrestle him. He throws them off violently. I'm going to be ripped to shreds. All that stands between him and me now is Marianne.

'Brian, leave him alone. He doesn't deserve it, not any more,' she says, her voice full of fear.

'Who the fuck are you, and how come you know my name?' Brian spits at her.

'I'm Niko's friend.'

'He doesn't have any friends,' Brian says without the least hesitation.

'Yes, he does. He's our friend,' Jeppe barks belligerently behind him.

Bike and Kink come back, bruised and battered, and stand up next to Marianne, scared but ready. Brian looks at them with surprise, then snorts contemptuously. He turns around and leaves us with brisk steps.

I visit Sis's grave every day while we're in Copenhagen, but I always have Jeppe with me. He keeps a lookout for Brian, while Sis and I chat. We talk about all the things we didn't dare talk about when she was alive. I realize how much it hurt her when I tortured myself. If I were her I would hate me, but she doesn't. I'm still her sweetie, and her death can't change that.

Tonight we party

Shocked at the sight of Kink's battered face, Anita jumps out of her chair and scurries, bewildered, from one of us to the next.

'What happened? Why does Kink have a black eye?'

She turns around and faces me, noticing for the first time that I have a swollen upper lip, which only increases her bewilderment. We're all so shocked at how scary Brian is in his hatred of me that we can't find the strength to reassure her. So she's left standing, confused, in the middle of the room, while we root in the freezer for bags of frozen peas to put on our bruises.

For a while we're just sitting, silent and broken, by the kitchen table. Then Kink – who's still holding a bag of frozen peas to his black eye – says, 'Fuck this. I want a beer tonight.' We quickly agree that we need to go on a proper bender.

*

We start out at Tjili Pop, and from there we do the grand tour of Nørrebro. At 4 a.m. we're all bladdered, but Funke is still open, and we'll keep the pints coming as long as possible. Jeppe has wet himself a little. There's a small wet patch right in the centre on his trousers. Bike makes sure we all notice it, but Jeppe is so drunk he doesn't care. Pointing in the direction of Sankt Hans Torv, he just leans towards me, whispering fondly, 'That's where we met.' Anita is nodding off in a corner. She tries to keep her eyes open, but they keep shutting and staying shut for longer and longer each time. Bike and Kink are in a heated discussion with a couple of FCK-supporters about whether Esbjerg is a better football club than the bastard Copenhagen team. They're trying to get into a fight, but the others only deal in verbal punches. Marianne is sitting outside on the doorstep, her head between her knees. I stumble out of Funke and over to her.

'Are you feeling poorly?'

'A little.'

'Have you been sick?'

'A little.'

I sit down next to her and put my arm around her. I pull her in close.

'You've held up better than I thought you would. Jesus buggery Christ, you've done some serious drinking.'

'Language, please.'

'Sorry.'

'You really should mind your language.'

'I said sorry.'

She puts her head in my lap. It feels nice.

'My ex could drink like nobody's business, and I never could tell from his behaviour. For a long time I'd be sick if I so much as sniffed a beer.'

'I didn't think drinking was allowed in the Jehovah's Witnesses.'

'He wasn't a Jehovah's Witness.'

'He wasn't?'

'No, he was an Albanian.'

'Oh. They let you go out with an Albanian?'

'Not really, but I did it anyway, and he was a heavy drinker.'

She turns around, so now she's on her back and not on her side. That means her face is turned towards me. She gives me a small smile as her eyes meet mine.

'Thanks for forcing to me to go and see Sis,' I say. 'We talked about you. My sister said you were pretty.' My heart is beating nervously.

'That's sweet.'

She strokes my cheek affectionately. I lean forward to kiss her, but my gut is in the way, and instead I lift her head up a bit. She lets me kiss her, but doesn't kiss me back. Her lips taste bitter because of the vomit, and my lips are hurting a bit. Nevertheless, it's a long kiss, because if I keep my lips pressed against hers, she'll have to reciprocate and kiss me. Instead I get two hands on my chest and a gentle press telling me to stop. I lean back, and she strokes my cheek affectionately once more.

'We can't be together.'

'Why not?'

'Because it'd make for an awful mess, and right now we should-n't make things any messier than they are.'

'I think you're gorgeous. Sis thought we were going out.'

She takes my hand and gives it a fond squeeze.

'But we're not, Niko, and right now that's all there is to say about it,' and then she gets up. She smiles at me fondly.

'No, I'm going to stay here for a bit,' I say, and try to return her smile, even though I'm disappointed.

I watch her as she staggers back to Funke, and that's when I see Anita staring out of the window at me. She has sad eyes that seem to be watering.

Anita wants to go home

We're having breakfast; that is, the lads are. Marianne is in the shower. We're all hungover, and Kink and I are suffering from other ailments as well. My jaw is still making a strange clicking noise. We're sitting silently and eating, and all of a sudden Anita is standing in front of us with her bags packed, and her shoes and coat on. We're looking at her, confused.

'Are you going anywhere?' I wonder.

'Home.'

'Back to Tarm? Why?'

'Because there's nothing for me to do here.'

Bike snorts.

'Oh for Christ's sake, Anita, you can't just go home because Niko doesn't want to shag you.'

Kink gets up resolutely and yanks Anita's bag out of her hand, opens it and swings it round, scattering her clothes all over the room. A pair of her knickers end up in Jeppe's cornflakes. Anita tries to stop Kink, but he pushes her aside until the bag is completely empty.

'What did you do that for?' she cries.

'We're all in this together, and we're all staying together.'

Anita doesn't say anything. She just turns around angrily, goes to her room and slams the door. The entire flat shakes. Two seconds later the door opens. She sticks her head out, bellows 'Shitty arseholes!' and slams it with a resounding boom, and once again the flat is shaking. Marianne comes out of the shower. She has flung a towel around herself.

'What's going on?'

'It's Anita. She's upset because Niko won't give her a bit of todger,' Bike says.

'Why don't you want to give Anita some todger?' Kink asks me.

Anita is pretty, and I'm fat. I ought to be grateful.

'Why should he? You may as well give her some yourself,' Marianne says.

'She wants Niko's todger,' Bike says.

'Well, she can't have it.'

'That's your decision to make, is it? Reserved it for yourself, have you?' Bike teases her.

She blushes. 'No, of course not.'

Marianne knocks on the door. She wants to be let into the

185

room and get dressed. The door remains not only shut, but locked. Anita makes sure to tell us all how stupid we are. Marianne is stupid too.

'I was in the shower. Why am I stupid?'

'You just are!' Anita shouts through the door.

'Come on, open the door and let me put some clothes on.'

Marianne is getting annoyed, because it's her room too, and now she has to sit here in a pair of trousers and a jumper that I've lent her. She looks far better in my clothes than I do myself.

It's a confused morning, as we realize we don't have a plan. We've come to Copenhagen in the hope of having an epiphany. We don't even have the element of surprise any longer, because Brian already knows what my friends look like, and next time around he won't spare them. We move the table right up to Anita's door and pretend that she's contributing to the meeting, and here we are now, looking blankly at each other. There's not the smallest cough to be heard from behind the door, and there's no sound out here either.

'Anyone have any suggestion as to what the fuck we do?'

No-one says a word.

'Then we may as well have stayed in Tarm.'

Bike says, 'Maybe we could sort Silje out first?'

I shake my head.

'No, it has to be Brian.'

'Why?'

'It just does.'

186

'I haven't met him,' Anita says cheerfully from behind the door.

So she is listening. The door is opened slowly, and Anita appears. She can't leave the room, because the table is blocking the door.

'He doesn't know who I am.'

We look at her excitedly, and she continues proudly, 'I can win his trust, and then I can talk him into meeting you. I can make him trust me, and then I'll plead your cause.'

'How?'

'I don't know, but he hasn't met me.'

'Does that mean you're staying?' I ask.

'Yes.' Her voice breaks.

Kink moves the table straight away – who cares about the stuff that's on it, mugs of coffee crashing to the floor   and we gather round her. Anita is a good girl; she's just not the one for me.

Nursery school

Bike, Kink and I want to cut corners. To put it very simply, we want Anita to get naked, and make sure Brian sees that she is naked. In times of trouble one should always rely on one's strengths. The girls say most definitely no, so we press them a bit. Anita is evasive, but her defence is growing weaker by the moment. We are slowly and surely talking her into the nakedness idea.

'WILL YOU SHUT UP?!' Marianne yells.

Straight away we're all silent, because she has a very loud and penetrating yell.

'What exactly do you think you're doing? Who do you think you are?'

'We're just talking,' I say warily.

'I said shut up!'

She throws a fork at me. It whizzes past.

'Do we have a deal?'

She looks at me furiously. I dare not do anything but nod silently. The others look at us, not quite understanding what just went on.

'I've promised Marianne that she can veto things.'

'That just isn't right,' Bike says resentfully.

'That's as may be, but that's just how it's going to have to be,' and Anita looks at Marianne with admiration.

There are hours of brainstorming, even if 'storm' is too big a word for what we're doing. Every once in a while an idea crops up, but it's immediately shattered by Marianne. Dejection starts to seep in, but Anita saves the day. Experience tells her that the road to a single father's heart is through his children, and in the end we decide that Anita is to work in the Ladybird Nursery School.

Karen comes to Copenhagen to help us out, and she, Anita and I go to see Gitte and Hanne. We're sitting at the half-empty Café Bopa on Østerbro, and Hanne asks us yet again, 'Could you explain it one more time?'

'We're going to help Brian. I'm his brother-in-law, and Anita is a good friend of mine. Brian is feeling really shite.'

Hanne and Gitte nod.

'I can help him, but Brian won't let me help him, because he's so aggressive. Anita is going to make him soften up to allow me to make my move. Do you see?'

They shake their heads simultaneously.

'We don't want to hurt him,' I say, and then I show them the contents of my bag: 300,000 kroner. It looks impressive, and Hanne and Gitte both go pale.

Karen says, 'Gitte, we know you're struggling with stress.'

'I'm what?'

'If you report ill with stress, Anita could fill in for you. We're thinking... maybe a three-month period, and we'd be paying you 200,000 kroner for it.'

Gitte peeps inside my bag again.

'And Hanne, if you could guarantee that Anita is chosen to fill in, we'd give you 100,000 for your trouble.'

They're ashamed of themselves, but they accept the money. Anita starts at the nursery school the following week.

The first day we're waiting excitedly for Anita. It's almost six o'clock. She ought to have been back an hour ago, but we'll be kept waiting for another fifteen minutes. When she finally gets there, she doesn't even make it through the door before we assault her with questions. She merely smiles, takes off her coat and lies on the sofa. She looks tired. We've been watching films and, unlike her, we've got energy to burn. She exhales.

'Do you want to hear about it?'

'Yes, dammit.'

'It's been the best day ever. I fixed a little girl's hair, and suddenly they all wanted me to do their hair – even the other teachers,' she says, looking happy.

'But did you talk to Brian?'

'No.'

'Then what do you mean it's been the best day ever, if you didn't speak to him?' I wonder.

'I love working in a nursery school.'

That surprises us. She was very uneasy when she left, but now she has a calm that really becomes her.

'But you didn't talk to Brian?'

'No. He's very introverted. But I will. It's just going to take some time. I spoke to Allan. He's adorable,' she says with a quiet smile.

Karen dismantles the rumours

My leaving Tarm out of the blue sets off a tidal wave of rumours. Karen decides to sort it all out by having Nadja Jessen from the *Skjern-Tarm Daily* round for a chat.

Goodbye to the old life

By Nadja Jessen
nj@skjern-tarm-dagblad.dk

Even his worst days in Tarm are better than his best days in Copenhagen, says Karen Juhl, close friend of Nikolaj Okholm.

When Nikolaj moved to Tarm, I did a candid interview with him. He made no bones about the fact that there are many things in his past he isn't proud of having done: stupid decisions, violent acts, foolhardiness. He hoped his coming to Tarm would be a turning point, but he is a thoughtful person, and he couldn't help reflecting on the pain he has inflicted in the course of his life. He's not a full-speed-ahead lad, and that's why we have all become so fond of him.

He has for a brief period of time chosen to move back to Copenhagen, and with him is a number of his new friends from Tarm. I'm sure I'm not the only one to think that Tarm feels strangely empty now that Nikolaj has left so shortly after moving here, taking with him a select group of Tarm's inhabitants. Rumours have a way of springing to life very quickly in these parts. He was the head of a religious sect. He had formed a rock band and was now touring Germany. He was on the run from the po-lice. Each rumour seemed more outlandish and silly than the next. Until, that is, Karen Juhl, who is Nikolaj Okholm's next-door neighbour, called me up and offered to acquaint me with a story that simply has to make Nikolaj even more beloved in Tarm than he already is.

'Kaj (Karen Juhl's husband) and I simply laughed at those rumours. They were so far-fetched we couldn't believe anyone would credit them. But then I was speaking to Bitten (Kaj Juhl's sister). She was terribly upset because Nikolaj had turned out to be a wolf in sheep's clothing. That he was a drug baron from Christiania. That's when I decided it was time to put a stop to all this nonsense.'

Karen Juhl tells me that it's a simple matter of friends helping each other out. Nikolaj is not a drug baron, a cult leader or a rock musician.

I can hear the warmth in Karen Juhl's voice when she speaks about Nikolaj. She's been in touch with him daily since he moved to Tarm, and as a consequence she has been able to see first hand what a splendid young man Nikolaj really is.

'He's a Copenhagener and a bit more lively and upbeat than we timid Jutlanders tend to be. There's certainly never a dull moment when you're Nikolaj's friend.'

They're a small, close-knit group of friends who meet on a regular basis to eat and enjoy themselves. Nikolaj does the inviting and the cooking. They always have chilli con carne, because it's the only thing Nikolaj knows how to cook. Among themselves they are known as NATO. The real life NATO is all about countries protecting and helping each other out in times of conflict. There's a pact between these countries. There's a pact between these friends as well. Nikolaj has got to know them all individually, and that's why he's the one they all rally around.

'He asked us over and said, "You are all my friends, and I need your help." It was that brutally honest. He told us his entire story, grim and tragic as it was. It was upsetting, but also uplifting, because the reason he told us was so that we could help him move on. He's a sweet, funny lad these days, but he has some things in Copenhagen that he needs to resolve.'

Essentially, it is to do with not being able to move on as long as he is still being plagued by the memories of what was. Once those things are resolved, he'll return to Tarm.

'Moving here means a lot to him. If you ask him, he would say that he is pretty close to being perfectly happy. Even his worst days in Tarm are better than his best days in Copenhagen,' Karen says, and reassures those of us who were beginning to fear that Nikolaj's stay in Tarm might be of short duration. He intends to grow old here, marry and have children and contribute to making Tarm an even lovelier place than it already is.

I should never have come

We spend hours every day going over Anita's workday. Every little detail could potentially be important, perhaps even crucial. We discuss rumours, what Brian and Allan wear, what Allan had for breakfast. We are convinced that we are gathering ammunition to arm me for the day when Brian lowers his guard.

Anita still hasn't had a complete conversation with Brian, but he speaks to her more than he does to any of the others. Primarily because she forces the issue. It baffles him that she isn't deterred by his angry grunts, but he doesn't let her get too close, and we resign ourselves to having to wait for a real breakthrough.

Of course, the wait means that my thoughts have time to grow and become big and brutal

I hide my stomach ache as best I can. Only Jeppe knows that I'm sick all the time. He and I go for walks together every day – often after I've been to the cemetery to speak to Sis. We find some where abandoned, and I yell and scream to vent my stomach ache, while Jeppe keeps a lookout. Of course, there are frequently people who interfere, but we're quite good at finding isolated places where I can scream without being disturbed. And when I'm sick, I turn on the radio in the bathroom. I'm very good at hiding it, because I've done it since I was thirteen. I don't want the others to be bothered by my weaknesses.

We focus all our attention on Brian. It's a matter of security. That's not to say that we don't discuss Silje, because of course we do. We're working every day, planning and researching a number of alternatives – the most ambitious involving all of Tarm, being in fact a full-fledged festival in Mum's honour. Of course, Grith Okholm Jam is to be one of the headline acts with a string of concerts spanning Mum's entire career. It's the plan I'm the most excited about, and not just because it'll mean Silje will get back onstage again. It's also about what we would be doing for Tarm.

I still remember the disappointment in the mayor who came to see Mum. I can't give them Mum, but I can try to lessen the disappointment.

We are, in other words, preparing for the battle to come, but that's all we do. We don't want to fall between two stools. If Anita gets in over her head, we have to be there for her. We have an understanding: we can talk about Silje, but none of us will get in touch with her.

Unfortunately, I go ahead and do it anyway, because I need to see her beautiful face. Last time I saw it, I had beaten it to a bloody pulp. The knot in my stomach tells me it's a stupid idea, but I do it all the same, because I'm an idiot who doesn't pay attention to obvious warnings.

Standing here at the Music Faculty, I can't believe I haven't told any of the others. She's happy. It's really nice to see that. I keep my distance to prevent her from seeing me. I've no intention of speaking to her; I just want to see her. She's as beautiful and lovely as ever. She has a small scar on her chin, but apart from that it's impossible to see that she was once bloody and wrecked.

Shit, they're coming this way. I can't bloody get out without their seeing me. Tits and fucking arse! I'm so stupid! I'm so stupid! I'm so stupid! She's going to walk right past me. I turn my back to her and hope it's enough. She's talking about a song she's written herself – apparently it's called 'Boyfriend'. She's proud. She feels that it's really significant, and then she stops in mid-sentence. The next thing I hear is Camilla's voice saying, 'Get Silje out! Now!'

It all takes place behind my back. It's a long time before I turn around, expecting them to be gone, but instead there's a very angry Camilla.

'I'm sorry. I shouldn't have come.'

She doesn't say anything. She simply glares at me angrily. The longer she holds my gaze like that, the more my stomach cries for help. Suddenly, the knot tightens in a violent jerk, and I cower in agony. Camilla takes a couple of steps back in surprise, while I try to stay upright, but – fuck me – it hurts so badly. I have to get away from her accusing glare, and I hurry out. She allows me to pass. I manage to get probably about a hundred yards down the street before I tumble to the ground outside a Fakta supermarket, roaring with pain. I can't seem to force the air into my lungs, and I lose consciousness. Before I know what's hit me, I'm lying in an ambulance.

woo-oo-oo-oo!

I try to convince the paramedics to stop and let me out, but they won't. When we reach the hospital, they want me to come in, but I refuse because there's nothing physically the matter with me. They pull at me, and I pull in the opposite direction. They talk to me as if I were retarded, and I tell them to piss off. I can feel a familiar aggression returning, so I make sure to leave as quickly as I can. They can't detain me. That would be illegal. I'm pretty sure of that.

When I get back, Anita has been back for more than an hour, and I'm met with a wall of disapproval. We agreed that we'd all be home when Anita gets back from work every day. I apologize, but I don't tell them about Silje. I tell them I fainted and was taken to hospital, but I soon wish I had chosen a better excuse, because now I've made them all worried. They're skipping about in agitation.

'Will you calm down? Nothing's the matter with me.'

'But you fainted,' Jeppe says, all upset.

'The doctor said I was as right as rain.'

'He's not a very good doctor, then. What's his name?' Marianne asks.

I search for a name in vain, but nothing comes to mind and they can tell.

'You haven't even had yourself looked at, have you?'

'Yes, I have.'

I don't even sound convincing to myself.

'All right, if you say so, but we're going to have to get you to another, better doctor, now that you go about fainting for no reason.'

She can be a real pain sometimes.

And it's a really awful day to be late, because Anita has made her great breakthrough.

Brian reads Spiderman

From the moment Allan arrives to the moment he leaves, she's there with him. They do whatever he wants to do. She plays ball with him. For all of three hours she runs around with a ball and gets tackled by a small boy with fair hair. She falls over and is bruised, and her trousers go green from rolling on the grass, but she laughs it all off. The girls in the nursery school pull at her, but they can pull as much as they like; today it's just Allan and Anita. At five o'clock they're the only ones left in the nursery school.

Brian doesn't get there till half-past five. He has a look around; the nursery appears to be deserted, but then he discovers Anita and Allan sitting in a corner, propped up with cushions. Anita is reading Spiderman to Allan. Brian holds back and contemplates his son's happy face. Anita looks up and sees Brian. She smiles; she has discovered that Brian possesses a unique kind of beauty. There's something beautiful about a man who grieves so intensely for the woman he loved. If he can love that passionately once, he might be able to do so again, and then who cares if he looks like a pudgy gnome? He's still attractive. It's the first time Brian notices Anita. I mean really notices her. He sees his son in her arms, and he knows it is a good thing. He doesn't say anything for a while. The moment is too precious to be disturbed. Once Spiderman has beaten up Vulture Anita says, 'Your dad's here.'

Instinctively, the smile disappears from Allan's face.

'Hi there, Allan. Shall we go home?'

Allan doesn't say anything. He simply takes another comic

book and hands it to Anita.

'You can't. We have to go home. The nursery's about to close.'

Anita takes the comic book and says gently, 'There's no rush. Come and sit.'

Allan and Brian are both taken aback, but after some hesitation Brian does sit down.

'Shall we read another comic?'

'Yes,' Allan says happily.

'Then I think your dad should read it.'

Anita hands Brian the comic book. This time the surprise is even greater. Brian and Allan look at each other sceptically, but Brian does the right thing. He reads, and he does it with such enthusiasm that Allan forgets to be afraid of his dad and becomes completely absorbed in the story. When Brian has finished, Anita hands him another comic straight away, then another one, and after that yet another. Brian becomes so immersed in the stories he's reading to his son that he forgets everything else.

It's dark, and Brian has read some thirteen or fourteen Spiderman comics. His throat is dry, and his eyes are blurry, but it's all good. Anita doesn't hand him another comic, and for a moment he's confused. She looks at him tenderly, but he can't see Allan. Where the hell is Allan? His heart starts pumping anxiously, but then he's conscious of something touching his leg. He looks down and there is Allan, sleeping with his head on his dad's thigh. His heart beats even faster. Anita rises and picks up Allan. She settles him carefully on the cushions, walks over to Brian, squats down and looks him warmly and reassuringly in the eyes.

'I wish you weren't so sad.'

Brian realizes that he wishes that too. He doesn't stop being sad. He just decides that he would like not to be any longer. He'd like more days like this one. Nothing more happens that day. They say goodbye, but it's a goodbye that contains so much more than just a bye for now.

A strong foundation has been built, and we're damned proud of Anita, but none of us stops to think that there might be more to this for her than just the mission, that she is in fact falling in love big time. We put her excitement down to pride in a job well done.

At the doctor's

I have a body fat percentage of 30.7, which means I need to loose two stone, but that doesn't explain why I fainted. As fat men go, I'm in pretty good health, certainly too good to account for any fainting fits. I'm grateful when the doctor stops prodding me, but it only gets worse. He starts asking about my stomach ache and not about how it actually feels, but about what is going on in my head when my stomach is screaming. I hesitate, but there's nothing for it. I have to be honest, because Marianne will detect any lie, and she insists on hearing every single little thing the doctor says. She is sitting quietly behind me, listening carefully.

'I'm scared.'

'What are you scared of?'

'Everything. Nothing. Just scared.'

'How often have you felt like that?'

'What do you mean?'

'How often have you had that stomach ache?'

'Oh. Every day since I was thirteen.' I hear Marianne gasp. I turn around and look at her. She's pale, and she looks at me in a very worried manner.

'What's up with you?' I wonder.

She looks like she might burst into tears at any moment, sighs and makes a small squeaking sound. She looks from the doctor to me and back again, then she hurries out of the door. She doesn't come back for some time.

After waiting for her for a couple of minutes the doctor says, 'Shall we continue to wait, or shall we move on?'

'We'd better wait. She'll be very cross if we don't.'

We sit and wait for another couple of minutes, and then the doctor gets up and goes out to look for her. They return, and she looks at me with a strange mixture of fear and anger.

'Are you afraid all the time?'

I shrug and mutter, 'I suppose.'

'All the time?'

'I wasn't afraid those first couple of months in Tarm, but that wasn't a good thing.'

'But over here you're afraid all the time?'

'Yes, it's much worse when we're here. I did tell you I was afraid of Copenhagen.'

'I know, but so afraid that you'd faint? What's the matter with you? You have to tell me these things, so I can help you,' she says, and her voice breaks as she speaks.

'What do you want me to say? This time I couldn't breathe. There's no reason why you should all be bothered with that.'

She looks at me with astonishment, turns to the doctor and says, 'Do go on. I don't get him. He scares me and he upsets me,' and she looks like she's about to blub again.

She sits down and presses her lips together firmly. I don't understand why this means so much to her.

'When you fainted, had you been doing something unusual? Were you more afraid than usual?'

I try to come up with a plausible explanation, but the truth will out.

'Yes, I had just looked up my old girlfriend.'

Again there's a gasp from Marianne, but this time she's not only afraid, she's angry.

'Silje? You total idiot!'

We have a row, which goes on for ten minutes with her attacking me and me trying to defend myself. I explain to her that I needed to see Silje, so that I wouldn't have her bloodied face in my mind all the time, and Marianne tells me that I must stick to the plan. We have to be able to trust each other. She's right. I know that, but I refuse to yield, because I'm sort of right as well. In the end, the doctor interrupts us and tells us to be quiet, and that it's very rude to quarrel in front of other people. We save the argument for later.

After an awful lot of questions the doctor tells me that I probably suffer from anxiety attacks. I'm surprised to hear that it has a name. I just thought I was scared, but apparently it's a condition that can be treated with pills and therapy. The doctor recommends a combination of both, seeing as I've been stupid enough to postpone getting help for so long. He says I ought to be ashamed of not having come sooner, but I'm not ashamed, at least not because of that.

'I'm not going to.'

'What aren't you going to do?'

'Therapy or drugs.'

They look at me, clearly not getting why. Surely I can't be serious!

'If I take pills to make it go away, I won't know when I'm happy.'

'What are you on about?'

'My knot will disappear when I'm allowed to be happy. I have to leave it be.'

Marianne gives me the you-are-such-an-idiot look.

'That makes no sense, Niko. It's an illness, that's all it is.'

Of course, they come at me with intelligent arguments, as well as a lot of abuse, but I'm not budging. I want the pain to disappear, but I won't do it the easy way. It's too easy to fix with drugs or therapy, because it's about doing the right thing. I'm proud of my decision. Jesus would agree with me, which means I must suck up the pain.

We don't speak on the way home. We're walking silently next to each other until Marianne suddenly turns and hits me hard on the shoulder. She gives me a thump and I jump away in pain. I moan, because it really did hurt, but I can tell that hitting me has lessened her anger a little bit.

'You have to talk to me every day.'

I frighten her.

'I do talk to you every day.'

'No, you have to talk to me every day about the things that scare you. The things that make you make such stupid decisions that you go and do things like this. I want to know everything. Everything! Get it?'

'I get it.'

'Everything.'

'Stop it. I get the picture,' I say, feeling annoyed.

We sit down every day from now on. She comes and gets me, saying, 'It's time.' Mostly some brutal thought pops up. A memory of my fist against Silje's face, and the crunching sound that comes hard upon it. The sound of Sis's voice on the phone as she tries to talk me into coming home instead of hanging out with Satan. Brian spewing vomit on my stairs. I've got plenty to talk about, and she's a good listener.

When I talk to Marianne, it makes me feel healthy. There are days when I forget that I ought to have a stomach ache. She doesn't tell me anything, but I tell her loads, and we build this intense intimacy. At first I tell Jeppe to go away when we talk, because he does tend to sneak in. It makes him feel insecure when I tell him to keep away, so in the end I decide that it doesn't matter. He just sits a couple of metres behind me and listens attentively. He realizes quite quickly, however, that he is not part of the intimacy between Marianne and me, so he stops coming along when

Marianne comes to get me. Marianne gradually starts to touch me a little bit, stroking my cheek; once in a while she even kisses me – only on the cheek, or the forehead or on the hand – but the sadder and more needy I seem, the more she touches me. I wish she'd tell me something as well, so that I might give her something too, but she's shut off, and while I know she speaks to the others, she doesn't say anything to me. She still doesn't trust me, because I haven't proved anything to her yet.

It's not just Marianne who is keeping secrets. Karen has a secret as well. I can hear it in her voice when we talk. Something's waiting for us in Tarm, something peculiar and lovely.

Kink lets his hair down

I've had to tell Kink and Bike off, because they've often not been home on time. Each time they've promised not to let to happen again, but the next day we're waiting for them in vain once more. Bike is embarrassed, because he takes this seriously, but he just can't get the better of Kink's fascination with Copenhagen.

Kink is thrilled that Nørrebro is such a jumble with trash lying about on the street. He's thrilled that there are so many wogs. He's thrilled that so many people are yelling at night. He's thrilled that the house on the corner has been occupied by squatters, simply because it was abandoned for five days. He's thrilled by the number of people. He's thrilled with Copenhagen for the simple reason that it's not Tarm.

Bike promises us that it's just a phase Kink needs to go through, but right now Kink is wildly enthusiastic about everything. Copenhagen is amazing, and everyone he meets in Copenhagen is amazing. Bike tries faithfully to follow Kink about. They're mates, and mates keep an eye out for each other, but Kink doesn't wait for him. He either doesn't care, or he is actually trying to shake Bike. He frequently goes AWOL with a little green-haired anarchist chick he met in a squat, which leaves poor Bike standing alone and bewildered in a house full of teenagers wearing Che Guevara T-shirts.

There's obvious friction now between two friends who never used to have any friction before. Jeppe notices it as well, because Bike suddenly starts talking to him. It confuses Jeppe, but he likes it. Bike sits down next to him and just talks about everyday trivia, oozing friendly camaraderie.

Jeppe doesn't say much, but he listens, he smiles and he nods. At one point Bike mutters, 'I'm sorry, I haven't been very good at speaking to you nicely.'

It's not a very big apology, but it's something.

The butterfly

I've started running as a way of getting some exercise. At first I feel stupid, because my running is actually more like walking, but I can tell that I'm making progress quite quickly. Within a week I can lumber around two of the three inner-city lakes.

It starts with me thinking, 'Crikey, she's got a butterfly on her bottom.'

I see her naked, but it's only by chance. She might have locked the door, and I didn't know she was in there. Maybe I shouldn't have stared quite so intently, but I just couldn't believe she was standing there naked in front of me. A tattoo on her bottom! Is that even allowed when you're a Jehovah's Witness? She's coming out now. She's blushing so hard that it's difficult to tell where her face ends and her hair starts. Kink looks at me with curiosity.

'Why are you looking so smug?'

I lean forward, signalling him to come closer, and then I whisper, 'I've just seen Marianne naked.'

'You're taking the mickey.'

'No, she'd forgotten to lock the bathroom door. She has a tattoo on her arse, a butterfly.'

'No, she bloody hasn't,' he says, clearly not sure what to think.

All of a sudden I'm being yanked out of the chair. Marianne has got hold of my ear, and she is cranky. My ear is being twisted to the point of almost coming off. Kink hurries away to escape the approaching storm. I look into her flaming eyes and stammer a pathetic, 'I didn't m-m-mean to.'

She lets go of my ear. The anger is slowly draining out of her.

I have to ask. 'Why do you have a tattoo?'

She considers for a moment whether I deserve to know, but finally she tells me a little bit.

'We've got the same tattoos, my ex and I.'

'The Albanian? Has he got a tattoo on his bottom as well?'

'No, on his chest. I wanted mine somewhere no-one else would see it.'

'I've seen it,' I say, remembering her perfectly formed bottom. 'Congratulations.'

'Thank you. Do you still see him?'

She chooses her words carefully, but says, 'No, he couldn't wait for me.'

'Oh. That's sad.'

'Yes, it was sad. And that's as much as I'm going to tell you.' She looks at me inquisitively. 'You like me, don't you?'

I'm immediately on my guard. I can tell she has something in mind. Still, I'm honest.

'Yes. I think you're hot.'

She comes up close to me. Her nose touches my cheek. Is she going to kiss me? Her voice is tender and insinuating, 'If you pull this thing off, I'll sleep with you.'

I look at her, absolutely dumbfounded.

'But you wouldn't let Anita use sex,' I say, baffled.

She smiles as she retreats.

'No, I wouldn't. This is different.'

'How's that?'

'It just is. But if you don't pull this off, then today is the first and the only time you'll ever see me naked. And Niko, you've got to lose weight. I can't be bothered to sleep with some big old walrus.'

I'm not a bleeding walrus!

When I return home from my run, dripping with sweat, she looks at me happily and with warmth, and I let her know that I'm doing it for her. She laughs it off, but she can't hide her pride. Making a difference means a lot to Marianne.

Running with Satan

I'm out jogging with Jeppe. At first he chatters away, but I don't answer, because I'm not fit enough to speak while running. Now we're side by side. Suddenly, I notice that Jeppe isn't next to me any longer. I turn around and look for him. It takes me a while to spot him, because he's some fifty metres behind and standing in the lake. He's moving further out into the lake, rather than coming closer to the shore. I lumber back towards him and look at him with confusion. By now the water's up to his groin. It must be freezing. It's early December, and I can see my own breath.

'Jeppe, what are you doing?'

He turns around and looks at me with real fear. It seems like he's forgotten about me, and then he screams, 'Run, Niko! Run!'

He's standing thigh-high in Peblinge Sø, acting odd, and people snigger as they jog by.

'I was running just now. What are you doing?' I yell at him.

'Run!'

I notice he's looking at something right behind me. I turn around slowly, but Jeppe screams, 'No, no! Don't look! Just run!' but it's only when I've turned all the way around that I understand his panic. Right behind me is his older brother with two seventeen-year-old lads.

'Hi there, Nikolaj.'

I don't say anything.

'I said, "Hi there."'

'Don't hurt him,' I say.

'Do you want me to come out there, you little punk?'

Jeppe has made it ten yards into the lake, but I can hear him whimpering loudly. He doesn't dare say anything.

'Can't you say hello?' Satan comes up close to me. 'Say hello. It's not that hard.'

He enjoys having me here. I wish I could outrun him, because I don't stand a chance against Satan, but I can't. I'm one fat slug. Out of the corner of my eye I see Jeppe, sneaking closer to the embankment – only a little bit, he's too scared to come near to us. In a way I'm relieved. Jeppe can't do anything but hurt himself. Satan's too strong.

'How are you?' he asks me.

'I'm doing well.'

'You certainly look like you're eating well. And here you are running about with my baby brother again.'

'Satan, who's this?' asks one of the boys

'You don't know who this is?' Satan asks, surprised. 'He's from before your time. Nikolaj Okholm.'

'*The* Nikolaj?' the lad says with obvious admiration.

'Yes, the Nikolaj. Son of sodding Grith Okholm.'

'Who's she?' the kid asks, stupidly.

He doesn't even know who Mum is!

'The singer Grith Okholm! If you don't know who she is then why do you say *the* Nikolaj?' Satan asks, annoyed.

'I've just heard all sorts of stuff about him. He's supposed to be way cool. He doesn't look way cool.'

'I heard he once beat you up,' the other kid says.

It's not true. I would never have dared to try. Satan turns to the kid.

'He beat me up?'

'Yes, you had a fight about which one of you was meaner, and he beat you up.'

Why doesn't he shut his stupid mouth? A bit further down the lake Jeppe has made it back to the shore, and now he's running hell for leather towards Rantzausgade.

'We're going for a walk here,' Satan says.

I shake my head. Satan grabs hold of my arm.

'I didn't ask you if you wanted to,' and then he drags me off.

I follow him like a whipped dog. He even tells me to come to heel when I'm lagging behind. We don't walk for long, only as far as the first backyard where we won't be disturbed. I'm surprised to see Satan withdraw. He looks at the lads with a challenge in his eyes.

'Beat him up. Then you'll see how tough he really is.'

They look from him to me and back, then walk over to me. They're standing anxiously in front of me, and then they look back at Satan one final time to have confirmation of what they're to do.

'Hit him,' Satan says, but they hesitate, and I react instinctively.

FLRBBBBB! The punch I land on one of them is so off that it borders on being just a clumsy slap, but they jump back, frightened. Satan, on the other hand, comes at me with fists that hit their target. I try to defend myself, but my punches hit nothing but air. Unlike mine, Satan's blows are scary and precise. Everything goes black.

When I come to, Jesus is bending over me.

'You all right?'

I nod and look around. The two lads have gone, and Satan is lying on the ground, quite still. I can taste blood in my mouth, and I'm rather sore, but other than that I'm okay.

'Did you do this?' I ask, pointing at Satan.

'Yes, this time I came with the sword.'

'You stabbed him?'

'No, of course I didn't, but I didn't come bringing peace.'

I feel dizzy. Jesus supports me and stops me from falling over.

'Are you sure you're all right?'

'It's nothing.'

He looks at me searchingly, but seems to decide that I'm the best judge of how I'm feeling.

'So, how are things?'

'Things are good. We're working on the master plan,' I say, proud and contented.

'I know. Anita's at the nursery school.'

That takes me aback. 'How do you know?'

'I know things, because I am who I am.'

He's just beat up Satan, and that takes real strength, but right now my body's hurts too much for me to be able to contemplate the fact that he might be divine. Instead, I point at Satan and say, 'He's not dead, is he?'

'No, but he's not doing well, and he'll never come near you again. He's not as tough as you think he is. Are you sure you're okay?'

'Yes, dammit. I'm just a little beat right now,' I say, still dazed from my encounter with Satan's fists. 'It's good having friends.'

'Of course it is. You ought to have given that a try long ago. I've got to go now. They'll be here soon.'

'My friends?'

'Yes. Jeppe went to get them,' and then he squats down and looks me in the eyes. 'Look after them. No matter what, look after them. I want you to promise that you will.'

'I promise.'

He's exacting a promise from me. I look at him, searchingly. He knows something. Something bad is going to happen, and he already knows.

'Good. You have to be there for them. You have to protect them.'

I nod, eagerly. I have to protect them?

Me?

Sod it, yes! I'm ready.

It's no more than thirty seconds from when Jesus leaves and they appear. When they see me, they all come running over and hug me. It's an amazing feeling. The lads then turn around and scout for danger, while Marianne holds me tight. She's blocking my view. That's why I don't see it when they discover Satan lying unconscious on the ground. All I hear is the sound of feet stomping on flesh, and Bike and Kink pulling the furious Jeppe off Satan. Marianne helps me get up, and we walk back to the flat in silence.

'I thought we were going to find you dead. I didn't think you could take him on,' Jeppe says happily.

Jeppe knows what his big brother is capable of.

'I couldn't. I was getting such a beating, but Jesus saved me.'

'Jesus?'

'I didn't beat up Satan. Jesus did.'

She's in love

Anita's insecurity disappears and is replaced by a calm, happy anticipation. For a long time we simply assume it's because she's good at her job. However, all of us notice the excited tone of her voice whenever she mentions Brian, and we begin – ever so slowly – to be suspicious. None of us dare say it out loud. Maybe we are reading things into Anita's behaviour simply because we know her. She speaks fondly of all men.

It's Marianne who brings it up. We're at home watching a film, while Anita is at some parent-teacher thing at the nursery school. We're watching *Notting Hill* with Julia Roberts and Hugh Grant. I chose it. I have a weak spot for romantic comedies, because violent films make me feel sick. Suddenly, Marianne says, 'Do you think she's in love?'

'Well, it's a rom-com, after all,' I say.

'I'm talking about Anita, not the film.'

'Who would she be in love with?' Kink asks.

He's the only one not to have noticed, because his thoughts are otherwise engaged.

'With Brian, of course.'

I can tell that there's a 'yes' hovering on both Bike's and Jeppe's tongues, and I can feel it on my own as well, but it sticks and doesn't want to come out, so instead we make Marianne say it for us.

'I'm absolutely certain.'

Bike tries to make light of it.

'She's always falling in love. Before Brian it was Niko, and once she's through with Brian, it'll probably be Jeppe.'

This idea seems to scare Jeppe, who starts to rock back and forth in his chair.

'There wasn't the same thrill in her voice when she spoke about Niko.'

'So she's in love with Brian, but wasn't in love with me? You know I'm like a hundred times better looking than Brian.'

'You're such an idiot when you say things like that.'

The evening is ruined, because now all we can think about is that Anita's in love.

When Anita tells us about her day, all we hear is Brian, Brian, Brain, followed by an enormous throbbing loveheart. She makes him smile. They hug each other. They talk about all sorts of stuff. He even tells her about Sis, and not just the terrible things. They clown about. He laughs, and is surprised by the sound of his own laughter. He asks her about all sorts of private things. She lies, of course. I don't think he believes her capable of those feelings, because she doesn't know him, but she knows him through me. I've been jealous and angry at Brian, but I've never pretended that he's not a good person. If he wasn't such an ugly bastard, I'd like to be him. He tells her he isn't angry any longer. He's stopped being angry. He doesn't know why, but all of a sudden he's smiling. She's winning his trust, and a lot more besides. None of us say, 'Watch out. This could backfire terribly.' We just nod eagerly, because we're afraid not to, and we leave her to nurture her love in peace.

We start getting ready for Christmas. We shop for gingerbread and tangerines like there is no tomorrow; Bike and Kink smuggle in presents; Marianne serves rice porridge on Wednesdays and Sundays; and Anita talks to Brian about their plans for Christmas.

'I'll be at home with Allan,' he says.

'No one else?'

'No, my parents will be at Tenerife. They go there every year. How about you?'

'I don't really know.'

'You don't know where you'll be for Christmas?' Brian sounds surprised.

'No, not really. I'll probably stay in Copenhagen.'

'But are you going to be spending Christmas with anyone?'

'Yes, I think so. Just some friends.'

'You think so?'

Anita doesn't say anything. She simply smiles sweetly and nods ever so slightly. Brian doesn't say anything for a bit, then he stammers nervously, 'If you haven't got anyone to celebrate Christmas with, you could come celebrate it with Allan and me.' She blushes.

'Do you think Allan would be okay with that?'

'Allan would love it. You're his favourite person in the whole wide world, and that's not my choice of words – it's his.'

'He's a sweetheart.'

'He's been so much happier since you've been here.'

'And how about you?'

This time Brian is the one who blushes. 'I've been a lot happier too.'

'No, what I mean is, would you be okay with my spending Christmas with you?'

'Oh. Yes, of course I would.'

Anita gives his arm a little squeeze, and says, 'You're making me really happy as well,' then she hurries away.

She can feel Brian looking at her for a very long time, but she pretends that she is so busy with some wailing child that she simply doesn't notice. She's nothing short of ecstatic when she comes home. She skips about the sitting room, and she doesn't try to hide the reason for her skipping about. Marianne catches her mid-air, brings her down to the ground and whispers, 'We all know. Be careful. Remember who he is, and who we are.'

Anita's elation is lessened, but it doesn't go away.

He is in love

The next day I talk to Sis about Brian's intentions. I'm worried, and my worry is in no way lessened when Sis says that he doesn't talk about Anita in that way. He mentions her often, but mostly

216

because Allan is so fond of her. But then, I don't talk about Marianne in that way either.

'There's nothing going on between us. We're just good friends.'

It happens every time! I can't have a conversation with Sis without her talking about me and Marianne.

'Liar.'

'I can't be bothered to do this again.'

'Liar.'

'Sis, could we please talk about Anita and Brian? It's important.'

'I'd like to talk about you and Marianne, so what should we do first?'

This is when Sis does something really mean. She goes silent, and the silence spreads like a wildfire. I don't like it, because if I can't hear Sis then she's gone. Then it's no longer Sis. Then it's just Sanne Okholm Jensen's grave, and it doesn't help that I tell her, 'Stop being so fucking stupid.' It's only when I say, 'I've seen Marianne naked,' that she speaks again

'You have? How?' Sis says, sounding surprised.

'She forgot to lock the bathroom door. Sis, please don't ever, ever do that again.'

'Do what again?'

'Don't ever give me the silent treatment.'

She can tell from my voice that I'm scared.

'I'm sorry, Niko. That was stupid of me. (Silence.) You've seen her naked. Was she attractive?'

'Very. She has a butterfly tattooed on her bottom.'

'Wasn't she a Jehovah's Witness when you met her?'

Sis is confused. So am I.

'Yes, she came to my door to convert me.'

'And then you ended up converting her instead?'

'I suppose so.'

At this point we are interrupted by an elderly man, who asks me gently if I need help. Jeppe is coming towards us belligerently, but I give him a small nod to indicate there's nothing to worry about. I smile, and say, 'Thanks, but I'm all right really. I'm just talking out loud to myself.' He doesn't seem to believe me, so I add, 'It's my sister,' and point at Sis. He nods, empathetically. I thank him for his consideration. When the old man leaves, Sis erupts in a fit of laughter.

'Come on, it wasn't that funny.'

'You should have seen yourself. You looked completely lost.'

'You know, I think I did a pretty good job of saving that one.'

'You did, sweetie, you did. You have no idea how happy I am that you are the way you are now. There was a time when you would have yelled at him.'

It starts pissing down, and I have no cover. Our conversation is nowhere near finished. I call Jeppe over. He comes running at once. He protests fervently. He's already wet, but that's not why I'm sending him home. I want to be alone with Sis. It takes me all of five minutes, before I get through to him, but he finally leaves. I'm cold and wet through, but I still lay down on the ground and hold Sis. The ground gets muddy very quickly, but it still feels comforting and almost like old times. We whisper intimately to each other.

'I think I might be in love with Marianne.'

'You think?'

'I'm not sure. It's not as intense as with Silje.'

'There are other ways of being in love. Sometimes it starts off as something small and then it just keeps growing.'

'Yes, maybe that's what it is. She'll sleep with me if I lose weight.'

Sis grunts with surprise.

'Are you sure she used to be a Jehovah's Witness?'

'Yup, absolutely positive. I really do have to know what Brian said about Anita.'

'He speaks about her a lot, but not about being in love with her.'

'Shit, that's not good. Anita's really in love with him.'

'Don't worry, sweetie. He's in love with her too. He talks about absolutely everything except how he feels about her. It's always Allan who's fond of her, never him, but I can tell by his voice. Do be careful. He wouldn't survive another big blow.'

'I promise he won't get one.'

After that we don't say anything more. I stay lying next to Sis, and she lulls me to sleep while the rain pours down over me. I haven't slept for very long when I'm roused by a hand, gently shaking my shoulder. I look up and see Brian with an umbrella. I jump up, scared, but I realize he means me no harm. If he did he wouldn't have woken me up so gently. We don't say anything to each other. I brush off the worst mud.

'She's all yours.'

'Thanks. Would you mind only coming in the mornings, so we don't bump into each other like this?'

I manage to mutter a quiet 'Righto'. I'm almost about to chatter on, because he is so mild, but I manage to stop myself before the words tumble out. I turn around and slosh homewards. No doubt about it: he's in love.

Netto, and Marianne peeing

I've gone down to Netto on Rantzausgade with Marianne. We're shopping for a Friday night in. Marianne has gone to pick out the sweets, while I play at being the wine connoisseur. I decide on a couple of bottles that are slightly more expensive than the others, and hence probably slightly better. When I turn around, Silje is standing right in front of me.

She drops a bottle of red, and it smashes on the floor between us. The wine sprays us both. It doesn't matter much as far as I'm concerned, but she's all dressed up in a pretty pink dress, which has now been splattered on. She looks at me, filled with anger and fear, but also with something strangely like desire, and then she darts out of Netto. I don't get a chance to say anything to her. It all happens much too quickly. I just stand there, splashed in red wine, while I try to subdue the stomach ache I know is coming.

'I couldn't find the ones with sour cream,' and then, once again, I'm confronted by an angry Camilla. She sees me first, then the puddle of red wine, and then she looks around for Silje.

'What the hell did you do?'

She looks thunderous.

I shake my head and mutter, 'I didn't do anything.'

Camilla comes up close to me, then spits in my face. It's every bit as humiliating as it always was, but she's not finished with me. She makes more gobbing noises, but I give her a shove and she slips in the pool of red wine. She falls and almost cuts herself on a large piece of broken glass. I flee while I can, but just before I leave the shop I turn around to see if Marianne is coming. She isn't. She's actually helping Camilla get up.

She doesn't come home for another half hour. I'm worried, of course, and I have a go at her as soon as she returns.

'Where have you been?'

'I was talking to Camilla.'

'What about?'

'About you and Silje, of course. I'm meeting her tomorrow night at Tjili Pop.'

'You're meeting her without me?'

She nods.

'But she spat at me!'

'And you pushed her. We're just going to talk, Niko. Maybe she can help us, and maybe we can help her.'

That's all there is to say about it.

The following day I'm all a-flutter. I want to go with Marianne, because I want to hear what they say about me, but I stay home, waiting impatiently for her to get back. She's gone all night, and when she finally comes home, she goes straight to her room. I knock. She doesn't answer. I open the door anyway. She's lying very still in the dark.

'Marianne.'

She doesn't say anything.

'Marianne.'

'Not now, Nikolaj.'

'How did it go?'

'You need to leave me be for a bit,' she says, sounding annoyed.

'I just want to know how it went?'

'Nikolaj, I need to be left alone for a while.'

I don't get it, and I switch on the light. She turns her face away from me.

'Turn off that light, and go away,' she says, sounding very decided.

'Has she hurt you?'

I'm worried. Camilla frightens me.

'Nikolaj, go away. It's you I can't face right now.'

I shut the door and hurry to the bathroom, where I'm sick with terror. I haven't managed to turn up the radio, which makes it audible and apparent to everyone. I've probably been going for a couple of minutes when Marianne knocks on the bathroom door.

'Niko, please let me in.'

I flush, spray deodorant around the room and let her in. She locks the door. We're standing awkwardly in front of each other.

'I need to wee.'

'Oh. Do you want me to go?'

She shakes her head, pulls down her trousers and sits on the loo. I can't help looking on in wide-eyed wonder. She smiles at me and starts talking while she's weeing.

222

'It just overwhelmed me, Niko. Hearing about what you did to Silje, it was very intense.'

'I'd already told you!'

'It seemed more frightening coming from Camilla. Maybe because she also told me about how Silje's been doing since. Just give me some time to digest this, and we'll talk about it later. Okay?'

I nod.

'Niko, nothing's changed. I still feel the same way about you that I always did.'

She stands and pulls up her trousers. I get a small glimpse of the butterfly, and my heart takes flight. She unlocks the door.

'You'd better stay in here.'

'Why?'

She puts out an arm, and I feel her gentle hand on my cock.

'Because you're bulging,' and with that she leaves me, hot, bothered and bewildered, but also feeling very encouraged.

Grith Okholm Jam splits (for now)

The band is offered a lucrative gig, playing at a Christmas party at a large consulting agency, but Silje doesn't want to. This time the others decide that enough is enough: they're fed up with only playing in the practice room. Camilla is pleading with them, but it's no good. They just can't be bothered any more. Camilla is afraid to tell Silje. As a matter of fact, she waits until they're standing in the empty practice room, then she tells Silje that the others

223

aren't coming. Silje weeps and wails, because now she's doesn't even have this.

Marianne sees it as our chance, and she tells Camilla about our plan to have a big festival in Mum's honour with Grith Okholm Jam as one of the headline acts. Marianne makes a big point of saying that it's just an idea we've been toying with. We want to make Silje a star, if nothing else then at least for a couple of days. Camilla listens with interest. She's excited by the idea, because – like us – Camilla is convinced that Silje needs to get back onstage. But now this isn't about whether I'm a bastard, or about how fragile Silje is, but about being able to actually do something. Of course, nothing has been decided when they leave Tjili Pop, because Camilla isn't convinced yet. She just isn't entirely dismissive, and they both think things might actually turn out all right in the end.

The truth will out

Tonight's the annual Christmas party at the nursery school. They've been at it for some time; spirits are high, and Anita's nineteen-year-old male colleague has already made a pass at her. She has politely declined the offer and moved on. She's enjoying the evening, and she's well and truly plastered. They all are. Headmistress Hanne has pulled her to one side and told her affectionately that she's so happy to be able to trust Anita. She's been so nervous since accepting the money. She just couldn't turn it down, but Anita's lovely. Anita smiles proudly, but anxiously. She doesn't feel quite comfortable with Hanne bringing this up now.

Time passes, and Anita's anxiety wanes. She's outside smoking when she hears Hanne bellow, 'I was offered a hundred grand to hire Anita. Would you guys have turned that down?'

Anita can hear how surprised the others are.

'I was a bit worried she might turn out to be a psychopath, but she's not. She's lovely, don't you think? I just don't feel guilty any more.'

Anita hurries back in. The snatches of conversation she overhears tell her that Hanne is speaking without thinking. When Anita is at the door, they all turn and look at her. Hanne has told them just enough to make them question Anita. She realizes that she is starting to cry very quietly.

'Did you pay a hundred grand just to be near Brian?' someone asks her with surprise.

Anita shakes her head, and manages to mutter, 'I don't know what she's talking about. She's drunk.'

Hanne gets up quite huffily. She's drunk to be sure, but Anita has no business saying it.

'I got a hundred grand just for letting you work here, and Gitte got two hundred grand,' she yells resentfully.

'I haven't got that much money. I've just filed for bankruptcy.'

That confuses Hanne, until she gets her muddled memory straight.

'It wasn't you, come to think of it. It was that Nikolaj character, Brian's brother-in-law,' she says triumphantly.

Anita's standing at the doorway, feeling exposed.

'That's not true.'

'What is it you want with Brian?'

They've all noticed that she's constantly circling him.

'I don't want anything with Brian. It's not true.'

They don't believe her, and Hanne – unfortunately – is so drunk that she doesn't realize how badly she is fucking up.

'My entire family is going off to Crete on that money. I'm not kidding.'

It's no use protesting. Maybe Anita herself has convinced them because she is so terrified. She hasn't considered how hard she is crying until the silent staring makes her flee. She runs, as fast as she can, and when she's standing outside in the cold she realizes her face is wet. She wants to disappear. She's so in love. It used to make her strong, but now it is making her crumble.

When she gets home, Kink and Bike are still up, sitting in front of the telly watching the latest Steven Seagal film, and looking half-asleep.

'Hey there, good party, was it?'

She doesn't say anything. She snuggles up to Bike and hugs him tightly. She even tries to kiss him and unbutton his trousers, but Bike, despite his terror, manages to push her off.

'What is it? Anita, what's happened?' Bike says, almost panicking.

Something's very wrong.

'Dammit, say something.'

Bike is in a frenzy. Anita isn't speaking, and all Bike can manage is, 'There, there,' while he gently strokes her and at the same time prevents her hands from getting anywhere near him.

'Get Marianne.'

Kink storms into Marianne's room and yanks her out of bed. She peels Anita off Bike with a steady hand, and takes her back to their room. Anita still isn't speaking. Neither of them is. Right before the door closes Marianne turns to Kink and Bike.

'We don't want to be disturbed, so don't wake up Niko.'

They nod in agreement, although all they want to do is kick my door down.

Choking and then blushing

When I wake up, Kink and Bike are staring at Marianne and Anita's door. I stand next to them and look. There's nothing to see. It's just a door.

'Why are you staring at the door?'

'Because Anita's in there,' Bike says without even looking away from the door.

'Yes. Where else would she be?'

They're silent, and it's only now I realize that something's not right. I get scared.

'What's happened?'

'We're not allowed to say.'

'You're not allowed to say what?'

'We can't tell you that, see?'

I start imagining all sorts of things. Brian knows, and everything is ruined. Maybe he's hit her. He got furious and couldn't

227

control himself, and now she's in there with her face beaten to a pulp and her heart broken to pieces. I walk up to the door resolutely. It's locked, so I knock. Bike puts his hand on my shoulder.

'Better not, Niko. They don't want to be disturbed.'

I shake the hand off with an irritated shrug and knock again, harder this time. My stomach is yelping at me, 'Do something, you tosser! Everything's falling apart!'

I promised Sis that we wouldn't fail, and now we bloody well are. I feel a hand tightening around my throat, and I turn to Bike furiously to tell him to come off it, but Bike is at the other end of the room. No-one's touching me, and yet I'm feeling every single finger of this powerful hand, which bears me no good will. Once again I can't breathe. I want to beg for help, but where there's no air, there can be no words either. My eyes are almost popping out of my head, my face turns blue and the veins in my neck are pumping like mad.

'Niko, what the hell is happening to you?'

They scream for Marianne to come. I'm out for a minute, tops. I come to with a gasp, and once again all my friends are looking at me with worry.

'You really must do what the doctor tells you.'

Marianne is sitting, bent over me, gently wiping sweat off my forehead. I shake my head stubbornly. Anita is standing at the door, looking at me with concern. She hasn't taken a step out of the bedroom. She's all in one piece. There's not a bruise to be seen anywhere. Still dizzy, I get up and walk towards her. She shakes her head and shuts the door in my face. Her face may not be beaten to a pulp, but I recognize the look of a heart that has been broken to pieces. I turn and face the others.

'What happened?'

'Hanne said you bribed her.'

'Damn and blast, that's not how bribes work. Brian can't know!'

'She didn't tell Brian. She told the other nursery school teachers.'

That gets my hopes up. Marianne seems to read my mind.

'He knows,' she says.

'Not necessarily, he doesn't.'

'Don't you think they'll tell him? We should never have done it.'

'Of course we should. We're doing it for his sake. Maybe they'll wait until Monday when he brings Allan.'

I go to my room and put on some clothes. I'm conscious of a will power in me, quite unlike my usual self. I feel strong. The others are following me as I put on my shoes and coat.

'Where are you going?'

'I have to see Brian.'

I say it without the least hesitation. Jeppe immediately starts getting dressed.

'Alone.'

He looks at me blankly.

'It's not safe. He'll beat you up.'

'Then that's the way it has to be.'

It's strange, but in the midst of this disaster I'm feeling optimistic. I've never been able to imagine what would happen with Brian and Anita. It was too unruly and unrealistic by far. Now the end is here, and yet all is not lost. As I leave, Marianne pulls me in close. She's holding me and whispering in my ear, 'Be careful. Promise me you will,' and I whisper back, 'I promise. Why are we whispering?'

She's smiling at me. 'I'm proud of you.'

That takes me aback.

'Why are you proud of me?'

'Because you're doing this for Anita and Brian.'

I blush. I blush for the first time since I've been an adult, but I'm filled with courage when I walk out the door.

Heavy drinking

He's still living in Peder Skrams Gade, and I try the old code on the front door. It works. That surprises me, given what I did last time I was here. I'm too fat by far to climb four flights of stairs, and when I'm standing outside the flat I need to catch my breath before ringing the bell. I sit down with my head between my legs, panting so loudly that I never hear the door being opened.

'You okay there?'

I twitch with confusion. Brian is standing at the door, looking at me. I try to get a grip, take a deep breath and get my voice under control.

'Sure. I'm just really unfit.'

He bends down and pulls me up – it takes some effort.

'Want to come in?'

I nod, relieved. I feel like I'm sullying his flat with my presence. I have a bit of a wander about. Nothing has changed.

Everything is the way it was when Sis lived her, except her shoes and coat are no longer in the hall.

'Where's Allan?'

'With some friends. Have a seat,' he says, pointing at the sofa.

He surprises me, because he sounds so relaxed and affectionate. I sit down, and he puts a bottle of whisky and two glasses on the sofa table. As it's only just past twelve, I decline. He shakes his head.

'You've come to apologize, so the least you can do is get drunk with me.'

I nod, pour myself a glass and toast him. He drinks as if it were a shot, despite its smoky flavour. I feel like I should keep up, so I do the same. He refills our glasses.

'You really have got fat, Nikolaj.'

He makes no attempt to hide his pleasure.

'I suppose so.'

He kicks back another glass, and I do the same. He pours us two more.

'How the hell did you manage to get yourself friends?'

'I've changed.'

'You have: you've got fat.'

'I've changed in other ways.'

'How did you get to be so fat? You used to be so slim, and now you're as round as a beach ball.'

Apparently he'd rather talk about that.

'I don't know. It just happened. Why?'

'I'm curious. Cheers,' he says cheerfully.

I don't drink this time, because I can't keep up with him. He pours himself another.

'I said cheers.'

He drinks again. He pours himself one more.

'Come on, Nikolaj, drink. We've got to get drunk.'

'Why?'

'Because you have well and truly shafted me, and now we're going to drink it out of our systems, so that I don't end up tearing you to pieces.'

He says it with an affectionate smile. I say 'Cheers' straight-away, and I no longer have any doubts that he knows what we've done.

He got a call at 2 a.m. from what used to be Allan's nursery school.

'Idiots,' I mutter. 'At least they could have waited a couple of days.'

Brian looks puzzled. I feel like I ought to explain, so I say, 'It's just that I would have liked to tell you myself.'

'Oh, you wanted to beat them to it. Why?'

He fills my glass again. I can already hear my speech getting slurred.

'I don't want you to ruin everything. Anita's crazy about you.'

'No, she's not. She's a liar. Cheers.'

We drink again.

'She's wretched, much more than you are.'

He doesn't interrupt me with a 'Cheers'. He listens carefully, so I continue.

'She's crazy about you and Allan, and she's pretty and lovely. That's not a lie, either. Yes, I paid for her to get a job at the nursery school, but I didn't do it to harm you. I did it to help you. Cheers.'

It seems to be my turn to drink alone. He looks at me curiously, then sips his glass thoughtfully.

'So you bought a girl for me to cheer me up?'

'If I did, would it really be such a bad thing? You're visiting prossies all the time.'

That really knocks the stuffing out of him. He coughs, confused, into his glass.

'I most certainly don't,' he stutters. It's true, he doesn't any more. It's been a couple of weeks since he told Sis proudly that he wouldn't do that any more.

'I speak to Sis every day. She tells me everything you tell her, so I know that you have done.'

'She's dead, you berk.'

'Yes, but I still talk to her. Our relationship is better than it ever was before. We're equals.'

'She's dead, you're alive, that doesn't exactly make you equals, does it? It's not like she's talking to you.'

'She's talking to me all right. She's doing far more talking than I am. I know that you don't have sex with those prossies either.'

He tries to make sense of it, but the only way it makes sense to him is if I'm a headcase. He looks at me to see if he can discern the madness in me, but I'm far more well and sane than I ever was before.

233

'I didn't buy her for you. She's my friend, not a prossie. I didn't mean for Anita to fall in love with you, she just did.'

He still isn't saying anything, and then I tell him the whole story. All the while, we kick back whisky. He replaces the bottle at one point, and we keep going at the same steady pace. He doesn't say anything, he just listens with interest. When I'm done, I'm both tired and drunk. He can drink a lot. I, on the other hand, stumble out into the bathroom. I'm not sick, but it comes close. Jesus titty-fucking Christ, this is hard! I want to hide out here until I no longer feel sick.

When I come back, he's sitting calmly in his chair.

'So in other words, you've grown a conscience.'

'I've always had one.'

'You've grown one that nags you.'

'I've always had one of them as well. These days I just do something about it.'

'Whatever you say, mate. Cheers.'

'Cheers.'

I knock back the whisky and am immediately and explosively sick. There's sick on the table and on the floor, and Brian just laughs.

'Nothing like a drink to make it better,' he says, and pours me another.

I'm not sure how long we keep going, and I'm not at all sure what I tell him. I'm probably trying to convince him that I'm a good person, and that Anita is doing wonders for him. I'm sick more than once. He just keeps the drinks coming. I don't know why. I just know that I fall asleep on his sofa, and that he lets me sleep.

When I wake up, the stench of vomit is drilling into my nostrils. I'm covered in it. So is the sofa, and I have the worst headache in the history of man. Brian is asleep in the easy chair. I wake him up gently. He opens his tired eyes slowly and looks at me sleepily. He smiles.

'You'd better go now.'

'What?'

'You've got to go. I don't ever want to see you again. Got it?'

I shake my head, feeling confused.

'Last night was my test, and I passed it. I don't hate you any more. I just can't be bothered with you.'

'You can't tell me to go. I've changed.'

'I don't care. You're nothing to me. You're crazy little Nikolaj who's found Jesus, because no-one else wants to have anything to do with you.'

That's not true. I've got friends, good friends. Nevertheless, I take it to heart, because Jesus came to me in my hour of deepest loneliness. I swallow my pride and remember Anita and her broken heart.

'What about Anita? Are you going to throw that away?'

He hesitates, then doesn't look me in the eye as he says it. 'I don't want her to ever get in touch with me again.'

I look at him sadly. It's such a wretched waste. He loves her, and she loves him. It doesn't have to be any more difficult than that.

'Go. Now!'

'Anita will make you happy.'

Brian gets up and comes over to me. He puts his hand on my back and pushes me forward gently, and I leave, protesting pathetically as I go.

I'm standing on Peder Skrams Gade, feeling less than settled about the whole thing. Suddenly there's a hand on my shoulder.

'How did it go?'

I turn around, and there's Jesus.

'Not quite according to plan. Not horrifically, but not all that well.'

'Wow, you stink, Nikolaj. Have you been sick all over yourself?'

'Yes.'

'Ugh. What did you do that for?'

'I didn't do it on purpose!'

We go round to the nearest bar that is open in the morning and have a hair of the dog. They look at us rather sceptically. I'm covered in sick, and Jesus is wearing sandals, even though it's a couple of days short of Christmas. Luckily they're not so sensitive that they refuse to serve us our beers.

'I can't believe he let me in, if he'd already decided what he was going to do. Why did he get drunk with me?'

Jesus shrugs. 'I don't know, but he wouldn't have done it two months ago, now would he?'

'No, but what does that mean?'

He's smiling smugly. 'It means that you're pulling it off.'

I gawp at him in surprise. Anita and Brian are both heartbroken, but it would seem that Brian has moved on. Two months ago he was filled with a rage, which left no room for anything else. Now there's room, and then it's really up to him. I can't make him happy. I just have to give him a chance to become so.

'What about Anita?'

'It's up to them now,' Jesus says. 'If they want it badly enough, they'll work it out.'

Is it really that simple? I don't much like it, but I've got to accept that I can't make them love each other and be happy. I have another couple of pints with Jesus, while we talk about this and that. He says he's proud of me. I've come a long way in a short period of time. I thank him. It means a lot to me that he should think so, and I tell him that. I want him to know that I'm grateful that he bothers with me. I don't much like leaving him – it's always reassuring to speak to him – but the others must be getting worried about me. I had better get home.

I've been gone a full twenty-four hours, so I'm greeted with relief. Marianne gives me a happy hug. Then she realizes I'm covered in vomit as the stench hits her nostrils, and she pushes me away in disgust. Anita has come out of her bedroom. She is sad but present. I sit myself down and explain what's happened, and what Jesus said. All is not lost yet. She nods, but I can tell that she's too scared to do anything about it.

'Does this mean we are no longer focusing on Brian?' Bike asks.

'Yes. Jesus said that it's all taken care of. It's up to them now.'

They don't understand, but I can't explain it more clearly than I already have.

'So now it's on to Silje?'

'Yes, but before we deal with that, we're going home,' I say, feeling profoundly relieved.

I need to go home. Copenhagen is wearing me down. I need to recover my strength. Marianne nods, as if she understands, even though I offer no word of explanation. She knows why. That's really all I need to be certain that I'm making the right decision.

We'll lure Silje to Jutland with Camilla's help. I'm sure of it, and once we've got her to Tarm, we'll make sure she's so successful that she'll have the strength to listen to me. That's our plan. It's that simple, and I know it's not bulletproof. But how can I plan for another person to forgive me? I can only apologize, then hope she believes me.

After several conversations we've finally convinced Camilla. She said no at first, even though she was tempted, but she won't allow me to meet Silje, least of all on my own turf. We resign ourselves to staying in Copenhagen, but then Camilla calls Marianne.

'She's holed herself up.'

'Silje?'

'Yes. She won't even answer my text messages. I can't take it any more. It's just too hard.'

Marianne holds her breath in anticipation.

'We absolutely have to do something,' Camilla says.

She has no alternative, and in the end she agrees to help us. From this point on there's a lively correspondence between Marianne and Camilla.

It's two days until Christmas Eve, and it would be too much fuss to move just before the holiday. We're all kind little secret Santas to Anita, and her spirits improve a little, because we manage to distract her. She'll live – she's got us after all – but it would be better if she also had Brian.

A very merry Christmas

It's Christmas Eve. We've put presents under the tree, and rice pudding on the table. No-one's found the almond yet. Spirits are high, but nobody's absolutely ecstatic. And then the phone rings. We look at each other, confused. Karen has already called, so who the devil can it be? The phone's about to stop ringing, but Jeppe picks it up just in time.

'Hello?'

As no-one says anything at the other end of the line, Jeppe repeats his hello.

'Who is this?' someone asks, timidly.

'You're the one who's calling, aren't you?'

'Who are you?'

'Who are you?' Jeppe says, ready for a battle on the phone.

'Brian Birkemose Andersen.'

He's got the number from Hanne. He promises he won't file

charges against her if she gets him Anita's number tonight, on Christmas Eve. Hanne doesn't have the number on her private phone, and she's spending Christmas with her husband's family in Odense. Brian leaves her no choice. It's come up with the phone number or face a police report. There's nothing for it but to drive back from Odense to the Ladybird, lock herself in, get out the number and, hey presto, here's Brian on the phone.

Jeppe makes a lot of queer gestures we can't make out.

'Do you know who I am?'

'Yes, I met you at the cemetery.'

It's only now we realize he's speaking to Brian. We all look anxiously at Anita, who has gone very pale.

'Is Nikolaj there as well?'

'Yes.' Jeppe signals for me to stand up.

'I don't want to talk to him. I'll hang up if you put him on.'

Jeppe signals for me to sit down again. Anita gets up and walks over to Jeppe. He hands her the phone, but first he puts it on speakerphone, so we can all listen in.

'Hello.'

Not a sound from Brian's end.

'Are you there?'

'Yes.'

We almost can't breathe.

'Is there something you wanted to say to me?' Anita asks.

'Yes,' but that's all he says.

'What did you want to say?'

'Allan's mad at me.'

Anita smiles, faintly.

'Why is Allan mad at you?'

'I promised him you were going to spend Christmas with us. And now he's locked himself in his room, and he says I'm a poo.'

'I'd like to spend Christmas with you.'

'I know,' he says, obviously ashamed of himself, and then there's another awkward silence.

'Was that all you wanted to tell me?'

'No. Won't you please come over?'

Anita bites her lips, nervously.

'Because Allan wants me there?'

'Yes.'

This is the big gamble.

'That's not enough for me.'

'What do you mean?' the voice at the other end of the phone says anxiously.

'You have to want it too. I'm very fond of Allan, but it's you I'm in love with.'

This is when Bike starts sobbing like a happy little girl. Kink moves away from him slightly, and that leaves Jeppe as the next person to do something. Jeppe looks with bewilderment at the tears that are rolling down Bike's cheek. They are happy tears, but they are tears nonetheless, and he extends an arm very gently, and puts it around Bike, who immediately cuddles up to Jeppe, sniffling as he does so. Jeppe looks at me for a second to check my reaction, and when I smile proudly he decides that he's doing the right thing. Brian doesn't say anything for a long time, but we can tell by his breathing that something big is in the making, and when he finally says it, it's like fireworks.

'I do want you here. I'm in love with you too.'

Anita can't hold it back any longer. She's bawling with relief and joy. We all get up to support her, but she pushes us off. We leave her to sit with the phone and have a little cry, and then she says, 'I'll be there in a tick.'

She puts down the phone and looks at us. We're suddenly very quiet, until that first gigantic yelp of happiness has been let out. We're all jumping up and down. Anita remains sitting by the phone, exhausted. She smiles happily at us loonies, tumbling about in a joy-induced stupor, bumping into furniture, the Christmas tree, into each other, until we collapse into her arms.

Ten minutes later, and she's gone. We're a bit perplexed, but there's still rice pudding to be had, and none of us have found the almond. It later turns out that Jeppe accidentally swallowed it when the phone rang.

This time she really does leave us

We have a marvellous Christmas Eve. We all have a really cool feeling that nothing can possibly go wrong now, and that's exactly the feeling you need on Christmas Eve. It makes us feel like giants who drink, overeat and bellow carols at the top our voices. It's the only Christmas ever when I've got drunk because I was happy.

I wake up on the sofa with my arms around Marianne. She's the one who snuggles up to me. I'm here first, then she muscles in, takes my arm and puts it around her. At first she actually puts my hand on her breast, but she only lets it stay there for two seconds, then she moves it down to her stomach instead. I try to put it further down still, but she won't let me.

She's still asleep. I've got her red hair in my mouth and a slight headache. I look around the room sleepily. There are bottles, dirty plates and wrapping paper all over the place, and Anita is sitting on a chair. She is smiling and looking at once happy and melancholy as she watches us. She's packed her bags once more. I look at it in surprise, and then at her face which is so calm. She lifts her hand in a silent farewell, gets up and, grabbing her bag, she leaves. There's no time for me to react or register it all, before she's gone; and, because I'm hungover, I end up snuggling up to Marianne again. That's why it isn't me but Jeppe who finds the note on the kitchen worktop.

> *Hello all. I can't see you any more. There, I've said it, and this is when I'm going to start crying. I hate this, I really hate this. I wish I could be around you lot all the time, but Brian says I have to choose between you guys and him, and I'm choosing him. Maybe that'll change one day, but today it's him or you, and it makes me so unbelievably sad and unbelievably happy at the same time. Do you know what I mean? I miss you already, but Brian wants me. He wants me! You all know how much that means to me. I hadn't even made it through the door before he kissed me. It was*

the best Christmas Eve ever, and I know that I'll never be
alone ever again because he's promised me I won't. I made
him swear, and he'd never lie. I just know that. I care so
much about you all, but he's the one I choose, because he's
the one I've been waiting for all along. This is not a goodbye.
At least I hope not.

Anita

Jeppe wakes Marianne and me gently, then we rouse Bike and Kink quite abruptly. None of us is irked or angry. We understand Anita's decision, but we all feel rather amputated, as if we were missing an arm or a lung. It's a weirdly quiet day, characterized by hangovers and a strangely happy longing. It's the first time I lose someone I'm fond of without it involving blood and gore.

Another one down

Our bags are packed, and it's time to say our goodbyes to Copenhagen. I've noticed that Kink is pacing the flat restlessly, and I'm only partly surprised when he asks me warily if we can talk. I know it's serious when he signals that we need to do it outside, so no-one else will hear. When we get out in the cold, he says almost desperately, 'Can I stay in the flat?'

'What do you mean?' I ask. After all, we're leaving to go home in just a few hours.

'Can I stay here?'

'Aren't you coming back to Tarm?'

He shakes his head, silently.

'Why?'

He tries hard to find the right words. 'The way you feel about Tarm, that's how I feel about Copenhagen.'

He's thought it through. This isn't something he's doing on a whim. This is the way it has to be. My stomach tells me that.

'I'm sorry to hear it, Kink, I really am, and the others will be too. You're an important part of the gang.'

He's struggling to hold on to his decision. The big oaf is close to tears.

'But if you really want to stay in the flat, then you just go right ahead.'

"Thanks.'

'You haven't told the others, have you?'

He shakes his head.

'When are you going to tell them?'

'Can't you do that? I'd rather not say anything,' and I know it's because of Bike.

'We'll think of something.'

He comes with us to the Central Station. We lag behind the others, then we hide in a corner until they've gone down to the platform.

'Are you absolutely sure?' I ask Kink, hoping he's changed his mind.

He nods. I give him a hug and the keys to the flat.

I run to make the train. The others have sat down, and I make it, panting, into the crowded train with two seconds to spare. They all look at me with surprise, because there's just the one where there ought to have been two of us.

'Where's Kink?' Bike asks.

I signal that I need to catch my breath and sit down. The question is repeated with increased intensity.

'He's staying in Copenhagen.'

Much to my surprise it's Marianne and Jeppe who are shocked, while Bike simply nods. He had an inkling. Now Kink's gone, and Bike is all alone. His eyes seek out Jeppe instinctively, and Jeppe gets up and sits down next to him.

Part Four

THE FESTIVAL

We're back in Tarm

When we arrive in Tarm, Karen is waiting for us; giving each of us in turn a welcome-home hug. Enveloped by her arms, I know why it is I love Tarm. Even Jeppe is enjoying her hug now.

It takes us more than an hour to get to 22 Poppelvej, as people keep stopping us to welcome us home. Several people mention that I've lost weight. I'm almost a stone lighter than I was when I left. I make sure to speak to everyone, and I give them a no-holds-barred account of our trip.

'But have you come back to stay?'

'Yes, I have. Tarm is my home.'

'Golly, you couldn't be more right,' they say enthusiastically.

I say the same things many times over. Why I went to Copenhagen. How things panned out. Why we've come home without Anita and Kink. There's an air of warmth and delight, and I ask Karen if she has set this up. Is that the reason she seems so secretive? She just shakes her head, smiling, and says, 'No, Nikolaj, they're just happy to see you home, that's all,' but she's keeping something from us. She doesn't try to hide it, because really she's as proud as punch, but she doesn't tell me why until we get back to mine.

Granny's in my kitchen.

What Karen got up to while the rest of us were in Copenhagen

We've been in Copenhagen for a week when Karen spots Granny in the supermarket. She's standing in the dairy aisle, almost in a trance. Karen looks at her askance, but Granny seems to have ground to a halt with a litre of full-cream milk in her hand. After a couple of minutes, during which Granny never moves, Karen carefully takes the milk from Granny's wrinkled hands, and Granny slowly starts coming to. She smiles sheepishly at Karen, but she can think of nothing to say, though she seems to search quite anxiously for words. She's just standing there, smiling sheepishly, against a backdrop of cheeses and milk.

'I know Nikolaj. He's a great kid,' Karen says proudly to Granny.

Granny simply nods, but she continues nodding for a bit too long for it to be normal. Karen feels that she ought to repeat it, 'A really great kid.'

Granny still makes no comment. She just keeps nodding. Karen is irked by Granny's lack of response. The least she could do is ask how I'm doing, but there's no reaction – except for that stiff nodding of hers.

'Come along,' Karen says, and starts walking.

She's convinced that Granny needs help this very minute. It can't wait until we come back from Copenhagen. Granny seems so frail that she must be at death's door. Granny stays where she is. She's not going with Karen. Why would she?

Karen repeats, 'Come now,' and Granny asks her warily, 'What is it you want?'

'Come,' and this time it is a command, though still a gentle one. That doesn't leave Granny a choice, and she follows Karen all the way back to 22 Poppelvej, and why shouldn't she? Karen only wants what's best for Granny. Granny seems to know that, even if she does think Karen is behaving oddly.

'This is where Nikolaj lives,' Karen says, showing Granny around my home. Karen has to do all the talking. Granny still isn't saying anything.

'Jeppe lives here as well. That's Nikolaj's oldest friend, you know. They've known each other since they were fifteen.' Granny smiles a little. The thought that I'm not altogether without friends makes her feel relieved.

'Right now he's in Copenhagen with Jeppe, Jonas, Lars, Anita and Marianne. They're all his good friends from Tarm. Do you know why they've gone to Copenhagen?'

Karen decides to be quiet and force Granny to say something, and, in the end, Granny mutters, 'Why have they gone to Copenhagen?'

'Nikolaj has a plan. He wants to turn his life around, and he has things he needs to put right. Among other things he needs to do is to help Brian move on. Have you ever met Brian?'

Granny shakes her head.

'He's Sis's husband.'

'Who's Sis?' Granny asks, sounding surprised, because Karen never mentioned someone called Sis before.

Granny can see from Karen's reaction that she's said something quite wrong, and suddenly it dawns on her. The shock of it seems to jolt her back to life. Ashamed, she hides her head in her hands. She peers out between her fingers, and says in a shaken voice, 'She's my granddaughter, and here I am asking who she is. I'm so ashamed.'

Karen hesitates for a bit, but she does say, 'Yes, and so you should be. I think it's terrible that you've never been there for Nikolaj and Sis, but now's your chance to make it all better.'

'How could I ever make it better?' Granny says without a flicker of hope.

Karen looks her squarely in the eyes.

'You have to be there for him.'

But a terror has hit Granny, and the terror has a name. 'What about Leif?'

'What about him?'

'He's very angry, you know, about Nikolaj moving to Tarm. Did Nikolaj tell you that they bumped into each other right after he came to town?'

Karen nods.

'Leif thought it was so embarrassing that I hadn't told him Nikolaj had come to town. If I had told him, then, of course, he would have recognized him. He made me sleep in the kitchen all week.'

Karen says, 'You had to sleep in the kitchen?'

'When Leif is angry, he wants me to sleep on the kitchen bench, because he doesn't want to have to look at me. It's not as bad as it sounds. Leif would never let me see Nikolaj.'

Karen refuses to give in to despondency. She merely says, 'Well, then you'll have to choose, won't you?'

Granny looks at Karen anxiously.

'But I can't. He's my husband.'

Karen says with all the conviction she can muster, 'Let me tell you what a husband is. A husband makes his wife feel proud. He doesn't make her feel ashamed of herself. A husband loves his children. He doesn't beat his daughter with a belt.'

This is when Granny starts crying quietly.

'A husband worth his salt forgives his children if they do something stupid. He doesn't keep his daughter at a distance. A real husband loves his grandchild, he doesn't call her a floozy. My Kaj is a real husband to me. A magnificent, lovely husband whom I love dearly. Can you really say that Leif is your husband?'

Granny shakes her head.

'Then what are you going to do about it?'

They meet six times after that, and Karen keeps working on her. She introduces her to Kaj as well, and Granny thinks he's a lovely man. They talk about memories, and Granny has to cast her mind back a long time to find any that she likes. All Karen has to do is

253

think about yesterday when Kaj called her 'Snuggles' and pecked her on the cheek. Granny says she hasn't been kissed for ten years. Karen also lets her meet Jens, and she makes Granny tell Jens about her life with Grandad. Afterwards Karen has to calm Jens down – otherwise he would have gone over to Grandad's, giving him a bit more than a few cautioning words. Jens gets very angry when elderly ladies aren't treated well. His mother was assaulted five years ago. Granny is surprised by the strength of Jens' reaction, but it does make her think. The sixth time she and Karen meet up, it is Granny herself who asks timidly, 'Karen, will you help me? I'd like to leave Leif.'

Karen hugs her, and says, 'Of course I will.'

Granny calls Karen the next day when Grandad is out for his daily two-hour walk. Karen, Kaj and Jens rush over. They throw everything she'll need into the car and hurry away. Granny moves in to my house and feels hopeful for the first time since God knows when. Grandad reports her missing the next day when she hasn't come home, but Jens pops round to his and tells him that she has left him, and that Granny doesn't want to be in touch with him at all. Grandad has been humiliated and is furious, but what can he do? He has no idea where Granny is, and no-one wants to help him.

Karen convinces Granny that it's better if they don't tell me until I return to Tarm. Then Granny is waiting with a table full of cakes when we walk wearily through the door. I stare at her in an off way and, feeling a bit befuddled, I turn to Karen and say, 'Is that the reason you've been acting so secretive?'

She nods, proudly. Out of one ear I half hear Marianne hurrying to say hello to Granny to prevent her from flailing, and I focus my attention on her again. Granny is waiting for me, and I walk over to her, holding out a hand, saying, 'Have you moved in?'

'Yes, I hope it's all right. Karen told me I could,' she says nervously, while she shakes my hand shyly but happily.

'Of course,' I say, as if it didn't matter much.

Marianne's eyes tell that it matters a great deal. I do know that, but how am I supposed to react? Am I supposed to be happy? Sod it, I'm mad at Granny. Am I supposed to be angry? Sod it, I'm happy my granny is here. I have a lot of conflicting emotions right now, but I pull out a chair for Granny and say, 'Right then, time for some cake, is it?'

'These are great cakes!' Jeppe exclaims, crumbs spraying out of his mouth.

Granny nods happily and sits down at the table with the rest of us. My life is fucking weird.

I've got a nagging resentment inside me, which makes it impossible for Granny and me to relax around each other. When we talk, we deal only in platitudes, because that's all we know to do. We are polite and sociable, but no more than that and it's frustrating. The others try to sort me out. They all fall for Granny's frailty. Granny is tiny and delicate. They all want to protect her. Bike, Karen, Marianne and especially Jeppe talk to her, and they talk to me about her. Do I know how much she has suffered? How much she has longed? How lonely her life was with Grandad? No,

I don't know, but in the end, it's her own fault. What do they expect from me? That I love her, because they say she's lovely? Because she's family? I love them because they're here for me, but Granny? I can't just chuck away my resentment because they want me to.

Marianne kisses me, and Granny tries to tell me something

Bike and Marianne both move in with me. They're at their own homes for just one day, then they come lugging a couple of bags. Living alone is lonely, and they've got used to living with us, so why change it? It's fine by me. I want to be with them as much as possible. The only thing that irks me is that they are all on such friendly terms with Granny, and I feel excluded again. I vent my frustration silently, but they can't help liking Granny. Am I supposed to forbid them to talk to her? I can't do that.

We've embarked on a new year. New Year's Eve was low-key, just a dinner in the company of friends and a shitload of fireworks. Today is 8 January, and I'm standing in the hall, steaming from having just been out running. It was cold and lonely, because Jeppe can't be arsed to come along any more. Since Bike lost Kink, Jeppe hasn't been out running with me once. I can hear him and Bike guffawing in the sitting room. They laugh in the same way and it's the same things that make them laugh. These days they hang out all the time. I'm a bit jealous, but I do see that their relationship is more equal than ours. It's no biggie. I'm not losing Jeppe. I'm just sharing him with Bike.

In other words, I haven't got Jeppe to make me go for a run when it's cold and rainy, but luckily my motivation has increased dramatically. It's no longer just about sex. It's about love, and not just the love I'm feeling either. Two days ago Marianne kissed me and not on the cheek, but full on the mouth. We are wrestling for fun, and I've pinned her to the floor. I'm big and I'm heavy, and I force her to the floor, putting myself on top of her. She's moaning as if in pain, while I grin smugly. My face is a hand's breadth from hers, and I want to kiss her, but I don't. Nevertheless, I feel her lips against mine, but it's not me kissing her. It's her kissing me. I almost go blind. When my sight returns, I can see that she's in shock. She's regretting it, and I let go of her. She scurries out of the room. I let her have some time to think.

A couple of hours later I look in on her. She's lying in her room, reading

'Do you want to talk about it?'

She shakes her head.

'Why did you kiss me?'

She doesn't say anything; instead she tries to focus on her book.

'Marianne, you've got to say something.'

I sit on the edge of her bed. I never get as far as touching her, before she tells me not to. She's still not looking at me.

'Why? You like me.'

'Are you a total spaz? I'm in love with you, but I don't want you to touch me. I still don't trust you.'

I stay on her bed, not touching her. As I sit next to Marianne, I feel the knot in my stomach loosening. It's never been as loose as it is now, and I realize that it will only take a very little bit for it to disappear completely. It's three-mile runs every day from now on.

That is why I'm standing, steaming, in the hall after my run, when Granny comes sneaking up on me almost without a sound.

'You are so like your mother,' she says in a whisper, as if it were dangerous to say out loud, and I twitch in surprise.

Because of her tone I can't work out whether she's insulting me, so I don't say anything. I just stare at her confused, but as she doesn't say anything else, I mutter, 'I've got to take a shower. I'm sweating.'

I leave Granny in the hall.

Jeppe knocks on the door while I'm showering.

'Niko, your granny's crying.'

I turn off the water, dry myself quickly, get dressed and go to her. She's my granny. She's an old lady, and she's crying. Of course I have to comfort her. She's sitting in the small sitting room. I shut the door behind me and sit down across from her. I'm searching for the right words, but I don't find them before Granny says, 'I've been so worried about you.'

I nod, but I don't take her seriously. If she's been so bloody worried, why hasn't she done anything about it till now? For eleven years I haven't heard from her, and then she expects me to appreciate how worried she's been. Worry should be noisy. She's searching for my hands once more, but this time I'm not startled and I allow her to hold them as tight as she can. We're sitting in silence for a long time, and I'm thinking about whether it'd be all right if I left when she finally speaks again.

'Do you think you'll ever be able to forgive me?'

'I don't know if I can.'

She nods, as if that's what she expected me to say.

'I wish you could.'

'So do I, but it's not that simple.'

'No, but it's too late with the others,' she says, sadly.

Once more she's sitting without saying anything. And once more I'm on the verge of leaving when she speaks again.

'I was so proud of your sister when she set those bikers on Leif. He got really scared. Of course you shouldn't be parted from your sister, but Leif wouldn't listen to me.'

I mutter that I'm sure her intentions were good, but that it doesn't really help me. She nods, sadly, and tells me yet again that I'm like Mum.

'No, Sis was like her.'

She shakes her head stubbornly.

'No, Sis was like your father. You're like my girl. Nikolaj, I'm so ashamed.'

Granny doesn't say anything else. She's just sitting there, tiny and frail. She doesn't want to talk about it any more; it's too painful. I get up, but before I go I bend and give her our first hug, because I want to. She laps it up.

*

Granny is constantly pondering her betrayal, and how she can make it up to me. I have to comfort her every day and tell her, 'What's done is done. It can't be helped now.' She's made up her mind that in some way or other, she must come to my rescue like Jesus said, but I'm fine with her just being here. It is the way it is, and she's an old lady who needs my protection, not the other way around.

I expect Jesus to turn up and say, 'Well done, Nikolaj,' but he doesn't, and I wait patiently for several days. I don't read anything into that except that apparently I can't tell when he's going to appear.

My talk at the local library

I can't let fear slow me down, so I contact the local library to see if they'd be interested in setting up a talk with me. The little librarian is so excited about the idea that she's almost afraid to agree. I smile to put her at ease, and she manages to stutter, 'We'd be delighted to have you. When?' I suggest a date in two weeks' time. Fortunately, Tarm is a small place, so the rumour of my first public appearance spreads like wildfire. On 27 January I give a talk at Tarm Library, entitled 'Nikolaj Okholm – His Mother's Son.'

When we arrive at the library, we see an enormously long queue, and we look at each other nervously. There isn't going to be room for all those people in the library. We sneak in through the backdoor, greeting the head of the library and the mayor of Tarm – his name is Mogens. He's a mink farmer and a decent fellow. He volunteered as chair as soon as he heard about the event. He peers out at the queue with visible envy.

'Just goes to show that showbiz has a greater appeal than politics. I've never had that long a queue for any of my election meetings.'

The front seats have been reserved for NATO, who sit down straight away. I need to be able to see them at all times. The librarian tells me that they've moved half the books out into a shed behind the library to make room for two hundred and twenty-five people.

'Is that going to be enough?' I ask.

'No, there's more than three hundred out there, and they just keep coming,' the librarian says.

I get up next to my little podium, and they open the doors. There's a terrible pushing and shoving, and Tarm Library isn't at all equal to it. There may only be two hundred and twenty-five seats, but there's a lot more people in the room than that. When the doors are finally shut, it's only a very few people who have to go home disappointed. Everyone is completely squashed. I hear arguments erupting here and there across the room. The mayor and the librarian try to smooth ruffled feathers, but in vain. In the end I grab the microphone and say, loudly and forcefully, 'If you can't be quiet and nice to each other, then I'm going to leave without saying a single word. Is that understood? There are a lot of people in this room, but we're going to have to learn to live with that for the next couple of hours, okay?'

The room is completely silent; not a sound. Unfortunately, the large crowd means that my view of NATO is restricted. I can only see them when the people in front of them shift about, but I decide to be brave. I clear my throat, take a sip of water and embark on my talk.

'I have hated Mum's songs ....
....
....
....
....
....
....
....
....
....
....
....
.... and that's where I am today. I'm looking forward so much to being Mum's son. Thank you.'

I have been talking non-stop for an hour, and my throat is parched. I'm not paying much attention to how it's being received – all my attention is on getting through it – but it's going down a treat. In any event they applaud me with almost hysterical excitement. Making an extra effort I manage to make eye contact with the members of NATO, including Granny. There's pride in their eyes. I, too, am proud. I never would have dared dream of such a triumph. It takes me all of twenty minutes to calm down the audience enough to be able to ask if there are any questions, and now about a hundred hands go flying up. It's too hard for Mogens to get around with the microphone, so instead it's just sent from one person with a question to the next.

'Why did your mum never play in Tarm?'

'Mum wanted to play here, but she was afraid that she wouldn't be able to do it well enough, and then it was easier just not to do it.'

There's a collective sigh of relief. It wasn't that she didn't like them; it was because she liked them too much.

'So, she had performance anxiety?'

'Yes. Though there was also something else she was afraid of in this town, but that doesn't matter.'

They know I'm talking about Grandad, the testy old man who barks at everyone and everything. I've mentioned him several times, but I haven't told them that he whipped Mum, only that he drove her out of town. I've also mentioned that Granny has left him, without saying that she's moved in with me. It gets everyone very excited.

'Do you have a favourite song?'

'Yes, Mum's only ever rock song, "Storm". It was her favourite as well. Mum never listened much to pop music. When she wanted to unwind, she always put on hard rock. She loved AC/DC and Metallica.'

People gasp. Now that's news.

'Have you ever considered a musical career?'

'No, I should bloody well think not. I can't even sing "Itsy-Bitsy Spider" without murdering the spider.'

People laugh, not a lot, but more than my joke really warrants. And then I hear Grandad. He's hidden in the crowd, and he's heard everything I've said about him.

'Do you know where my wife is?'

The laughter stops short, and the confusion from several hundred people is buzzing loudly. I search for Granny, and I get a glimpse of a pair of very frightened eyes. She's hiding as best she can. I can't see Grandad. He's standing behind a wall of people. I motion for them to move aside so I can see him, and there he is.

'Hello, Grandad. Yes, I do, but she's not coming back to you.'

He's a sorry sight. He's absolutely filthy, and his thin hair is a mess.

'She has to. I need her.'

'No, she doesn't have to do anything at all.'

Two hundred and fifty people hold their breath and eavesdrop on our conversation excitedly.

'I'll find her,' he says grimly.

'You'll leave her alone. You've ruined enough as it is.'

I look out at the crowd, and say, 'I'd like to tell you all about my mum's last day in Tarm. On that day she was whipped by my Grandad until she bled, and the only reason he stopped was because my dad intervened.'

The atmosphere changes abruptly. People are shocked and furious. Grandad hurries out. He has no choice. The entire room starts applauding him mockingly, and people yell at him, some of them even pushing him. What a bastard, whipping his daughter – although it's still better than that paedophilia rumour that has been going around for a couple of months. Everyone now understands why Mum never came back.

When all the questions have been asked, the mayor wants to round things off. He thanks me and tells me how fond the entire town is of me. Once again the applause goes through the roof.

'We're hoping that you will continue to make Tarm an interesting place to be for many years to come.'

We'll never get a better occasion than this to get people involved. I take the mike and thank the mayor, the library, everyone who's come out tonight, and then I thank Tarm itself.

'I'd like to thank Tarm in more than just words, because I really feel that you've given me a lot. I belong here. That's why I'm so excited that so many people are here tonight, and that you are here,' I say to Mogens, 'because I need your help.'

The room is now completely quiet.

'Are you excited?' I ask, cockily.

There's another roar.

'I'd like to set up a festival this Easter in Mum's honour.'

They're applauding already.

'Music everywhere in Tarm throughout Easter. Every band that's ever made a cover version of Mum's songs will be invited. Thomas Helmig, Lis Sørensen, everyone, and we'll get Denmark's best cover band, Grith Okholm Jam, to come as well. It'll be a thank you from me and my mum to a fantastic town. Are you with me on this?'

Massive roar.

'Will you help me? I'm going to need help. It's not long till

Easter. We're going to need tents, beer, sports halls, schools, permits. Everything. What do you say?'

Once again there's a massive roar. I hand the microphone back to the mayor. He looks at me with surprise, and we all wait excitedly for him to say something. He mutters, 'Thank you. That does sound great, but surely we can wait until autumn, so we won't have to be in such a rush.' There's a big, disappointed sigh, and several people bellow, 'But Grith was born in Easter!' That was going to be my argument, but it sounds better coming from a stranger. It's a coincidence. Easter is simply the first opportunity to have a festival. We don't want to wait until autumn. Mogens realizes that there's no getting out of this, and promises that there will be a festival during Easter, and that nothing is going to stop it!

Karen has positioned herself at the door. She makes sure that no-one leaves the library without having been assigned a job. The entire town is put to work in the following months under Karen's supervision. We've spent months planning this in detail. Now's the time to put it into practice. Everyone's keyed up by the bombshell I've dropped, but only a few days later they get another one to contend with.

Jeppe isn't harmless

I'm washing up, and Bike and Jeppe are drying the dishes. Washing up is a man's job in our house. Granny and Marianne are doing all the other jobs. The house would be a dump if they weren't living here. In the last week Marianne has told Bike three times to remove his skid marks from the loo. The only job we lads have is the dishes, and here we are then. It's always me washing up, and always them drying the plates. They're swishing each other on the arse with the tea towels. Outside Granny and Marianne are chatting. As I look at them puttering about in my garden in the wintry sunlight, I catch myself thinking that everything is good, and everything is quiet. Then, suddenly, it isn't any longer. It seems like Grandad comes out of nowhere. He's standing in front of them, looking furious, and they don't have time to run. He hits Marianne hard in the face with his fist, and starts dragging Granny away. I'm the fastest; I'm there in ten seconds flat.

'You stay away!' he screams at me, but I yank Granny out of Grandad's grip, catch him by the belt and the neck and hurl him headfirst – and hard – into the hedge. He tries to get up, but I push him back down. He's crying.

'You're leaving. You're not going to come here ever again. You're going to get fucking lost. Is that understood?'

I turn my back on him, and ask Granny, 'Are you all right?'

She nods, and then she squeals. Grandad has got up. He has picked up a log from the ground, and he's swinging it at my head. Jeppe wards off the blow with his left arm just in the nick of time, while bashing Grandad over the head with my cast-iron saucepan, and then everything is quiet.

We're all in shock. We're just standing there, staring at Grandad, who's fallen over. I can see right into his brain. I turn to Jeppe and I say, 'You've killed him.'

'He was going to hit you.'

'Yes I know, but you've killed him.'

I hear Marianne crying, and I shake off the shock and walk over to her. She's still lying on the ground, battered and frightened. I smile at her reassuringly and help her up. I'm holding her.

Granny's moving over to Jeppe ever so quietly, taking the saucepan out of his hand. At first Jeppe doesn't want to let go, but Granny insists, and suddenly Jeppe lets go. Everything he's ever hoped for is falling apart now. He's screaming out in agony, but Bike grabs him with a strength and a ferocity I haven't seen before. He almost tackles him and holds on to him as if the earth were trying to spit Jeppe out. Jeppe feels like running away, but Bike won't let him – not because he needs to be punished, but because we can't do without him. He tries to wrestle his way out, but Bike resists until Jeppe has no more strength left in him.

'I'm going to put him on the sofa,' Bike says, holding the limp Jeppe in his arms.

We nod, and there we are then. I notice that Granny is smiling happily, which I think is seriously off. No doubt the man was a gigantic twat, but that's no reason why she couldn't show a little bit of fear or remorse.

'We'd better call the police,' she says, smiling faintly, and goes in to wash the blood and brains off the saucepan.

It starts snowing, and I stay for another couple of minutes with Marianne in my arms. I want to go back in to the others, but she lets me know that she needs me to hold her a little bit longer.

We don't actually call the police; we call Karen, who in turn calls Jens. She comes rushing over and is as shocked as the rest of us. When Jens arrives we're all sitting paralysed in the sitting room – except for Granny, who is keeping to herself. We haven't said a word for more than half an hour. Jeppe is hiding under a blanket. Jens and his young colleague look baffled as they see my dead grandfather, who is by now half-covered with snow. We haven't told them why they had to come, and it's rather a surprise for them to see Grandad lying dead on my lawn. They come in. They don't seem agitated. On the contrary, they are quite calm, as if they're worried that we are okay.

'What's happened?' Jens asks gently.

Karen says humbly that Grandad got hit on the head with a saucepan.

'How did he get hit on the head with a saucepan?'

None of us says anything, and then Jens repeats the question calmly, and I look around at all of them. I've promised Jesus to protect my friends, so I say, 'I hit him. I didn't mean to, but I hit him.'

They all look like I've just hit them hard in the stomach, and Jeppe throws off the blanket and screams, 'That's not true! I did it!' as if they were the most important words he had ever screamed.

I shake my head and say, 'You don't have to protect me, Jeppe.'

Jeppe has gone quite blue in the face, but there's no time for him to protest any more, because of Granny, who suddenly interferes. She's come in to the sitting room.

'Jens, Jens.'

Jens turns around to face her.

269

'Yes, Ulla.' His voice becomes soft and soothing. Jens is very fond of Granny. He's been to see her several times lately.

'It was me who hit him. The saucepan is in my room. They're trying to protect me, but Leif came, and it frightened me. At first he hit Marianne (Marianne's cheek is swollen and purple); then he hit Jeppe (he's got a bruise the size of a hand on his arm), and then he wanted to drag me off. I got so scared and angry and then, well I hit him with the saucepan.'

Jens nods, and he escorts Granny into her room to fetch the saucepan. Jeppe keeps protesting, but the younger officer tells him that it's pointless trying to protect her once she's confessed the deed. Jens returns with the saucepan and Granny.

'I'm sorry, but I'm sure nothing much is going to happen, because that bastard had it coming.'

Karen gets up and gives Jens a hug. He smiles at her and says, 'We're going to call for an ambulance now, and then we'll take Ulla into the smaller sitting room and have a bit of a chat with her. Once we've done that, of course, we'll have to talk to you lot.'

He winks at Karen to let her know that he's doing us a big favour. In the span of the next ten minutes we manage to get Jeppe to calm down, and we get our stories straight. Grandad came; Grandad was violent; Granny hit him – because that's the way she wants it. She's doing this for us.

Of course, there's a to-do all day. Ambulance, more police, journalists, the usual nosy crowd, the snow falling and shitloads of stress, but in the end it's all over, and they take Granny off. I say goodbye to her with a really bone-breaking hug. When they've driven her off, it stops snowing.

Once everyone's left, and we're alone again, we all exhale with relief. We realize that it isn't over yet, but right now, we're just us, and we can relax. They all look at me with surprise.

'Why did you do it?' Jeppe asks, not comprehending.

I weigh my words, but there's no better explanation.

'Because you're my friend.'

They don't say anything, and Jeppe looks at me gratefully. I notice that he and Bike are holding hands, and I'm glad that Bike is still looking out for him. Marianne is looking at me in a way she hasn't looked at me before. It's confusing.

'What?'

She says nothing. She simply drags me into her room.

Marianne's story

I can see in her eyes that something momentous is about to happen. She pushes me down onto a chair and, sitting down astride me, showers me with hot and heavy kisses. I decide to risk it and let my hands find her breasts. She doesn't try to stop me, and I allow my hands to slip under her top. She's still isn't trying to stop me, which baffles me so much that for a moment I'm hitting rather than fondling her breasts. Once I regain control of my hands, I undo her bra and pull off her top. And then I grind to a halt, because the sight of her tits makes my heart beat uncontrollably. She smiles and moves back about four inches, leaving my groin exposed. She gives me a steamy look as she unbuttons my trousers. My cock makes a grand appearance. She gets up and pulls off her trousers and knickers. She's standing stark naked in front of me, and the sight of her red pubes alone is almost enough to make me come. She wants to sit down on me, but I say, 'No, please stay there for a bit. I need to look at you.' She obeys.

'God, you are so beautiful!' I say, and lean forwards to touch her very gently. I let my hands run from her tits, down her stomach, which I'm kissing, down to her bottom, which I'm holding on to. I take a deep breath and let a hand slip up between her legs, but not all the way. She is shaking a little, and I look into her eyes just to be on the safe side. She is smiling happily, and saying, 'I love the way you touch me. You're so gentle.'

My hands slide back up to her breasts. I half get up and let my lips encircle her nipples. Her hands search for cock, but she can't quite reach, so I stand up and kiss her. She's got a good grip on my cock now and she gives it a few good tugs, which make me gasp. I'm not done touching her, and I allow my fingers to find the cleft. She's shaking a bit more now, and I slip a finger into her. She is soaking wet and open. She lets go of my cock and removes my hand brutally. For a moment I think I've done something wrong, but she gives me a hard shove back to make me fall into the chair. Then she sits down on top of me, and we shag with pent-up intensity.

In the midst of it all Bike knocks on the door and asks if I want to talk to the *Skjern-Tarm Daily*. They're on the phone, but I can't concentrate enough to string words together, and the upshot is that I don't answer. He's standing by the door listening. Suddenly he bellows, 'They're fucking shagging!' Immediately I hear Karen yelling, 'Jonas, step away from the door,' and then, ten seconds later, 'Jonas! Now!'

Afterwards, Marianne stays sitting on top of me, holding me tight. It's an amazing feeling, and I want to just sit here and play with her bottom.

'Now I'm going to tell you everything,' she whispers and bites my ear.

She looks at me to see if I'm listening, but I've never listened this intently to anyone ever.

She's thirteen when her mum decides that becoming a Jehovah's Witness is the answer to absolutely everything that has been amiss up until that point. The decision is an easy one; Marianne's aunt and cousin are already members.

'I have these huge rows, because I can't be arsed to be a Jehovah's Witness. It's embarrassing, but then Mum falls ill and gets really sad, and I feel guilty and promise to give it a try. I do try, but then I row with Mum again, and she falls ill and gets sad again, and I feel guilty. In the end, I just give in.'

Ever since Marianne was born her mum has suffered from severe depression and failing health, but the Jehovah's Witnesses make her feel noticeably better – physically as well as emotionally – and in the end Marianne accepts her new life despite it all; the loss of friends, dress sense, interests. She makes new friends; gets new clothes, new interests, but it's all a sham. She's only herself when she's alone.

Mathias is the first boy she kisses. She's twenty when they kiss for the first time, and she has a rep for being unattainable. He walks her home, and then he kisses her. It's a bit of an ambush kiss. Nothing has led up to it.

'We sneak in a snog every now and again for the next year or so. It's completely innocent, but kissing feels good, even if it is kissing Mathias.'

She's twenty-one when they become engaged. Everyone says they're perfect for each other. It's a long engagement, driving Mathias to a horny frenzy, but Marianne doesn't want to get married until he makes just a little bit of an arse of himself. He has to show her that he is not ever-so-perfect; and that's when Marianne meets Emir.

She knocks on his door, and Emir opens. Emir is Albanian, the only Albanian in Tarm. He's a trained engineer, but he can't find work in Århus, where his family lives, so he moves to Tarm. Marianne asks if Emir would like to talk about the Bible. Emir really wouldn't, because he's a Muslim. He doesn't say that to Marianne though; she's a good-looking girl and Emir is lonely. He listens to her, nods attentively and gawps at her tits.

'Of course, I notice, but I decide to ignore it, just like I did with you. I've got great tits, haven't I?'

'You've got perfect tits,' I say without the least hesitation, grabbing a firm hold of one of them.

'Thank you,' she says, happily.

Marianne talks to Emir about Armageddon and Jesus as the king of the earth. After a while Emir gets up restlessly. She can tell that he is working up the courage to do something. He stands behind Marianne and then he lets his hands run down to her breasts. Startled, she jumps out of her seat. He looks just as startled, as if he can't believe what he's just done. She rushes home. For an hour or so she is scared, but then she starts fingering herself. The next day she returns to ask if Emir would like to hear about the Bible.

They are together secretly for the best part of a year. Marianne spends all of her time planning how she can be with Emir and not be found out. When she goes for a walk in the woods, she does so to meet Emir behind a tree, and up against a tree. It is frequently cold and wet. When she visits her cousin in Copenhagen – which she suddenly takes to doing four times in a year – she stays an extra four days in Copenhagen, and she and Emir drink, shag, and have butterflies tattooed on their arse and chest. The tattoo is a promise to herself to do something. She can't marry Mathias with a tattoo on her arse. Marianne and Emir are close, but only as close as they can be while it has to be a secret. Emir is willing to let everyone know about them, but Marianne is still afraid to. It's a shit situation, because Emir has fights of his own to contend with. His mum and dad want to bring him closer to the family and have him marry a Muslim woman. His parents have introduced him to the daughter of some of their friends. She is neither dumb nor ugly, and Emir can easily see himself marrying her – that is, if he wasn't going out with Marianne. There's a tacit pressure and a lack of understanding that their son is still not married. Emir's mother asks him nervously if he fancies men. It is the single most embarrassing moment of his life. Emir begs Marianne to come clean, but she can't.

Of course, people notice that she is different. Her mum and Mathias both have long conversations with her. Is something bothering her? Then why is she going for all these long walks alone? Why doesn't she want to get married? After all, they're such a perfect couple. Everyone says so. She can't explain why, and then she uses a word she knows will work – the word her mother always used to make Marianne realize she was in a bad way.

'I tell them I'm feeling sad.'

It frightens her mother, because she knows what the word signifies. She protects Marianne and makes sure she gets some quiet and privacy. Mathias doesn't understand.

She really has made up her mind to do something; that is, break away. She just needs to work up the final bit of courage, and then Emir goes and ruins it all. For some weeks he has seemed distant, and then one day he doesn't turn up. Marianne waits for more than an hour at their secret hide-out. It's cold, and she feels very alone. He has moved back to Århus, to his family and a real girl-friend. He hasn't had the courage to say goodbye, but he sends her a letter, which Marianne's mother decides to open.

'I come home, and there's Mum with the letter in her hand. She gives it to me. She doesn't seem cross; on the contrary, she seems sad for me. I read the letter and start blubbing. Mum comforts me.'

She tells her mother everything. There are no cross words or reproaches, just comfort. When she's all talked out, her mum tells her calmly, 'You will burn in Hell for this.' She calls Mathias straight away and tells him everything, word for word.

'I'm banned. I have to sit at the very back at prayer meetings, and I can't talk to anyone, and no-one can talk to me. Even Mum doesn't talk to me, although I can see she wants to. It pains her, and then she gets sad, depressed and ill, I mean really ill. She dies just four months later.'

At this point Marianne hugs me tighter.

'I can trust you. You'll fight for me, won't you?' she whispers in my ear.

I nod intently. I can't believe how fragile she has become in my arms. She's always been strong, and here I am sitting with my hands on her arse, feeling like Superman. I kiss her softly on the forehead.

Marianne sits at the back of prayer meetings and is pierced by silent, reproachful looks. Why doesn't she run away? Because it's all she's got. Where would she go? So, she stays. Mathias enjoys lording it over her, protecting her, against the others and against herself. It's only been six months since the ban was revoked and she was allowed to evangelize again. It's Mathias's doing: he has 'fought' for her, promising to keep her on the straight and narrow. She's not allowed to go anywhere without him.

'I know that one day I'll get away. I just don't know how, and then you turn up. You seem mad, but you also seem honest and wrong in just the right way.'

I get up, while she stays sitting on me; I turn us around and put her on the chair, pulling her lower body hard against mine. She giggles happily, and then we're shagging again.

Granny's dead

I can't fall asleep. There are too many in thoughts in my head for that. This is big, maybe even bigger than with Silje, because I'm in a different place in my life. Marianne is resting her head against my chest. She's snoring in her quiet, girly way; it's adorable. She had no trouble falling asleep. She just settled against me and shut her eyes. I pull back the duvet a bit to reveal her luscious bottom. There's the butterfly. I hear the front door being opened. For a brief moment I worry that we've forgotten to lock it, and that we're being invaded in the dead of the night, but it's Karen who's snuck in. What's she doing here so late? It must being going on three. She knocks on the door quietly, and whispers, 'Nikolaj? Nikolaj?' Marianne rouses a little as I peel her off me carefully and put her head on the pillow. She's a good sleeper. She's good at a great many things. I get up, put on underpants and a T-shirt and go out to Karen. She's got her worried face on, but it's the middle of the night and I'm tired, so I can't quite work out why.

'Why are you here so late?' I mutter in my night-time voice.

She's looking for the gentlest way of putting it, but there aren't all that many ways of saying these things.

'Nikolaj, your granny's dead.'

Because I don't say anything, Karen keeps talking. Granny's dead, and I don't feel sad. There's no pain. On the contrary I feel a strange kind of pride.

'She passed away in her sleep. She didn't suffer.'

I nod, and Karen gives me a hug.

'There now, Nikolaj. Don't be sad, will you?'

I'm still not saying anything, because I know I can't say that I'm proud. It would sound cynical, but it really isn't. Jesus said she mustn't die weighed down by guilt, and she died happy. Karen lets go of me.

'Go back to Marianne, and I'll take care of everything.'

I snuggle up to Marianne and try to find some sort of peace of mind. She complains a bit in her sleep, because I fidget so. I lift her head gently from the pillow and put it back on my chest again. She isn't awake, but she isn't asleep either. In her sleep her mouth finds mine. We kiss. She's kissing me in her sleep, and I'm kissing her wide awake. I slip away from her and let her head fall rather clumsily on the mattress. She's lying on her stomach, and I'm pulling the duvet off her. She's muttering sleepily that it's cold, but if it is so cold, then why am I feeling lovely and warm? I scramble on top of her.

'Niko, you're heavy,' she says sleepily, but I'm not going to let her sleep.

Suddenly she gasps; I'm inside her. She lifts her pelvis to give me better access, and I go at it hammer and tongs. I just want to come as quickly as possible, so my mind will be easy, but for some reason I can't. She's on all fours now, banging her arse against my pelvis. I'm sweating and crying all over her, but I'm not coming and I pull out my cock. She turns around, her legs wide open, and pulls me back into her. When I finally come, I collapse on her, panting, saying, 'Granny's dead.'

I fall asleep immediately, and I dream that Marianne and I have tender sex. It's a lovely dream, but it doesn't measure up to the real thing.

The next morning I wake up alone. I potter out to the others. Jeppe is still asleep. He had a rough time of it last night, and Bike had to get him drunk to get him to sleep. He doesn't yet know that Granny is dead. It'll crush him, because he'll think it's his fault, but really it isn't anyone's fault. It's just as it's meant to be. The phone has been ringing all morning; local and national papers alike have been trying to get a hold of me. It's a big story – after all, how often are celebrities involved in murder? Neither Granny nor I are celebrities, at least not nationally – but we're only one link removed, and in a country so short on real celebs, we'll do. Karen has been protecting me to ensure I slept after getting the sad news. Kaj is standing outside, making sure no-one is pressing the doorbell. I kiss Marianne lovingly; Bike giggles.

'You two woke me up last night.'

'Oh.'

'You're a screamer.'

Marianne blushes happily, even though it's a strange thing to say when Granny has just died. I sit down and have a cup of coffee.

'She just passed away in her sleep?'

Karen nods, relieved that I'm speaking in my calmest voice.

'In a cell?'

'No, on a sofa in the office. She needed to rest for a bit, and ten minutes later Jens found her dead.'

'What happens now?'

'What do you mean?' Karen asks.

'What do we do, about funerals and all that stuff?'

Karen will sort it out. She's got a handle on all those practical details, the funeral – Grandad's as well – and I don't have to worry about anything except working out how I feel about it. She assures me that nothing is going to fall apart, least of all me.

The funeral is in five days, and they're five long days during which we're assailed by the media. Newspapers, radio, television, they all come at us relentlessly, but also without any success whatsoever. People try to besiege us, but we won't let them. From my hiding place behind my blinds I can see Kaj explaining to the journalist from *See & Hear* that parking in front of 22 Poppelvej is a daft thing to do. This is Tarm, and over here we behave with common decency. There's a photographer who hides out in my neighbour's garden, and when my neighbour wants to send him packing, they get into a brawl. Jens arrests the photographer on the spot. Radio Klitholm campaigns against the invading hordes. They think that all the out-of-town journalists and photographers ought to be forced out of Tarm. People yell at them on the street; some are spat on. *Skjern-Tarm Daily* is chock-full of letters to the editor saluting and protecting me. The *Daily* is the only newspaper I talk to. We invite them round the morning after Granny's death and give them her story. She was protecting herself, and violence was her last resort. We fill out any and all the gaps in our story with drama, violence and passion. They take a picture of Marianne and her bruised cheek to back up our story. Jens confirms our interpretation, even the bits of it that are sheer conjecture.

The funeral itself is a quiet do, apart from the fact that Jeppe is bawling his eyes out. The past five days have been harder on Jeppe than on anyone else. He's convinced he's done for. It's only the five of us, plus Kaj and Jens, at the funeral. No-one else knows Granny well enough to want to get involved, but nevertheless it's seven more people than were present at Grandad's funeral. We are left alone by the paparazzi and journalists – they're afraid of what will happen if they don't. As the coffin is lowered into the ground, I notice yet another guest, standing about 30 yards away, watching the proceedings. I lean towards Marianne and whisper to her, 'I've got to go. Jesus is here.'

Marianne quickly looks round, but he turns a corner before she spots him. I grab Jeppe by the shoulder.

'Come. I want you to meet Jesus.'

Jeppe is happy

Jeppe can't get his head round the fact that Jesus is here at Tarm's cemetery. His eyes are popping out of their sockets. There are thirty long seconds of silence as we wait for an opening, so we can move on. Jesus is visibly annoyed that I've dragged Jeppe along, but I'm as sure as eggs is eggs that I've done the right thing.

I clear my throat and say, 'She died without being weighed down by guilt. Are you proud of me?'

Jesus nods in an absent-minded manner; his attention isn't directed at me.

'How are you, Jeppe?' he says in his booming bass voice.

'Not too good.'

'You shouldn't be feeling good when you've killed a man.'

Jeppe looks at me nervously to see if I've spilled the beans, but I wouldn't dream of it. Jesus puts us at ease at once.

'No-one will know. You didn't mean to do it, and you're repenting. Am I right, Jeppe?'

He nods ardently.

Of course, Jesus can't ignore Jeppe's anguish. He goes up to him, grabbing hold of his head with his big paws. Jeppe's tiny head all but disappears in his big hands, and Jesus pulls him in close.

'Who am I?'

Jeppe says without the least hesitation, 'You're Jesus. I don't want to feel this way any longer. Promise me I won't have to feel this way any longer.'

Jesus turns his gaze on me.

'Nikolaj, would you give me some time alone with Jeppe, please?'

I'm taken aback, because after all Jesus is mine, but I can hardly object when it was me who dragged Jeppe along. I walk a few hundred yards away and sit on a bench, waiting. I stay there for a long time. At least an hour. In the end my arse is so cold that I simply can't wait any longer, and I go back there, but Jesus has gone, and Jeppe is delirious with joy. I look around not comprehending, but he isn't here.

'Where's Jesus?'

'He left.'

'Where did he go?'

Jeppe shrugs, and I curse with irritation. He can't just leave without talking to me. What a tosser. Suddenly I feel Jeppe embracing me from behind. His head is resting against my back, and he's giving me a good squeeze as if to say that this is a special hug.

'I love you as a friend.'

That's a queer way of putting it.

'You're my friend too.'

I've told him that many times before.

'No, that's not what I mean. I love you as a friend. I'm not in love with you any more,' and I stand quite still, not even my heart is beating.

I peel his hands off me and turn to face him with a bewildered look. As we stand face to face, he grabs me by the neck and kisses me. It's a hard, strong kiss – not at all bad, actually. I don't know why I don't push him off, but I let him kiss me.

Jeppe smiles as we head home.

'I'm not going to kiss you again. No need to be afraid of that. But I am going to kiss Bike.'

'Don't you think Bike will find it odd if you start kissing him?'

He shakes his head, smiling.

'No, I think he'll love it,' and that's when it dawns on me.

'You've already kissed him!' I say, astonished.

'No, he kissed me.'

*

When we get home, I can't help staring at Bike. He looks different now. He looks like a bum bandit. I hear Marianne speaking to Jeppe.

'What do you mean? I don't believe it.'

'He was there. I was talking to him.'

'I just don't believe it.'

'He's real,' Jeppe says, stubbornly.

Later in the evening when Karen and Kaj have gone home, I'm in the sitting room with Marianne when we suddenly hear a series of roars coming from Bike's room. It makes me feel uncomfortable, because I can guess what the roaring is about, but Marianne can't, so she hurries over to see if Bike has hurt himself. I try to say something, but the words won't come out of my mouth. She makes it to the door, presses the door handle down, and I think, 'Let it be locked', but it isn't. She screams, shuts the door, turns to me with a deeply shocked expression, and then she collapses in a gigantic peal of laughter. She tries to tell me what she saw, but I don't want to know.

LA LA LA LA LA LA LA LA LA LA LA LA LA LA LA LA LA LA LA LA LA LA LA LA LA LA LA LA LA LA LA LA LA LA LA

Half an hour later a sweaty Jeppe appears. He laughs smugly, and Marianne skirts the room, shouting, 'This is so cool! This is so cool! This is so cool!' She hugs him, tussling his spiky hair.

'How long have you been doing it?'

'What? You saw?'

'Yes.'

'That was the first time, but we've been kissing for a while.'

He goes to the kitchen and gets a drink of water.

'Do either of you have a smoke?'

I fish my smokes out of my pocket and throw them at him.

'Thanks. I'd better get back to Bike,' he says with a horny grin, and then the little sod makes off with my smokes.

I can't look Jeppe or Bike in the eyes from now on. It makes for an awkward atmosphere in the house, but it sickens me every time I hear Bike roar.

He's not Jesus

A couple of days later I'm out on a boyfriend-girlfriend walk with Marianne. We're holding hands, stopping to kiss, chatting about anything and everything the way boyfriends and girlfriends chat about anything and everything.

'Are you happy?' she suddenly asks.

I hesitate, because I know that saying 'no' will hurt her.

'No, not quite yet, but I'm as close as I've ever been.'

She nods.

'I'm happy.'

That's good. I'm pleased to hear her say it.

'Do you love me?'

I don't need to hesitate here.

'Yes, very much.'

'Then why aren't you happy?'

'Because I'm not allowed to be happy.'

'Not allowed? Says who?'

'Says me.'

She's disappointed.

'Well, you are everything I need. I don't need permission.'

She doesn't say anything for a while, and then she continues: 'Jeppe told me he met Jesus. That he's real. A big guy in sandals.'

She has tried to talk about this before, but she hasn't been able to work out how.

'Yes, Jeppe needed to see him, but I didn't think he'd turn him gay.'

'Don't you think that's strange?'

'Yes, it's disgusting.'

She gets annoyed. She didn't mean Bike and Jeppe, and there's nothing disgusting about love. I apologize straight away; of course, she's right, I'm just being squeamish. Don't I think it's strange that I'm being advised by a guy wearing sandals? I get defensive.

'It's no ordinary man. It's Jesus.'

'No, it's a man calling himself Jesus.'

'You haven't complained about this before.'

'That was when I thought you were bonkers. I think it's worse that you are taking the advice of someone who is bonkers.'

We walk for a bit in silence. I'm not angry. I understand why she's saying it, and I think she understands me. She stops and snuggles up against me.

'I didn't mean to make you angry, Niko.'

I lean forwards and kiss her.

'I'm not angry, but he does mean a lot to me.'

'He's not Jesus.'

'How do you know?'

'Because Jesus would demand that you believe in God, and you don't believe in anything.'

When we come home, Jeppe and Bike are in the sitting room. Bike has his arm around Jeppe, and I've never seen Jeppe look so peaceful. I walk over and slap at his legs to make room for me on the sofa.

'You do know that he was in love with me first, don't you?'

I've just gone and made the situation even more awkward. Marianne comes in and sits at my feet. I've got to make some sort of apology for being so uneasy. We can't live like this. I lean forward a bit and let my hands seek Marianne's to help me find some peace in bodily contact.

'I'm sorry I've been such a prat. It's me who's being a total spaz about it. It's great that you two are together. I just feel left out.'

Marianne gives my hands a gentle squeeze. Neither Bike nor Jeppe says anything.

We've gone to bed, but aren't sleeping yet when Jeppe knocks on the door. I open very quickly. He's got something he wants to say. Immediately, I start anticipating the worst. When he says that they are moving, I start blubbing uncontrollably. I don't hear him say 'into Bike's house'. I just think that they're going, and now I'll be losing two of my best friends. Jeppe and Marianne try to calm me down, but I just keep blubbering, which in turn makes Jeppe blubber, and then Marianne has to comfort both of us. Ten minutes later I understand that they are as much my friends as they ever were. They just want to be a couple and be alone now and then. That's why they are moving into Bike's house, which is just sitting there, empty, waiting for them. I'm happy that they won't move far, and I hug Jeppe, feeling relieved. When I'm lying in bed again, Marianne tells me, 'Now we can prance about naked all the time', and then she disappears under the duvet, and that's how I become grateful that Jeppe and Bike are moving out.

Every night I wake up for a brief moment and touch her tenderly to make sure she's sleeping soundly. She never wakes up; she can sleep through a tornado as long as I'm by her side. I run my hand over her back, then I move down and kiss her butterfly, and then I shut my eyes again. When I wake up in the morning, I wake up knowing that I've got something special which only she and I share. But that's not happiness, is it?

The end is nigh

For the past few months Marianne has been in touch with Camilla almost every day. It hasn't been easy for her to even start to persuade Silje, but Camilla has had it, and she wants the old Silje back. The first time Camilla broaches the idea, Silje stares at her as if she's crazy. She accuses her of being a bad friend, though she takes this back immediately when she sees how much it hurts Camilla.

'You know, it's just like when a victim of violence meets her attacker. They blow it out of all proportion in their head, and then, when they meet, it's really perfectly harmless,' Camilla says.

'There's no "just like" about it. I am a victim of violence. Why would I meet him now? You've never liked him.'

'No, and I still hate him. This is for you. He's going to be man-marked. He won't be allowed anywhere near you. I'll rip him to pieces if he tries anything funny,' and Silje realizes that this is important to Camilla.

Camilla also tells her that I've found Jesus, and that I've become a mild-mannered, easy-going Jutlander. My new girlfriend is going to be there as well.

'He's got a girlfriend?'

'Yes, Marianne. She's really quite lovely.'

'Are you mad? I don't want to hear that he's got a lovely girl-friend. I don't want him to be happy.'

'He's not. When he spotted you at the Music Faculty, he fainted. You scared him so much, he collapsed on the street. He was taken away in an ambulance.'

Silje smiles, happily. She hasn't heard anything this encourag-ing for more than a year, and Camilla feels bold.

'If you agree, we'll get everything our own way.'

Even Silje is surprised when she says, 'I'll think about it – but then what they offer us has to be really good.'

*

Their terms:

(1) Fee

They are to get 150,000 kroner per concert. They'll play three concerts – two of them with Mum's songs, and one of them with Silje's. That's a total of 450,000 kroner. Karen wants us to negotiate. It's a matter of principle, because people should be paid what they're worth and not a penny more. Grith Okholm Jam are good, but they're not worth 450,000 kroner.

'They are to us,' I say, and put a stop to the discussion before it begins.

(2) PR

'Oh, that's what you call yourselves now? All right then. That's what we'll call you.' Marianne hangs up and looks at the rest of us. 'They're not called Grith Okholm Jam any longer. They're called the Silje Kjær Band.'

Apparently, Silje has decided that if she agrees to this it'll be the very last time she performs Mum's songs. She offers no explanation, just insists that that's how it is.

We promise to advertise the concerts with the name Silje Kjær Band. I start talking about Silje in every interview I do. I call her the most talented singer in Scandinavia. We give them top billing on the poster that goes up nationwide. That's not a request of theirs; we just do everything we can to persuade her.

Silje is baffled when she sees her name everywhere, all over the poster before she's even agreed to do the concerts, but Camilla tells Marianne that Silje is flattered and that we should just keep at it.

(3) Practical arrangements

They don't want to play before an established group; that would make them seem like a warm-up band. They are to be the headline act, and their last concert will conclude the festival. As they don't want to stay in Tarm while they're playing, we make reservations for them at the Hotel Vestjyden in Skjern. We are also required to make sure they have a fully stocked tour bus to hang out in for the duration of the festival. We find one and make sure it has everything they could possibly dream of needing on a tour bus.

(4) Me

I'm not allowed to see the first two concerts: Silje would find it too stressful. But I must be there at the last one. Apparently, it's important that I'm present on the final night. Marianne asks why, but Camilla won't say.

'Is she going to tell everyone what Niko did to her?' Marianne asks.

'Maybe. You can't ask her not to.'

We are to meet in the tour bus after the last concert. If I try to see Silje before then, I can forget about ever talking to her. Camilla makes it perfectly clear that Silje is afraid of meeting me, and if I behave inappropriately in any way, the whole thing will end right there and then. They make the rules for our meeting, not me.

Even though we agree to all of Camilla's demands, Silje still has doubts. Two weeks before the festival, Camilla decides that a definite yes or no is required. She asks Silje in front of the other band members (who have come back knowing that there's oodles of money to be made) whether they're going to be playing or not. Silje is furious, because she feels ambushed, but she has to say something, and she makes it short and sweet: 'We'll play.'

The band members are ecstatic.

Camilla calls Marianne right away.

'She's agreed to do it.'

Marianne sighs with relief.

'Good. Are you okay with it?'

Camilla doesn't say anything, but Marianne can hear her breathe.

'Camilla?'

'I don't want him touching her.'

Tarm in ecstasy

We estimate that the number of out-of-town visitors for the festival will not exceed eight thousand (the actual number is just over fifteen thousand, which by Tarm standards is a lot). I have plenty of planning meetings with Karen and Mogens. Everything is going according to plan. We're booking bands, ordering portable toilets (but due to the unexpected demand we don't have quite enough, which means that Tarm reeks of urine throughout Easter), tents, beer kegs, and we get permits from the police and the fire department. I'm not involved in the practical arrangements. Karen and her army of volunteers are on top of that. I just approve the decisions and pay whatever needs to be paid. Apart from that I give an interview whenever I'm approached for one.

I'm the spokesperson for the festival. It's a good story. I mean, my setting up this festival in honour of Mum in the town where she was born; and all the radio and television networks, all the newspapers and magazines want in on it. Mogens is in fine feather because Tarm is mentioned in the news every day. They've never had such intense media attention, and Mogens speaks about it having the sort of advertising power that money can't buy. His happiest moment is when the national paper *Politiken* happens to write that there exists almost a sibling relationship between Tarm and Skjern, with Tarm being the bigger brother. Mogens cuts out the article and hangs it on his noticeboard. In an interview with the *Skjern-Tarm Daily* I call him a man of vision, and say that if Mum had ever received a visit from him, I'm sure she would have been persuaded to play in Tarm. The next time we meet, he puts the article in front of me, gives me a pat on the shoulder, and simply says, 'Thank you, Nikolaj.'

The entire town is excited in a strange way, because it isn't just excitement. It's a relief as well; that is, an excitement about feeling relieved. For many years they've nurtured a love for Mum that was never requited. The festival confirms to them that their love wasn't in vain. I am my mother's mouthpiece, and I'm telling them that I'm fond of them, to the point even of being willing to squander my millions on them. The closer we get to the festival, the more I experience an almost violent friendliness. People spontaneously hug me on the street without offering the least explanation. It's weird being a part of the excitement, when all my life I've tried to avoid Mum, but I can't be bothered to run away any more. The festival is my way of embracing Mum and letting her embrace me.

I don't feel my worth decreasing

My financial adviser gets in touch. He tells me cautiously that in a year I have spent fifteen million kroner.

'Oh. But I'm not going bankrupt, am I?'

He quickly says, 'No, of course not,' because I really hate it when the bank interferes, and they know it. 'I just thought you might like to know that your spending is out of control.'

'It's not out of control. I only spend what needs to be spent,' I say, annoyed.

I'm still rich, and, by the way, I'm thinking about getting a job when all this is over. I've received an application form from the Royal Mail. I want to be a postman in Tarm. I have no reason to be ashamed of being a postman, because I'm not my dad. Karen is ever so proud, because it proves that I'm one of them. She wastes no time in telling Bitten.

Excerpt from a radio show

There's a radio show right before the festival, and Mogens and I are in the studio. We've been going for some time, which means we've been introduced by now. It's about my motives for setting up this festival. Of course, we've talked a lot about Mum and her relationship with the town, but now it's about me and my relationship with Tarm. Mogens is there as my excessively chatty squire.

RADIO HOST:

But is it different because it's in Tarm?

ME:

Yes, it is, because Mum was born here. That – as I've already said – is the reason why I moved here.

RADIO HOST:

But is it different to you because you live here now?

MOGENS:

Of course it's different to Nikolaj. This is his town. We look after Nikolaj, and he looks after us. That's how it is in West Jutland. We care about each other.

ME:

Yes.

RADIO HOST:

So it's not just about your mum? It's about you as well, and how you feel about the town, is it?

MOGENS:

Of course it is. If I didn't know better, I'd think Niko-laj had lived his entire life in Tarm, but he's only been here a year. Has it really been a year?

ME:

Not quite. I moved to Tarm in June last year. It's also about Mum, you know.

MOGENS:

Yes, of course it is, but you're the one living here now.

RADIO HOST:

And you felt settled in right away when you moved here?

ME:

Fuck me, yes. Oh, sorry, didn't mean to swear.

RADIO HOST:

Not to worry. Why did you feel settled in?

ME:

I really can't say.

MOGENS:

Tarm has a lot to offer. A bustling business life, great landscapes, lots of things to do, a bowling alley. There are thousands of reasons to feel at home in Tarm.

RADIO HOST:

But surely that's not why you felt at home, was it?

MOGENS:

These things do matter, you know!

ME:

No, they actually don't, Mogens. It's to do with the people of Tarm.

MOGENS:

Of course. The people are what matters most of all. Nikolaj is part of a strong community now.

RADIO HOST:

What do you mean? How is it about the people?

ME:

I don't know. I just felt welcome.

RADIO HOST:

You felt welcome?

ME:

Yes.

MOGENS:

He was very welcome. No doubt about it.

RADIO HOST:

What do you mean, welcome?

ME:

Oh. Oh, I don't know. It's to do with the atmosphere.

RADIO HOST:

Is there a particular kind of atmosphere in Tarm?

MOGENS:

Yes, there is. Tarm may not be a big city, but we are quite something.

ME:

I agree with Mogens.

Bike loves Jeppe

I'm having dinner with my girlfriend and my two gay friends a couple of days before the festival. None of them has a clue about cooking, and even I know that rice shouldn't taste like charcoal.

Nevertheless, we eat it with a smile. Late in the evening Bike gets up. There's something he wants to say. He's got the Dutch courage he needs. The first bit of his speech is about me and Marianne, and about how lovely we look together, and then he turns to Jeppe, who's sitting there with a do-sit-down-smile plastered on his face, but Bike doesn't sit. For a full ten minutes he talks about Jeppe, and about everything that Jeppe means to him. I can't believe his courage! I can't believe that he can just stand there and be himself! That he can say, 'I love you', then stop for effect and look intensely at Jeppe.

'I love you.'

Jeppe looks feverishly around for help, but he doesn't need help. When we go home, I ask Marianne if I can stop looking out for Jeppe now. She smiles at me, and asks me, 'Do you want to stop?', and it suddenly dawns on me that not absolutely everything has to end.

The festival

I'm opening the festival with Mogens. I've never seen a middle-aged man this nervous. We're standing behind the large open-air stage, better known as the Football Stage, because it's really Tarm's big football pitch. He's sweating, shaking, and pacing up and down.

'Are you all right?'

He straightens up.

'No, I'm just a little nervous. You don't happen to have a cigarette on you, do you?'

'I didn't know you smoked,' I say, and hand him my pack.

'Not for three years. My wife will be very cross.'

His hands are shaking so badly he can't light it. I take the lighter out of his hands and light his cigarette. He takes an almighty puff, and it seems to calm him down. He undoes his tie and unbuttons his shirt. It's wet through. I let him finish his smoke, although we're already running late. He's trying to work up some courage before the opening speech. There must be a couple of thousand people on the pitch, come to hear us, which – strange as it may seem – leaves me quite unperturbed.

'It'll be all right, won't it?' he asks me, anxiously.

'The speech? Absolutely.'

'No, all of it. We're not going to look like fools, are we? Are we up for this?'

We've just realized that we've underestimated Mum's appeal. People from all over the country are flooding Tarm.

'Sure we are. It'll be fine.'

He exhales, relieved, and walks briskly on to the stage. I follow him. He speaks a bit about Mum and the town, and I speak about Mum as a private person and as an artist, and then we do a bit of verbal ping-pong. We've even put a couple of jokes in there. When we're done, Mogens hugs me with obvious relief. It's that hug which makes him mayor when the councils of Tarm and Skjern are merged. At least, it will be his official press photograph from now on.

We are followed by Thomas Helmig, and after him Silje is going to play, so I make good my escape. It would be downright stupid if I were to accidentally bump into her and ruin our plan.

I wander about town on my own. There are loads of things going on. Everywhere there's a concert, including several cover bands. A couple of them are decent enough, but none of them can hold a candle to Silje. I enjoy the festival, and I sign autographs until my hand hurts. There are people everywhere. Tarm has never been this full of happy people. It makes me feel proud. I sit on the bench by the stream and look with delight at the passers-by. I smile broadly, because I'm exactly where I'm supposed to be, and I start humming 'With You', thinking about Marianne as I do. It's the first time ever I've hummed one of Mum's songs. I close my eyes and let the song come to me. When I open them, Karen and Kaj are standing in front of me. I'm looking up at the broadest grin I've ever seen.

'What?'

'You're singing,' Karen says, surprised.

'No, I'm humming.'

'Nikolaj, you are singing loudly and happily.'

I can see in her face that she's right and I'm wrong. People are looking at me, and I blush. She bends down and caresses my cheek gently. She wants to pull back her hand, but I grab it before she can manage. She's startled, not because it's me, but because of the movement. Kaj takes a step forward, but I quickly say all that needs to be said. Right now the happiness is so great, that I can't hold it back.

'I'm so damned grateful to you for barging into my life. You're the best person I've ever met, and I just don't know where I'd be if you hadn't come round bearing cake. I'm so bleeding happy that I'm singing Mum's songs, and it's your bloody fault.'

I let go of her hand. Tears of joy are running down my cheeks, and I try to get a hold of myself, but I don't do a very good job of it. Karen is standing, looking at me in a state of shock, and then suddenly she starts blubbing too.

According to both Jeppe and Marianne, Silje did okay. She was nervous and very introverted, but she sang well. Bike, who has seen them playing before at Herning Congress Centre on the other hand, said that he had a feeling that they were a cover band of a cover band.

No-one is going without love

Kink arrives on the Friday in time for the festival. He's brought his little, green-haired girlfriend. She's sweet but naïve, because she thinks everything is intentionally kitschy. She laughs loudly when she sees the street teeming with drunken Jutlanders, clapping to the beat of the music. We pretend nothing is happening, but it's a bit annoying that she's staring completely unreservedly, while roaring with laughter. Later that evening, after the world's most tedious concert ever, which is what she calls Silje's second performance, she starts making fun of the dancing couples in the largest beer tent. It's obvious to everyone that she's pretending to be a dumb Jutlander, but luckily Kink is looking out for her. The more stupid she sounds, the bigger Kink appears. In the end, he gets control of her, gets her settled in and sat down at our table.

Karen, who has wanted to say something for a long time, leans across the table and takes her hands.

'It's not polite to poke fun at other people. I don't think you should do that any more.'

She becomes very quiet, but after a few seconds she apologizes. She settles in, and it's not long before she is slow-dancing with Kink.

It's a little bit awkward when Kink meets Bike, but only for a split-second, and then they're giving each other a proper hug. Bike is all over Kink's girlfriend, whom he says is enchanting. She's never been called enchanting before. Kink's girlfriend laughs like a drain when Bike mentions how Kink got the scars on his cock. Kink, on the other hand, gets cranky. She sees it, stops laughing, leans in close and whispers something that only he can hear. All crankiness vanishes into thin air. I look around the table with surprise. Kaj has his arm around Karen, Marianne has her hand on my arse, and Bike is nestling in close to Jeppe. I'm sitting at a table where no-one is going without love. I turn and look around the tent. People are singing, dancing, drinking, kissing and smiling. Later we all dance as Poul Krebs sings that people like us need someone to love.

As I walk home with Marianne, I tell her I love her very much, because I need her to know. She asks me again if I'm happy. I'm not allowed to be happy yet, but I don't want to live without her. She promises that she'll never leave me. That night we have sex so gentle that it almost feels like we're not touching. Afterwards, we're lying close together and talk about tomorrow. I've spoken to quite a few people who think that Silje's heart hasn't been in it these first two concerts. She's singing well enough, but she's not giving her all. Marianne thinks that she's hasn't dared to. Silje has seemed tiny and fragile on the big stage.

'So, what do we do about it?' I ask nervously.

'We wait until tomorrow. Right now there's nothing we can do. There's got to be a reason they want you to see her at the concert tomorrow.'

Of course there is, and I think I know why. Up until now Silje hasn't said a word about me, but I fear that tomorrow I'll be busted, and that Tarm will turn against me. I've fooled them into thinking I'm a nice person, but nice people don't beat up their girlfriends. Marianne promises that no matter what happens, she will always be with me. She snuggles up to me and falls asleep straight away, but of course I can't sleep for fear of what will happen tomorrow.

I push her off me very quietly, and go to the sitting room and turn on the television. I pour a glass of port, and there I am, then, drinking, smoking and watching *Gilmore Girls* to relax. My stomach isn't hurting as such, there's just a nervous stitch. I've been sitting there for a while, when I realize that there's someone standing behind me. I automatically assume it's Marianne.

'You couldn't sleep either?' I say, and turn around. It's blooming Jesus. 'Hello there. What are you doing here?' I ask surprised.

He's smiling.

'I've come to say goodbye.'

'What do you mean?'

'We won't be seeing each other again. You can manage on your own now.'

It takes me a couple of seconds to understand what he's saying. When I have, I get up and give him a real bloke's hug.

'I'm proud of you, Nikolaj.'

'Thank you. You've been a great friend.'

And then there we are awkwardly standing in front of each other, until we give each other another hug. He turns around and leaves, but just before he disappears, I have a question I need answered, and I ask him quickly, 'Are you really Jesus? I mean, *the* Jesus?'

He turns to face me.

'What do you think?'

'Marianne says that you're not, but I don't know what to believe.'

'Nikolaj, I can't prove it to you. You've got to either believe in me or not believe in me.'

That doesn't quite settle it, but I've got a nice feeling of calm in my body, because he's been here. I turn off the television and go back in to Marianne. I nestle close to her. Suddenly, I'm not afraid of tomorrow, because tomorrow everything is going to fall into place. It is also tomorrow that Marianne is going to die, but I don't know that tonight.

At the concert

Mogens is standing on the Football Stage. He is proud and he is very vocal about it, thanking a phenomenal audience for having ensured that we have had three phenomenal days of smiles and laughs. People are applauding each other enthusiastically. There have been a few minor cock-ups here and there, because of the large crowd; a bit too much urine on the streets, and Friday night we almost ran out of beer, but luckily we got the emergency rations here in the nick of time. Mogens is thanking all the volunteers as well. Karen, of course, is the woman of the hour. She's standing next to me, looking very happy. Mogens would have liked me to get up on stage with him. We opened the festival together, and we ought to close it together, but I'm not going along with that. It would be too risky, what with Silje coming on stage right after us. And for that reason I'm standing with NATO at the very back.

'Last but not least, I'd like to extend a big thank you to Nikolaj Okholm. He's standing down by the subs' bench. He didn't want to come up here on stage, because he didn't want us to make a big fuss, but I say let's make a big fuss anyway. I'd like you all to turn around and applaud him. He's standing right there – look where I'm pointing,' and Mogens points to where he thinks I'm standing, but to get a better view of things we've moved about fifty metres. Five thousand people bustle and shift and clap excitedly in the direction of the subs' bench. I turn and clap in the same direction.

Mogens calls us to order. People turn towards the stage again. He introduces Silje as being Mum's musical heir. I've told Mogens he has to really deliver the goods, because the more he delivers, the easier it'll be for her to win over the audience. Mogens calls them beautiful songs for the general public. We haven't heard her songs, but we assume they'll be tender pop songs. That's why it's primarily young families and little old ladies in the front rows. The band goes on stage and Silje steps up to the microphone.

'It's different today,' Marianne tells me straight away.

Silje has only been on stage for two seconds. She hasn't said a word yet; she hasn't even looked at the audience, but Marianne just knows.

'I can see it in the way she walks.'

I want to believe her, but I can't see it myself. Silje is looking at the ground, away from the audience, and she's usually switched on from the get-go.

'I just can't see it.'

'It's different.'

'In a good way?'

'Yes, she's stronger.'

Marianne is seeing something I can't see. She sees defiance where I'm seeing fear.

'Hello, my name is Silje Kjær. You'll know me as the lead singer of the band formerly known as Grith Okholm Jam. Tonight we're not playing Grith's songs but mine. I've been invited to play at this festival by my ex-boyfriend, so if you're not happy about tonight's gig, he's the one to talk to.'

She pauses for effect, and people cheer excitedly. Of course, we were a couple. People standing close to me turn around with great big smiles, and I smile back at them nervously. I squeeze Marianne, because I'm convinced Silje is about to spill the beans.

'You like him, do you?'

People cheer again. Some even shout, 'Nikolaj is God!'

'I think he's a bastard and a twat.'

She doesn't say anything else, but the music starts roaring at that very moment. The audience is paralysed, not just because of such foul language from such a nice-looking girl, but the music itself is a shock. Silje screams and screeches; the guitars whine, and the drums are shredded. The lyrics are violent and brutal. They're about death, fornication, violence and calamity. The young families and little old ladies make good their escape, but Kink's little green-haired girlfriend is jumping excitedly up and down.

'This is so cool! It sounds just like PJ Harvey!' she shouts, pulling Kink up with her. They are darting up in front of the stage with Bike and Jeppe in hot pursuit.

Silje scares off a lot of people, but quite a lot stay, and those who stay are thrilled. They gather in front of the stage in a big group, all bumping happily into each other. I stay at the back with Marianne and Karen, but Karen leaves us quite quickly, because the music gives her a headache. Mogens comes down to me, looking confused. He fears that this may be a colossal anticlimax for the festival.

'Did you know it'd be this sort of music?'

'No, of course not. If I'd known, I'd have told you, wouldn't I? But I think it's cool, because it gives people something to talk about afterwards.'

'Oh, right. I hadn't quite thought of it that way. So it's a good thing?'

'Yes, it's a good thing. We're not just going with the safe bets.'

Mogens isn't quite convinced, but he lets it go for now. It's only when the reviews of Silje's concert turn out to be monumentally positive that he calms down and becomes very proud of the fact that Tarm was where Silje made her big breakthrough.

Silje doesn't say a lot between the songs. In other words, she's not talking to the audience, and usually she's very talky and flirty. It's part of her stage persona. Today the music is doing all the talking, but the audience is still captivated. I need a while to get my head round the brutality of the tone, but the music's got verve. We all expect a nice, polished end to our festival, and instead what we're getting is a fist to the face. It doesn't ruin it for me. Maybe it ruins things for some of the elderly ladies, but not for me. I think it's great that Silje has finally found her own voice, even if it's an angry one.

'Blimey, she's got an intense air about her. Did she always have that?' Marianne asks.

'No, even when she got mad, she was meek. I can't remember she was ever really angry with me.'

'She never yelled at you?'

'No, certainly not the way you do. You hit me as well.'

We are the only two people watching the concert and holding one another. All the others are bumping into each other. I'm certain Silje sees us when the pitch is half-empty. I certainly feel as if she's keeping her eyes locked on us, while she screeches angrily, and I really don't mean singing. At one point she is screeching angry sounds into the microphone, and people go ballistic.

When the final song is over, Silje looks excitedly at the audience, and then at me. I can't imagine that she'll go offstage without exacting her revenge. There are large empty spaces on the pitch, but at the very front there are excited boys and girls screaming for more. She gawps at them in wonder, and I have a feeling that it's them who save me. She can't believe that she's being applauded so loudly. It would be too brutal to tell them the truth about me. She doesn't say a word, but steps off the stage silently, and I breathe a sigh of relief. Marianne turns around and gives me a reassuring kiss. I can always tell when her kisses are reassuring, because she holds a bit back.

'Let's go for a walk to help you relax,' and I realize that in my anxiety I've been pressing her too hard against me.

We go out into the forest where we can be alone. I'm happy that I'm meeting Silje here in Tarm, because if this had been in Copenhagen, I'd be lying on the ground gasping for air right now. I feel safe and scared at the same time. The next hour we don't speak a single word to each other. I don't need to talk. I just need Marianne to be there to stop me from exploding.

Review of the concert in *Gaffa* music magazine

Silje Kjær, The Football Stage, Grith Okholm Festival

Live – by Hans Henrik Fahrendorff

The former lead singer of Grith Okholm Jam has made a surprise coming out at Denmark's cutesiest festival as the saviour of Danish punk rock.

As *Gaffa*'s reporter at the much touted Grith Okholm Festival in Tarm I've experienced umpteen cover bands singing the same Grith Okholm songs, as well as an array of aging Danish pop stars: Thomas Helmig, Poul Krebs, Peter Belli, Ivan Pedersen, Gnags, Sanne Salomonsen, TV2. Pretty much every Danish pop musician who was part of the Danish music industry when Grith Okholm was alive was to be found at the festival. Some delivered passable performances, while others relied on their reputation to get them through the event.

The festival was intended as a tribute to Grith Okholm, which made for a rather unique atmosphere – amazing to a lot of people, but it gave me the creeps. It felt like a sect where everyone had to like the same things. Everywhere at the festival there was the same comfy feeling. People were hanging out, having a lovely time, and there's nothing wrong with that, but it did make me feel that not being well-behaved and nice was not on. Being wild at the Grith Okholm Festival was not on.

Personally, I've always thought she was overrated. In my opinion she's only made three or four great songs ('What the Heart Holds' is on par with Stevie Wonder's best work) and not a full catalogue of amazing songs. The rest of it has been pretty pop music, but because of her death she has been idolized by a growing number of fans, and nowhere more so than in her native town of Tarm.

That amount of niceness is simply cloying. It makes me feel claustrophobic. I was thus looking forward to getting back to Århus and experiencing something with a bit more edge to it. Before I could do that, however, I had to get through the final concert with Silje Kjær – the much-hyped former lead singer of Grith

Okholm Jam. She had been promoted by the festival as an epiphany of unheard of dimensions. She had been headlining on all the posters, and there have been ads in all the national papers touting her debut concert with her own tracks. I – like most others – expected a pale replica of Grith Okholm. Very few had heard any of her songs up until then. I wasn't one of them, and boy was I wrong!

She is introduced as the musical heir of Grith Okholm, but from the very first note she distances herself from Grith Okholm. Silje Kjær is the anti-Grith Okholm. Her appearance may be slight and fair, but her music is raw and dirty. Her weapons are simple but efficient. Intense, beautiful, frightening but very catchy songs with lyrics that are upfront and explicit about destructive relationships, betrayal and violence. Everything sung with a rage that one wouldn't associate with a former lead singer of a Grith Okholm cover band. The song 'Boyfriend' may be the

Photograph: Martin Dam Kristensen

best Danish song about a destructive relationship ever written! It may refer to Grith Okholm's son, Nikolaj, who has come up with the idea as well as the funding for the festival, and whom Silje used to go out with and for whom she obviously has no great fondness. I had expected an overdose of niceness; instead I was given the antidote: a dangerous and intense concert with an original and exciting new artist. The best concert I have been to this year! I'm looking forward very much to this year musically, when Silje Kjær will make a big breakthrough. The Queen is dead. Long live the Queen.

Thanks for the hype, Grith Okholm Festival. You got me in the end.

Seeing Silje

We knock on the tour-bus door for ten minutes before anything happens. It opens, but we're not asked inside. Camilla simply pops out her head and says, 'She needs another ten minutes.'

The door is shut once more, and we wait. Ten minutes become thirty, and I can tell that Marianne is thinking what I'm thinking: that they're playing us for fools. She doesn't say anything though; her only concern is whether I'm okay. We're standing on the parking lot where anyone and everyone can see us, and people come up to me, happy and drunk, and bellow, 'Dammit, Nikolaj, it's been three amazing days!' and I nod politely, but I'd really much rather be left alone.

Finally, the door opens. We hurry inside. The air's so thick you could cut it with a knife, and really unwelcoming to boot. It's teeming with tension. Oddly enough, I'm a bit turned on by it. Silje is sitting in one of the sofas at the very back of the bus. The bus suddenly feels very long, and getting to the end feels like making a very long journey. I can't quite work out how to say hello. I almost give her a hug, but stop myself, because it would be too intimate a gesture. Then I half hold out my hand, but take it

314

back quickly, because that would be too impersonal. In the end I settle for a small wave, while saying, 'Hi there. Good to see you again.'

Silje makes no answer. She merely turns her eyes from me and stares at the floor. I sit down across from her. It's a rock 'n' roll bus with tinted windows and funky furniture. Marianne remains discreetly behind me. Silje looks annoyed at her for a brief moment, then stares at the floor again.

At the very last moment Silje demanded that Marianne stay away, but that was the only demand they made that we couldn't accept. Camilla clears her throat. She is standing right next to Silje and she is holding a wine bottle in her hand as a weapon.

'Try anything funny, and I'll give you such a beating. Got it?'

I try to smile reassuringly at her, but it's only half a smile.

'Got it?'

'We'll just talk.'

I look back at Silje, who quickly looks back at the floor. She's shaking. At one point someone knocks on the door. It's the driver who wants to be let in, but he's being sent off instead. When he's gone, Silje takes a deep breath, and then she finally says something.

'What did you think of the concert?'

'It was amazing. You blew them away.'

'A lot of people left, you know.'

'Yes. They were shocked.'

She almost smiles.

'Thanks for making me do this. It means a lot to me.'

'You're welcome,' and I can't hide my relief.

For the first time her eyes meet mine. I smile at her with relief, but I feel penetrated by her eyes and my smile fades quickly. She doesn't say anything for a long time. We're not saying anything; we're just sitting there silently looking at each other. In the end the silence becomes overpowering and I say, 'I'm so sorry, Silje, and if I could, I'd make it up to you, but I just don't know how.'

She still isn't saying anything.

'Silje, I'm sorry.'

'I know you are, Nikolaj,' she says.

I want to smile at her again, but her face tells me not to. She works up the courage to say, 'I loved you very much. How could you do that to me?'

My stomach is screaming with fury, but I bite it back. I start sweating. The air is thick in here. I look away from her and at the others. They're not sweating. Marianne is smiling reassuringly at me. She can tell that I'm not feeling well, and it makes my stomach calm down a bit, but then I look at Camilla, and she is looking even fiercer than she did before.

'I loved you very much too,' I mumble.

'Then how could you do that?'

'I don't know.'

She needs an answer. I'm looking for an answer that won't hurt too much. Fortunately, someone knocks on the tour-bus door again. This time it's a group of teenage boys who want to talk to the star. They're very persistent, so Marianne goes out to calm them down. They're drunk, and they don't understand that we need them to leave. The door is open, and one of them nips past Marianne. He darts up to Silje and hugs her, shouting that this was the greatest concert he's ever seen. Silje just doesn't have the energy to cope with a drunken teenager, so I get up to remove him. Camilla is there in a jiffy. She shakes the bottle at me as a warning, and I sit down again, shaking my head at her. Luckily, the kid thinks it's him she's threatening and he hurries away, apologising as he goes.

We don't say anything until they've left, and Marianne has returned to her seat.

'I was scared. That's why I did it.'

We've lost the thread, and Silje doesn't understand what I'm talking about.

I take a deep breath and say, 'I didn't deserve your love. It scared me, and that's why I hit you.'

She looks down and says very quietly, 'But you don't get to decide that.'

'I don't understand.'

'You don't get to decide whether you deserve to be loved.'

Marianne has moved closer to me. She's stroking my back gently to make me relax. I turn towards her and smile gratefully. My blood is pumping, and I feel strangely flushed. Marianne smiles happily at me, and I want to shout that I love her more than I had ever thought I could love anyone. Of course, I don't do that because Silje's face has gone strangely hard. My love for Marianne is different from the love I had for Silje. Marianne makes me feel that everything is just as it should be, but surely that's not

317

happiness? It can't be, because Silje still hasn't been sorted out, and my stomach is still aching. I turn to Silje and smile a wide, astonished smile, because I'm suddenly not sure any more. Am I happy? She is annoyed with me for smiling, but I can't help myself.

I try to resume the conversation and say, 'I couldn't breathe, and you made it worse.'

She says angrily, 'I made it worse? How did I do that?'

It sounds unfair, but that's what it was.

'Because you scared me.'

'But you can breathe now? Because of her?' she says, and points at Marianne.

I nod, although I know it isn't going to make her happy. I tell Silje about my friends, about Jesus and the love that is in my life, but she isn't listening; she's just looking at Marianne who in turn is pulling back a bit to become less obvious, but it doesn't seem to satisfy Silje.

'Silje?'

'What?'

'Are you listening to what I'm saying?'

'Yes, you're talking about Jesus,' she snaps at me.

I stop saying anything. She gets up, goes to the fridge, opens it and takes out a bottle of coke. Marianne shifts to allow Silje to pass. They are standing very close to each other. Silje puts her coke bottle down and lashes out. Her hand only grazes Marianne. I jump out of my seat at once. Silje is taking another swing at Marianne. She still isn't hitting her, and Marianne is trying to keep her off. She isn't scared, because Silje being violent isn't scary.

I grab a hold of Silje to get her back in her seat and make her calm down, because frankly this is just daft. Apparently, it seems like I'm attacking her, because Camilla panics. The wine bottle swishes past my head. It scares the bejesus out of me.

'For Christ's sake, I just want her to sit down!' I yell, and I let go of Silje immediately, who starts screaming. 'I have let go of you!' I yell, and that's when I hear a strange noise behind me, like someone who's coughing underwater.

Marianne is swaying. Blood is gushing from her mouth. I feel like I'm standing watching her for a very long time, because everything happens very slowly now. My breathing is slow, my movements are slow, my thoughts are slow, and my eyes are slow to focus. Silje hits me hard on the back and screams, 'Niko, do something!' and then, next thing I know, Marianne topples over. She's spitting blood, and then she shuts her eyes. She's dead.

Suddenly, everything happens very quickly. I fall to the floor and pull her towards me, while I'm breathing shallowly. I start chanting, 'SAVE HER SAVE HER SAVE HER SAVE HER SAVE HER SAVE HER SAVE HER SAVE HER SAVE HER SAVE HER SAVE HER SAVE HER SAVE HER SAVE HER SAVE HER SAVE HER SAVE HER SAVE HER!'

Camilla is apologising hysterically at the top of her voice, while calling the emergency services. They can barely understand what she's saying. She's screaming, staccato-style, about blood, bus, blood, bus, blood, bus! My world is very small right now. There's just me and Marianne. That's why I don't notice that Silje is sitting next me, looking baffled. After a while she starts stroking my back reassuringly, exactly as Marianne was doing before, but all I can think about is my prayer. She then tries to get my arms to let go of Marianne. She speaks to me, gently at first, and then more forcefully, because I'm not listening; my own desperate voice is drowning everything else out. In the end she shakes me ruthlessly.

'Nikolaj, you have to let go of her, or she can't breathe.'

I look at her with confusion, and then I look at Marianne who is looking back at me rather groggily. I ought to let go of her, but instead I hold her even tighter. At this moment I'm experiencing a sensation I've never had before in my life. My breathing is strangely unhampered, because there isn't a knot in my stomach. Marianne is dizzy and bleeding, but she's alive. She and the doctors both claim that she never did die. They say that the blood was due to her biting her tongue badly, and that it was the shock that caused her to pass out, but I know better. It wasn't just that. I look deep in her eyes and say, 'I think I'm happy.' She doesn't catch on, though, because she isn't fully there yet.

The ambulance comes to pick up Marianne, while people gather around the bus. Silje explains to the paramedics that Marianne was hit on the head by a cupboard door. I'm falling about, and I want to go with her to the hospital, but Silje yanks me out of the ambulance. I do manage to kiss Marianne over and over before she's taken away, and I repeat, 'I think I'm happy.' She smiles. This time she understands it, partially. She tries to speak, but she can't say anything, because her tongue is swollen. She reaches out for me, but Silje pulls me away. The ambulance drives off, and I stay behind with Silje. I'm instantly aware that Marianne has gone because my body starts to feel uneasy. I look around.

'Where is she?'

Silje grabs hold of me and pulls me off in the direction of the tour bus.

'Where's who?'

'Camilla?'

She pushes me up the stairs and into the bus, shutting the door behind us.

'I sent her away.'

I want to beat Camilla to a pulp. I want to make her suffer for what she's done to my Marianne, but instead I'm cooped up with Silje, who looks at me. Why is she just standing there, gawping at me?

'Where is she?' I whisper, furious.

'I don't know, Nikolaj.'

There's a guitar on the seat next to me. I pick it up, waiting for Silje to do something, but she doesn't do anything, so I smash it on the floor. It makes an almighty racket, and the guitar breaks.

'You know, that wasn't Camilla's guitar,' Silje says.

Someone knocks on the door and asks, 'Are you guys okay in there?'

Silje says, 'Yes, we're fine. Please, just leave us alone.'

I'm standing there, huffing and puffing.

'I'm going out and fucking finding her,' but Silje gets in front me.

'No, Nikolaj, you're going to stay here with me.'

The air is strangely thick again, and I've got so much rage inside me that just has to come out.

'Why are you looking at me like that?'

I don't understand it, but her eyes are challenging me. She doesn't say anything. We're standing close together, and her hand brushes against my thigh. Just like that, I get an instant cramp in my calf, and I bend over to massage it. She laughs.

'What are you laughing at?'

'Still get those cramps, do you?'

I shake my head, which makes her stretch her hand teasingly towards me. Feeling annoyed I grab hold of her. She makes a frightened little twitch, and I let go of her straight away.

'You can't touch me, Silje, not now.'

I have to get out. I can't be cooped up with Silje, but she gets in my way.

'I want to leave.'

'I can't let you do that, Niko. I want you to stay here with me.'

There's only an inch of dense air between us. I'm sweating again. She looks me hard in the eyes, and I take a few steps away from her, but she comes after me. There's nowhere left for me to run to. She's waiting for me to do something. I'm about to explode. She's as close to me as she can be without touching me. She's toying with me. This is sexual.

'Silje, go away,' but she doesn't, and I can't take it any more.

With my left hand I grab hold of the back of her head, pull her face in close, kiss her hard and put my right hand down the front of her trousers. I try to get a finger into her, but I can't: she's squeezing her legs tightly together. She doesn't want to. I let go of her.

'I'm sorry, I thought you wanted to. I shouldn't have done that. I love Marianne,' I mutter.

Silje doesn't seem to be scared. She's just standing there with her trousers halfway down.

I'm disgusted with myself. She doesn't say anything. I want to leave again, but once more she gets in the way. I'm not angry any more. I'm ashamed and afraid.

'Please, let me go, won't you?' I beg her.

She shakes her head. Then she turns around, pulling down her trousers, holding on to two rows of seat and leaning forward a bit. I am huffing and puffing with confusion. She's standing there, flaunting her arse and blocking my escape. I get a bit closer, then I move away from her, and in the end I stand behind her, taking it out and sticking it in. I thrust as hard as I can. She's absolutely silent. When I come – and I come quite quickly she pushes me off at once. I sink to the floor, kneeling there, while she pulls up her knickers and trousers. I feel sullied and vile. She steps past me and sits down on the sofa with a deep sigh. She's looking at me with amusement, still sitting on the floor with my arse bare. She's laughing again.

'Nikolaj, for crying out loud, put your trousers on, will you? It's a bit off-putting to have you sit there with your spotty arse poking out.'

I manage to put my trousers back on and get up. I'm afraid to look at her, so instead I stare at the floor.

'Don't look so frightened. Nothing bad's going to happen to you.'

'Can I go now?'

'Yes, run on home to Marianne.'

She gets up from the sofa and walks past me. I cringe in fear, and then she opens the door of the bus. I scurry out. Right before she shuts the door, I turn around to face her.

'I don't understand this.'

She simply shuts the door, and I'm standing face to face with Nadja Jessen from the *Skjern-Tarm Daily*, who wants to know what it is that I don't understand.

The bus leaves half an hour later.

Marianne and me

I'm terrified of going home, and it's a long time before I start walking towards Poppelvej. I walk past happy, intoxicated people who are making the most of the last parties before Tarm returns to normal. I haven't decided what I'm going to tell Marianne when I get home. Luckily, she isn't back from A&E, and I dart into the shower. While I'm standing there, she comes home. She tries to yell at me. I hesitate, but I yell back that I'm in the shower. She comes to the bathroom and pulls back the shower curtain to see me. Her tongue is swollen, and she looks like a retard, standing there with her mouth half-open, because her tongue won't fit in her mouth.

'How are you feeling?' I ask her.

'I've had a few stitches in my tongue,' she lisps, then sticks it out so I can see the stitches. It looks horrid. Her tongue looks like it was almost bitten off. I have to try very hard to understand what she's saying. She steps into the shower with all her clothes on and holds me. She lets her head rest against my back.

'Are you really allowed to be happy now, Niko?'

She almost can't say it, but that's not just because of her tongue. I think I'm allowed to be happy, because my stomach isn't hurting, but I don't say yes. I say, 'I did it with Silje.'

It takes her ten seconds to understand what I mean by 'did it with Silje'. She lets go of me. I wait for her reaction, and then she starts slapping my naked back. THUMP! She keeps hitting me until my back is black and blue. I accept every slap, silently. She stops hitting me.

'You utter, utter idiot!' she lisps, and then she leaves me.

I stay in the shower. I can hear her kicking at doors and throwing around furniture, but then suddenly I can't hear her any longer, even though I listen really hard. I turn off the water, dry myself, and then I stand there hesitantly before I dare step out of the bathroom. I hope she's still here.

Acknowledgements

Thanks are due to:

Henrik Vestergaard, Simon Pasternak, Camilla Pedersen, Johannes Riis, Carina Kamper, Jette Christa Pedersen, Kevin Lytsen, Anne Dissing, Thomas Husum Jensen and all the other people who have helped me.

To find out more about our books, to meet our authors, to discover new writing, to get inspiration for your book group, to read exclusive on-line interviews, blogs and comment, and to sign up for our newsletter, visit **www.portobellobooks.com**

encouraging voices,
supporting writers,
challenging readers